D0174966

The purchase of this item
was made possible by a
generous grant received
from

Burn Me Deadly

ALEX BLEDSOE

Burn Me Deadly

AN EDDIE LaCROSSE NOVEL

TOR®

A Tom Doherty Associates Book
New York

This is a work of fiction. All of the characters, organizations, and events portrayed in this novel are either products of the author's imagination or are used fictitiously.

BURN ME DEADLY: AN EDDIE LACROSSE NOVEL

Copyright © 2009 by Alex Bledsoe

All rights reserved.

A Tor Book
Published by Tom Doherty Associates, LLC
175 Fifth Avenue
New York, NY 10010

www.tor-forge.com

Tor® is a registered trademark of Tom Doherty Associates, LLC.

Library of Congress Cataloging-in-Publication Data

Bledsoe, Alex.
    Burn me deadly : an Eddie Lacrosse novel / Alex Bledsoe.—
1st ed.
        p.   cm.
    "A Tom Doherty Associates book."
    ISBN 978-0-7653-2221-0
    I. Title.
  PS3602.456B87   2009
  813'.6—dc22

                                                    2009016458

First Edition: November 2009

Printed in the United States of America

0 9 8 7 6 5 4 3 2 1

For Hays Davis

Many years (and beers) ago, during one of those all-nighters in which we alternately solved the world's problems and decided what music belonged on our mix tapes, you made an offhand comment that stuck in my head and led directly to the writing of this book. For two decades' (and counting) worth of friendship, I dedicate this to you, pal.

SPECIAL THANKS TO:

Marlene Stringer and Barbara Bova
Tom Doherty and Paul Stevens
Jason and Jeremy
Grace West
and Valette, Jake and Charlie

Burn Me Deadly

chapter

ONE

The blonde dashed out of the darkness into the moon-light, right in front of me.

My horse, Lola, tried to bolt in surprise. I yanked on the reins and drew her up short. She reared and nearly threw me, but I held on and turned her away so she wouldn't trample the woman. We spun for a moment like a trick rider in a show, kicking up dust on the dry, deserted road. Then she found her footing; I pulled the reins tight and managed to regain control.

The cloud raised by our near accident momentarily obscured the woman. As it dissipated, I got a good look at her. She was young, with leaves and twigs tangled in her hair. She wore only an oversize man's jacket that hung past her hands and thighs. Scratches laced her slender legs and dirty, bloody feet. She stood with her eyes closed, face screwed up and arms covering her head as she anticipated the impact.

My voice was higher than normal when I demanded, "What the *hell*, lady? You could've killed us both!"

She opened her eyes and stared at my horse for a long, silent moment. Unscrunched, her moonlit features were very attractive. "Wow," she said softly, "that was close."

"No kidding," I snapped, still battling Lola's skittishness. The mare tossed her head and snorted, not convinced that all the danger had passed. If only I'd been as smart.

The woman's dirty face showed marks of recent tears. She grabbed Lola's bridle and said, "Please, sir, I have to get away from here." She looked over her shoulder toward the dark woods from which she'd emerged. "I'm in terrible danger."

"Uh-huh," I said dubiously. I followed her gaze and saw nothing, but unsnapped the catch on my scabbard just in case. Muscodia was still a pretty uncivilized country, and this road ran for miles through the dense, sparsely inhabited woods between Neceda and Tallega. At this time of night a lot of nefarious things could happen with no one the wiser, and I was too old and too experienced to fall for the frightened-damsel-as-bait bit. "How about you tell me what you're doing out here undressed like that?"

She met my skepticism with a well-practiced imitation of a hurt kitten: she dropped her chin, raised her eyes and pulled her mouth into a tiny pout. I think her lower lip even trembled. "I'm in *danger*, sir. Please, I'll explain everything later, but right now, I must get away from here." She turned her head and moonlight fell on the marks of big fingers around her neck. "Please. Look at me."

"Your husband get mad at you?"

"I don't have a husband. The men who did this did other things as well, but those things . . . don't show."

I scowled. I'd made an overnight run to a big manor house outside Tallega, delivering a sealed parchment and a bag of gold to some woman on behalf of a compromised nobleman. She'd taken the money, laughed at the note and slammed the door in my face. Her footmen made it abundantly clear I shouldn't wait for a reply. Now it was after midnight, and what I most wanted was to be home with Liz, in our nice soft bed with her nice soft body pressed against me. Also, every instinct screamed that *this* damsel was trouble the same way a hurricane was rain.

Still, I couldn't just leave her half-naked on a deserted road in the middle of the night. "All right, climb on," I said wearily. "I can take you into Neceda." Lola snorted with disapproval as I scooted back to make room for the girl on the saddle in front of me. She felt skinny and weak as she settled back, both her legs dangling off the left side, and clutched the saddle horn. I nudged the horse with my heels and we trotted off down the road.

The night was clear, and we stood out plainly on the road whenever the moon shone through the trees. I suppressed the urge to keep glancing behind us, or to spur Lola to a gallop. More than likely whoever had injured the girl was passed out drunk somewhere; if not, then I doubted they'd push for a confrontation. The kind of men who beat up women seldom had the stomach for a fair fight.

I said into my new companion's ear, "Okay, so what's going on? Who are you?"

"My name is Laura," she replied. "Laura Lesperitt. And you?"

"Eddie LaCrosse."

"Ah." She turned and looked back over her shoulder at me. The helpless maiden look had been replaced by something far more calculating. "From one of the minor noble families in Arentia, then. If it's the same LaCrosses."

She was right, but I saw no need to discuss it; I'd burned those drawbridges years ago. "You know a lot."

She nodded modestly. "A little *about* a lot."

When she offered no further information, I prompted, "And someone strangled you because . . . ?"

"Because I wouldn't tell them what they wanted to know."

"And what's that?"

Again she turned and looked up at me. The moon cast dark shadows that hid her eyes. Her smile was weak and sad. "Oh, Mr. LaCrosse, you think you can help me, don't you? You think you can ride up and save me, like a knight in a children's story. But these are bad, bad people. And if I tell you what they wanted to know, they might do the same thing to you to find it out."

"They might try," I said.

My confidence made no impression. She turned away, looked out at the passing trees and pushed the jacket sleeves up past her elbows. A livid, fresh injury that looked like the touch of a heated iron marred the insides of both arms down to her palms. The pain must've been awful. Her wrists were also rubbed raw and bloody from struggling against ropes or manacles. "They carried me to a small house in the woods three days ago. They took my clothes and kept me in chains. But I had to get away before they made me tell, so I picked the lock when they weren't around and fled. I stole this"—she indicated the jacket.—"from a farmhouse where everyone was sleeping."

"Why didn't you ask the farmer for help?"

Again the sad, wan smile. "They had children. I didn't want their blood on my head if I was caught again."

"But you don't mind mine."

She shrugged. "I'd prefer not. But I could live with it better."

"And so you're not going to tell me what this is about?"

She shook her head.

I took a deep breath, feeling like an idiot in advance for what I was about to say. "Look, *I'm* not some farmer. I'm a freelance sword jockey with an awful lot of hilt time behind me; maybe I *can* help."

Again her eyes rose to meet mine with slow, dramatic amusement. "A 'freelance sword jockey,' " she repeated. "So what does that entail? Saving damsels in distress for a fee?"

"Ideally, yeah. But since I'm my own boss, sometimes it's just because I feel like it."

"And you feel like saving me," she said. It wasn't a question.

"I don't know about 'saving' you, but I *am* offering to keep people from beating on you any more tonight. What you tell me after that is up to you."

Something changed in her face, and for a moment she looked ancient, with despair deeper than any I'd ever seen. And I'd seen a lot of despair. "The only way you can help me tonight," she said with slow, deliberate words, "is to get me to Neceda alive. Nothing else will truly help me."

We rode in silence for a bit. The trees began to thin out, and just ahead awaited the edge of the forest. Past it the road descended and snaked across miles of open prairie, as vivid in the moonlight as it might be on an overcast day. Scattered across the plain were small camps of travelers, a few with fires still lit.

In the far distance glowed the lamps of Neceda, and just beyond that sparkled the Gusay River. The waxing, nearly full moon lit the vista in shades of blue and white.

When she saw the distant town she sat up straight and tightly grasped my arm. "We may make it," she said softly.

"We'll make it," I said with certainty.

I was tense and alert and experienced in just about every sort of attack. So when the blow struck the back of my head, damn near hard enough to knock my beard from my face, I was so surprised it took me a moment to realize I was falling from my saddle onto the road. I'd heard no one approach, either on foot or horseback. These guys were *good*.

I landed awkwardly, too stunned to react but not completely unconscious. Sparks danced around the edges of my vision. My body pinned my sword to the ground; the hilt dug painfully into my side. I reached for it, but my limbs would not respond with any speed.

The dust from our pursuers drifted over me. Above the roar of blood and pain in my head, I heard Laura scream. We were too far for any of those camped on the prairie to come to our aid, even if they were so inclined.

A horse stopped beside me, and someone dismounted almost in my face. Expensive black boots, decorated with a silver dragon design that sparkled in the moonlight, hit the ground. Above them a stern, annoyed voice said, "Shut her the hell up. You can make her scream all you want back at the house, at least until she tells us where it is." Laura's screams were suddenly muffled, as if by a gag or a big hand.

"What about this guy?" another voice asked.

"Bring him along, too," dragon boots said. "We don't know what she told him. Oh, hell, he's waking up."

One of the boots rose out of my field of vision and came down hard on the side of my head.

I awoke, sort of.

My whole skull was numb. My fingers tingled, and when I tried to wriggle them I found my wrists were bound tightly behind my back. I tried to move any other body part, but nothing cooperated.

I lay facedown on a rough wooden floor. A fire lit the room, and I felt its heat from my left. Over its homey smell, I caught the tang of blood and the odor of scorched meat. Or flesh. The air hung with the echo of the sound that had awakened me: a woman's scream.

"Uh-oh," a voice said. "I, uh . . . I think she's dead."

"You *killed* her?" another voice demanded. I recognized it as the one associated with the dragon boots.

"No, I didn't kill her," the first voice said with professional annoyance. "I *do* know how to do this, you know. But look how burned she is."

"From *your* irons."

"*No*," the torturer insisted. "I didn't do this. Not on her arms and hands."

"How do you know?"

"Because I'm a professional. I have a *style*. See here on her tits? And here? I made these; they're very specific, they have a pattern and everything. These others are . . . arbitrary."

"What the hell does that mean?" a third male voice demanded.

"I'm so tired of you and your damn big words, like you're some kind of wizard or something."

"It means I didn't make those other burns," the torturer sighed.

A moment of silence passed. Again I tried to move, but I was still too foggy. It took every ounce of strength not to fade back into that nice padded darkness.

"No, that's not what it means," dragon boots said, his voice cold with fury. "It means she *moved* them. Sometime between her escape and the time we caught her, she hid them somewhere else. *That's* how she got burned."

"Where?" the clueless third man asked.

"How the hell do I know?" dragon boots exploded. He slammed his hand on a table I couldn't see. Rattling metal told me it held the interrogator's special tools. "We didn't know where she hid them in the first place, so how could we know where they are now?"

"The boss won't be happy," the third man said.

"Let me worry about him," dragon boots snapped.

"What about her boyfriend?" the torturer asked, and nudged me in the side with his foot.

Hands grabbed my hair and bent my neck painfully back so they could look at my face. I played dead, which wasn't hard. "This guy? You saw what he had in his saddlebags. He's just some dumb-ass in the wrong place at the wrong time."

"I could still find out what he knows," the torturer said. His eagerness really did scare me.

"He wouldn't last five minutes in this shape. No, we'll dump them both. Have to start from scratch. We know she hid them around here somewhere, so we'll just keep looking the old-fashioned way."

He released my hair, and my head thumped hard against the floor. That was all it took; I dove back into quiet, peaceful nothing.

WHEN I woke up again, I was bathed in moonlight.

The clear sky above was alive with stars, all twinkling happily at me. I blinked, waited for the dizziness generated by that movement to pass, and then blinked again.

I lay on my back on the ground. I was untied, my arms and legs thrown wide like I wanted to embrace the night. A rock dug painfully into my behind, but I lacked the energy to move away from it. With tremendous concentration I turned my head to the right.

Laura Lesperitt lay beside me. Most of her front teeth, one eye and half an ear were gone. She was naked, and her upper torso was a mass of poker burns, cuts and bruises. I saw what the torturer meant: his points of contact were small and precise, but something else had burned the insides of her arms from wrist to elbow. The scabbing told me she'd been alive when most of it happened, but the milky stare of her remaining eye said she was past the agony now. Insects had already collected around the injuries, and a shadowy canine form slipped through the darkness beyond her: a wolf or coyote, cautiously approaching a free meal.

I tried to rise. I managed a feeble finger-wiggle.

We lay in a gully or a dry creek bed, where the light only reached us because the moon was straight overhead. The sides of the ravine rose sharply and seemed to my befuddled brain as if they might snap closed over us, trapping us in darkness like those fly-catching plants.

Suddenly a shadow blocked the moon. A shape in the air above me grew larger and made a high, keening sound. I knew some birds of prey hunted at night, and I recalled childhood stories of giant owls that would swoop down and snatch misbehaving brats from their beds. I'd never seen a bird large enough to lift a human being, but then again, this night seemed to be all about bad surprises.

Then my brain cleared enough for me to comprehend what I was actually seeing, and I used every last bit of available energy to roll twice, just before my horse, Lola, crashed down onto the spot I'd occupied. Her equine screech of terror ended with the sharp, wet sound of impact. Big globs of something splattered over me.

Three men stood silhouetted in the moonlight on the edge of the cliff. Dust glittered in the air from where they'd driven Lola over the edge. I lay very still; did they realize she had missed me?

I heard their murmurs without catching any words. Then they turned and walked away, apparently convinced I was as dead as my horse, and the girl. Boy, were they in for a surprise, I thought grimly. Especially that bastard with the dragon boots. All I needed was time to catch my breath.

Then I coughed, tasted blood and got a fresh jolt of agony from my side. I realized the girl and I had *also* been tossed off that cliff. I tried to rise, knowing if I stayed put I'd be dead by morning. But just breathing exhausted me, and before I knew it the night wrapped me up and again took away the pain. If this was death, I wouldn't protest.

I shimmied back into the world. That's really how it felt, like different parts of me were yanked into consciousness and then shaken to make sure they were awake. It's not the best way to wake up, and it definitely affects your temper.

The air around me was warm and scented with medicinal incense. I lay flat on my stomach, one eye buried in the pillow, the other showing me a flat expanse of white wall. I took a deep breath, harder to do than it should have been, and said, "Anybody there?" My voice sounded thin and weak.

A blurry head-shaped mass appeared in front of me, at an odd angle because of my own position. "Back with us, then?" a woman's voice asked.

I blinked a couple of times, and her face resolved. She had gray hair and kindly eyes that belied her no-nonsense tone. She wore flowing robes and at her throat hung the crescent symbol marking her as a moon priestess, a religious sect that flourished in this part of the world. "I'm Donna Bennings. You're in the moon goddess hospital, just outside Neceda. Can you understand me, Mr. LaCrosse?"

"Yeah," I said, mostly into the drool-damp spot on my pillow.

"Can you repeat it back to me?" she asked.

"It back to me," I repeated. I began to roll onto my back, and she moved to help, cradling my head. The maneuver exhausted me, and I closed my eyes. My skull was three times too large, and a throbbing mass clung to the back of it. My chest felt too small for my lungs. "Okay, that's enough work for one day," I said.

"Do you *ever* put in a full day's work?" a familiar voice asked. Like mine, it sounded weak and tired.

I turned my gigantic cranium enough to see Liz Dumont seated beside me, bent forward with her elbows on the edge of the bed. She wore a tight tunic blouse and men's-style trousers with high boots. Her short red hair was matted and strands fell into her equally red eyes. The harsh light from the window highlighted the crow's-feet and smile lines on her face. She needed a bath, a change of clothes and some serious rest. I thought she was the most beautiful sight in the world. "Did you go out in public like that?" I asked.

"You're no picnic yourself." Her hand found mine in the tangle of blankets. "And watching you sleep is just as exciting as it sounds."

Liz was, for lack of a better term, my girlfriend. It seemed an odd word for a relationship between two people our age, but no other one applied. She was a freelance courier, moving everything from documents to livestock as needed. Two years ago she'd come to Angelina's tavern to deliver something to me, and I hadn't let her out of my sight since. Besides being beautiful, intelligent, tough and inexplicably smitten with me, she was the only other person in the world whose judgment I consistently trusted.

"Now *you* can get some sleep, too," Bennings said to Liz. The priestess lifted my eyelids higher than I expected. "Hm. Well, you seem to truly be on the mend. We've been giving you some elixirs and doing a few simple noninvasive spells for your recovery. But you'll be feeling that head for a while, I imagine."

"Better than not feeling it," I said.

"Yes. I'll leave you two alone to catch up on things, and check back later."

After she left, I looked around the room. The moon goddess hospital was well-known, if mysterious, to most of Neceda's population. It had been here for three generations, training apprentices as well as caring for the injured. The knot of small buildings was constructed over hot springs, and their heat could be channeled into the structures to keep the rooms at reasonably constant temperatures. The walls inside and out were whitewashed, while the door bore the universal red-pentagram symbol of the place's purpose. It could accommodate about twenty patients, two to a room if necessary. A fence surrounded the compound, crucial since a constantly rotating population of young females lived within it.

The priestesses, called "Mother" once they reached a certain rank, and their trainees were skilled in herbal therapy and pain management. Neceda, a wide-open river town, appreciated this service even if officially King Archibald frowned on the order, whose hidden rites were the source of many scandalous rumors.

I knew of the place by reputation, but luckily had never needed its services before now. Guess my luck had changed.

I turned to Liz. "How long have I been out?"

"A week."

"A *week*?"

She tenderly brushed a stray lock of hair from my eyes. "They brought you in the morning after you left for Tallega. At first they told me you were dead. They kept you on sleep herbs for the first four days. You were pretty much written off, and they didn't see any need for you to suffer. Then when you *didn't* die, they decided to see if you'd come out of it. I told them a blow to your head was the least likely way to kill you, since it couldn't hit anything vital."

I grinned. "You're a bitch when you don't sleep."

"Then scoot over," she said, and without waiting climbed onto the narrow bed with me. I put my arm under her neck, and she draped one leg over mine. I winced as the weight came down on my injured side. "Ow," I gasped.

"Oops, sorry," she said as she adjusted. "Is that better?"

"Perfect," I said, and meant it.

She rested her hand on my chest, a possessive gesture that made me glad to be possessed. I pulled her as close as my weakened condition allowed and kissed the top of her head. She was asleep within five minutes.

I lay awake and stared at the blank white wall. A week had passed, plenty of time for the trail to grow cold. But however long it took, I knew I had a date with three certain gentlemen, one of whom had dragons on his boots. Until I found them, that final image of what they'd done to Laura Lesperitt would be the first thing I saw in my mind each day.

★   ★   ★

I perfected the skill of playing dead and found out a lot. People always talk freely around the unconscious.

I learned from the gossipy apprentices who checked on me at night that a farmer had discovered me at the bottom of a ravine beside the corpse of a girl and a horse's carcass. The farmer threw me and the girl in his wagon and brought us into town; he didn't even realize I was still alive. He did not leave his name, and had not been back to check on me. Understandable, if he thought he was just dropping off two anonymous dead bodies.

Likewise, no one had come to claim the girl's remains. The hospital staff did not even know her name.

These teenage apprentices found all this very mysterious and sexy. Their speculation about me and my occupation ("He's a sword jockey, you know; you don't get to be one unless you're really good with women. . . .") made it a challenge to keep the smile off my allegedly sleeping face. I had a hard time picturing tough, matronly Mother Bennings ever being one of these giggly girls.

Although my rescuer was a no-show, I learned that someone else *had* stopped in to check on me. My second conscious morning I overheard Bennings tell Liz about "that man" who had been around to ask about me again. They stepped outside to discuss it in the hall, but since they left the door open, I still heard everything. My first thought was of the man with dragon boots, but this didn't sound like him.

"Did he leave a name this time?" Liz asked.

"No, he just asked if Mr. LaCrosse was going to be okay. I was with a patient and couldn't talk to him, but the girl who did said he seemed kind of squirrelly. Sound like anyone your friend might know?"

"Sounds like *most* of the people he might know," Liz said wryly. "You said he was an older man?"

"That's what the girls said. I told them to come get me if he shows up again, even if I'm with someone."

If Liz replied, I didn't hear it. Concentrating so hard made my head hurt, so I drifted back to sleep.

On the third morning Liz touched my hand and, when I opened my eyes, said, "You've got a visitor."

She stepped aside, and a wide-shouldered man with heavy eyebrows moved closer. He looked me over, then nodded at the bandages wound tight to my skull. "I've seen better heads on cabbage."

"Every time you look in the mirror," I said.

Gary Bunson managed a smile. It was not an expression his features accepted willingly. He was the local head magistrate, a king's agent content to let Neceda's vices run rampant as long as no one got hurt and he got his cut. He was younger than me, but his ravaged complexion and gray-streaked hair made him look several years older, and his uniform always seemed too large, as if he were gradually wasting away inside it. He could be as vicious as a snapping turtle, but preferred the tortoise approach: slow, steady and willing to withdraw into his shell if things got sticky. He said, "I would've hoped that a good blow to the head would've made you funnier."

"We can try a blow to *your* head next time." I slid up into something like a seated position. "So what happened to me?"

"I was hoping you could tell me. The fellow who brought you in said he found you out in the Black River Hills, but he left town before we could get any more details, including his name. What do you remember?"

"I was riding from Tallega to Neceda when somebody slipped up behind me and whacked me on the back of the head. Next thing I knew, I woke up here."

He nodded. "And who was the girl?"

I don't know why, but I decided to play dumb. "Girl?"

"The dead girl that was brought in with you. She'd been beaten up pretty badly. Or pretty well, depending on whose side you're on. The gals here told me when they looked her over that at least three of her injuries could've been the fatal one."

I shook my head slightly. "Not a clue."

"It's not the first time he's been coldcocked," Liz offered. "They said those things add up, and he might have some memory loss."

"Hm. The convenient kind, I suspect," Gary said. "But there's no rush. If it's bandits, they'll do it again to somebody else and we'll hear about it. If it's personal, *you* will. If you think of anything you want to add, let me know."

"That's your whole investigation?" I said wryly.

He shrugged. "No point in leveling my lance if there's no one to joust with. Give me a name or a description, I'll get on it. Otherwise . . ." He shrugged.

Gary left, and I watched out the door until he was far down the hallway. He stopped and chatted with a pair of apprentices in their striped robes, and left them giggling. When he finally turned the corner and was out of sight, Liz sat on the edge of the bed and took my hand. "Want to tell *me* about the girl?" she asked quietly, her face neutral.

"I picked her up on the road. She'd been beaten up and

needed a ride into town. I thought she'd been smacked around by some drunken husband or father. Turned out I was wrong."

"Did you get her name?"

"Laura Lesperitt." I looked up and managed a smile. "And that's *all* I got from her."

Liz's eyes narrowed playfully. "Well, let that be a lesson to you about seeing other women behind my back, Eddie LaCrosse." Then she kissed me.

THE next day I left the hospital. My ribs had pretty much healed, and the huge bandage around my head had diminished to a single circlet mainly protecting the thick scab under my hair. Mother Bennings said it could go, too, whenever I felt like it. My head still hurt and my side ached, but I could rest at home just as well. Besides, those blank white walls were starting to get to me.

My belongings, including my Jackblade KG-model sword, were returned to me when we checked out. So the guy with the dragon boots hadn't kept it; he meant for my death to look like an accident, as if I'd simply ridden off the cliff in the darkness. I checked it over, including the stiletto hidden in the hilt, but it was undamaged and had not been sabotaged. I did not buckle the scabbard around my waist; it had done me no good at all the last time I'd worn it.

Down the hill from the hospital squatted Neceda, happily going along without me. It was a small village on the Gusay River, a crossroads town where people stopped on their way to and from other places. The town's actual population was small, but at any given moment hundreds of strangers roamed its streets, drank in its taverns, fornicated in its whorehouses or languished in its jail. And for now and the foreseeable future, it was home. The people who wanted my services appreciated the fact that my office wasn't in a big, gossipy city where their friends or enemies might spot them talking to me.

Liz may have looked slender and shapely—which she was—but she was also ox strong, and came awfully close to carrying me a few times as I hobbled out to her waiting wagon. I was stiff, thick with too much rest and blinded by the fresh sunlight. Every bump in the road sent jolts through me, so she kept us at a crawl.

I scanned people's feet as we rode through town, especially those of men lounging against walls, standing in doorways or doing any of the other things people do when they're trying to fake being casual. I saw no dragon boots. One guy caught me checking out his feet and glared at me, then took in the bandage around my head. His expression changed to one of annoyance mixed with pity.

As the wagon rolled through town, I glanced down one of the side streets and managed a weak double take. A group of men and women unloaded furniture and other items from three overstuffed wagons. Two things were odd about this: the building they were moving all this into had been a popular whorehouse called the Lizard's Kiss before I'd been hurt, and the people all wore matching red head scarves. They also had the same general physical look: squat and thick bodied, with coarse features set in what looked, at this distance, like a perpetual scowl.

"What's all that?" I asked Liz.

"What?" she said, looking around.

"Back at the Lizard's Kiss. Looked like they were redecorating."

"Oh. That closed down. Joan, the owner, sent the girls packing and lit out for somewhere else."

"Why?" It seemed odd because Joan had been thoroughly well connected to the powers that be in Neceda, something that took a while to establish and was not lightly thrown away.

Liz shrugged. "Don't know. Might ask Gary."

"Yeah," I said. A whorehouse shutting down wasn't *that* unusual, but something about those red-scarved people stuck in my mind. Nothing shook immediately loose, so I pushed it aside for more immediate concerns. "Go by the tavern."

"What?" Liz said.

"The tavern. I want to check in at my office."

She did as I asked. Even though it was not yet noon, a half-dozen horses were tied on the street outside Angelina's establishment. The building was low and broad in the front, with a second-story attic in the back built directly over the kitchen. The main doors opened as we stopped, and a tall man with a scarred face wobbled out, squinting into the light. He froze when he saw us, his expression a mix of shame and surprise. I had no idea who he was, and after a moment his red-rimmed eyes adjusted and he realized he didn't know me, either. He stumbled off with a mumbled apology, his conscience apparently so guilty over something that even being blind drunk in the middle of the day couldn't quiet it. I checked his boots; dragon free.

"Just wait here; I'll go get her," Liz said.

"Uh-uh," I said, and swung one heavy leg over the side of the wagon. "I'll never live it down if I don't walk in with my chin high."

"That's silly."

"So is calling something a 'sharp curve,' but we still do it."

We walked in with Liz's arm around my waist, surreptitiously supporting me. Angelina came out from behind the counter and, without a word, put her arms around both our necks. It hurt when she squeezed, but I said nothing. My hand covered Liz's on Angelina's back. If I had a family anymore, these two women were it: lover/partner and sister/confessor.

Angelina pulled away and scowled at me. "Hit him in the head, huh?"

"No doubt there's a mace with a serious dent in it some-where," Liz said.

Angelina shook her head. She was middle-aged but still hand-some, with a form that in its day must've inspired plenty of young men to acts of passion or violence. She was well educated, road smart and honest, and could've done much better for her-self than owning a tavern in Neceda. But I never asked any ques-tions, and she never offered any hints about who or what she was hiding from.

Angelina returned to her spot behind the bar and said, "Cal-lie will be sorry she missed you."

Callie was Angelina's favorite barmaid, a sweet teenage girl with the figure of a goddess and the smarts of a horseshoe. "Where is she?" Liz asked.

"She fell in love. Ran off with some traveling conjurer. I fig-ure she'll be back any day now . . ."—she patted her stomach—". . . hopefully without a surprise in the works."

"Teenage girls never know what's good for them," I agreed as I lowered myself onto a stool at the bar. Liz took the one be-side me. The big square room had booths along the walls, four wobbly tables and a clear space for musicians and dancing. The wall behind the bar hid the kitchen, although the heat and odor of whatever was cooking always filled the place. There were no windows, so except for the table lamps it stayed perpetually dark, which suited the clientele.

"There's folks asking about you," Angelina said as she put two fresh tankards in front of us.

"Clients?" I asked.

"I'm afraid not, Mr. LaCrosse," a new voice said.

I turned as much as my stiff body allowed. A tall, well-groomed man stood beside me. He wore a cloak, and the tunic beneath it bore the royal seal of Muscodia. The insignia told me he was a captain, an awfully high rank for one so young: he couldn't have been more than twenty. His cleanliness told me he took himself and his position very seriously. His eyes told me I should, too.

The well-groomed young man said, "Daniel Argoset, King's Special Office of Domestic Security." He offered his hand, and I shook it. His grip was firm.

"Does your father know you stole his uniform?" I asked; I'd seen stable boys who looked older.

His smile was the patient expression of someone really tired of hearing jokes like that. "I'd like to ask you some questions about the incident on the Tallega road. Is there somewhere private we can talk?"

Another young uniformed soldier appeared at his elbow. This one was huge, with shoulders that strained the sash marking him as a mere private. He had the dull arrogance of someone used to applying force to any problem, and did not introduce himself.

Behind them, Gary Bunson hunkered down guiltily in a booth. So that's how they found me. The man had a spine of wet pasta.

"My office is upstairs," I said. "I haven't been there in a week, so I can't say what shape it's in, but you're welcome to come up."

"I straightened it up a little," Angelina said. "You're a tenant, after all. It reflects on the whole establishment." Her face was absolutely straight when she said this, but it was her way of assuring me there was nothing incriminating lying around.

I gestured toward the stairs. "After you, then, gentlemen. I'm still awfully slow at climbing things."

Argoset headed up the steps first; I checked for dragons on his boots, but there were none. I was pretty sure I'd know the guy's voice again when I heard it, but it never hurt to be overly cautious. Despite my warning, his muscle-bound companion dropped back to bring up the rear. He was about as subtle as a punch to the nose.

The stairs seemed to have grown steeper and higher since I'd been hurt, and without Liz behind me I would've tumbled backward down them quite ungracefully. I opened my office door and stepped aside to allow Liz, Argoset and Muscles to precede me, which gave my head time to stop swimming. The slab of beef balked, so I went in ahead of him. He followed, closed the door once we were all inside and then stood before it, arms crossed.

My office, in the attic over the kitchen, had once been used by workingwomen for functions not that morally dissimilar to my own. I'd put in a divider wall and another door to give me both a waiting room and a private inner office. I kept the front door unlocked, with a bench against one wall in case anyone decided they needed to wait. The dust on the bench was undisturbed, which said a lot about the recent demand for my services.

I unlocked the inner office, where I had a desk, two guest

chairs, a sword cabinet and a hidden bottle of rum. Argoset took all this in with a slow, methodical sweep of his eyes. I went behind my desk and gratefully fell into my chair. Liz sat on the edge of the desk to my right, and Argoset took one of the guest seats. He sat upright, his spine and shoulders straight enough to draw lines with. Muscles closed the inner door and again stood with his back to it. If he'd stared at me any harder, his eyes would've shot across the room.

"Would anyone like a drink?" I said as I took the bottle from a drawer. "I haven't had anything in a week that wasn't flavored like green tea."

Argoset shook his head. I looked questioningly at Muscles. He wrinkled his nose distastefully, although I wasn't sure if it was because of me, the booze or the surroundings. I decided to hold off on that drink for myself as well.

Argoset took out a small wooden tablet with vellum sheets clipped to it. He lifted the first one and read, " 'Edward LaCrosse. Nationality unknown, age unknown, no apparent family.' " He cut his eyes at Liz, but she said nothing. " 'Current occupation personal soldiery, investigations into domestic indiscretions and so forth.' I believe the slang term is 'sword jockey,' am I right?"

"When you call me that, smile."

Argoset did not smile. "Where did you come from before you landed in Neceda?"

That story would take longer than Argoset could imagine. The tale of how a teenage heir to minor nobility lost the girl he loved and abandoned his fortune and title to become first an anonymous soldier, then a vicious mercenary and finally a middle-aged guy who offered his skills to private citizens would sound as ludi-

34

crous to him as it sometimes did to me. So I merely shrugged and said, "Around."

"And how old are you?"

"Older than anyone else in the room."

He looked steadily at me. Completely at odds with his youth, he had the cold, vaguely reptilian gaze of the intrinsically dangerous. "Mr. LaCrosse, why were you on the road to Tallega the night you were attacked? And spare me the wit, if you can."

"I was doing an errand for a client."

"Who was the client?"

I shook my head. The motion made my eyes cross a little. "That's confidential. I'm sure you understand."

"This is an official investigation of a murder."

"And an *attempted* murder," Liz put in.

"Yes," Argoset agreed. "It was only luck that kept it from being a double homicide. We're not even sure if you, or the young lady, were the intended victim."

"Lots of people wouldn't mind dropping me off a cliff," I agreed. "But I'm pretty sure it was her."

"You told Magistrate Bunson that you had no memory of the girl."

He'd have to work harder than that to catch me out. "I didn't then. Now I do. Lots of things are coming back to me."

He closed the pad and looked at me. "I imagine, then, given your occupation, that you plan to conduct your own investigation based on some idea of personal honor and revenge."

"Me? Nah. I plan on sleeping off this headache, which the priestess up the hill says may take six months even with whatever spells she does. Otherwise, I've got nothing on my schedule."

Argoset tapped the tablet thoughtfully against his chin. "You really don't seem like that kind of person."

"He is," Liz assured him. "I've seen swatting a fly exhaust him."

Argoset put the tablet back in his pocket. "So you're content to leave the investigation up to the people the king assigns to do this sort of thing?"

I shrugged. "It's your job, not mine. I don't have a client."

He nodded again. His eerie, steady quality made me nervous, especially since it emanated from such a boyish face. I could imagine what it would do to someone who really did have a guilty conscience. Finally he said, "I don't believe you, Mr. LaCrosse, but I *do* believe that your injuries will slow you down considerably and keep you from getting in my way. So I'll leave you with this. A crime has been committed, and as far as we know, you are one of the victims. It wouldn't require much traveling to look at things from the other side and see you as a suspect. Do you understand?"

I nodded, very slightly this time.

A slow, knowing smile spread across his face. It was not reassuring. "Right." Argoset stood, nodded respectfully to Liz and left. Muscles fell in behind him. Liz followed, watched them descend the stairs, then closed the outer door behind them. She crossed her arms and said, "That was all kinds of strange, wasn't it?"

I sighed and sagged in my chair. Even sitting up straight was exhausting. "Yeah. A sword jockey and some farm girl get ambushed, and suddenly the king's security forces are all over the place."

"What do you think it means?"

Before I could answer there was a soft, furtive knock at the door. Liz palmed a knife from her belt and stood flat against the wall beside it. "Yeah?" she said.

"It's me," Gary Bunson said. Liz let him in. "Did you talk to Argoset?" he asked at once.

"And his charming gorilla," Liz said.

"Of course we talked to him," I said, annoyed. "After you told him all about us, how could we not? Thanks for being such a pal."

Bunson waved his hands in front of his face as if warding off bees. "Hey, Eddie, we're friends, but when it comes down to a choice of asses to watch, my own comes first. I don't know whose toes you stepped on, but this has to be serious. I didn't think King Archibald even knew Neceda existed, and I'd just as soon he forgets that it does. So you better lay low for a while."

"I'm getting that advice a lot."

"I'm serious, Eddie. Argoset is the golden boy up in Sevlow, and he has the king's ear. He whispers, and people go away permanently. And he didn't look happy when he came down-stairs." He looked from me to Liz and back, trying to impress us with his urgency.

"So why *is* he interested in this?" Liz asked.

Bunson shook his head. "I don't know, and I don't *want* to know. We all have good things going here in Neceda. I don't want to see any of us not around to enjoy them anymore."

"Well, I'm too tired to do much about it right now," I said honestly. "I'm going home and back to bed."

Bunson looked at Liz. "You make sure of that?"

She smiled. "Absolutely."

★ ★ ★

LIZ lay asleep beside me, naked, one leg draped over mine. A single candle on the table lit her skin in flickering waves of amber. Distant music from Angelina's tavern mingled with the street sounds into a rolling, tinkling buzz. Inside we were warm, safe and sated.

Liz shifted a little, and clutched me tighter. I grunted as my ribs protested, but Liz didn't wake and I wasn't going to disturb her. Nothing like nearly dying to make you appreciate things like sex with your girlfriend. I was too weak to participate much in the physical part of our reunion, but my enjoyment seemed reward enough for her. If the situation was reversed I'd feel the same way, so I accepted it. Luxuriated in it, in fact. It was a feeling I never expected to have in my life, and I tried very hard not to second-guess it.

Our place was on the second floor of a rooming house three buildings down from the tavern. The old lady who owned the building dealt in small-time tariff-free liquor on the side, which everyone knew about but no one minded; Neceda collected shady entrepreneurs like manure drew flies. It meant being awakened by the occasional loud confrontation in the middle of the night and stepping over fresh bloodstains on the stairs in the morning, but the rent was cheap and the rooms were cool in the summer and warm in the winter.

Liz yawned and raised up on one elbow. She traced a finger down the old sword scar on my chest and said, "You're not going to let it go, are you?"

"You know I'm not," I said.

"Another man in your position might count himself lucky and just put it behind him. It really had nothing to do with you; you just stumbled over it and got caught in it."

"That makes it my problem."

She firmly grabbed my beard and turned my chin so I had to look her in the eye. "*Why*, Eddie?"

What could I tell her? The truth was that too many women in my life had died when I should've protected them. When I was sixteen it had been Janet, sister of my best friend, raped and killed while I was forced to watch. Years later it had been Liz's twin sister, Cathy, a story I still kept from her. There had been dark Jenny, on the island of Grand Bruan. And now it was Laura Lesperitt.

But what I *did* tell Liz was also the truth. "A sword jockey who lets someone riding with him get killed, and then doesn't do anything about it, won't get much work after a while."

"Is that the real reason?"

I grinned. "It's *a* real reason."

She shook my chin with playful annoyance. "Okay, so what's our first move?"

"Hm. Well, I want to see where that farmer found me. Maybe there's a clue left lying around. That house where they took us to torture the girl can't be too far away."

"It's been over a week. By now they must know you're not dead."

"I know. But I have to start somewhere."

"What can I do to help?"

"Other than what you just did?"

She grinned. "That helped us both."

"If you feel like it, you could try to find out who else Argoset talks to, and what he's really doing here. He's looking into something, all right, but it's not me. And if he wanted to frame me for the girl's death, he would've done it already. He just wanted to scare me out of the way."

She nodded. "I'll ask around."

"But watch yourself. This isn't a simple thing."

"I know. That's why you need help with it."

I turned and looked at her. The soft candlelight smoothed out her lines and made her look much younger: as young, in fact, as my memories of her twin sister, Cathy, over fifteen years ago. Soon I'd have to tell Liz that story, because it hung over us like a sword only one of us could see.

But not at that moment. At the moment I only had to kiss her again.

THREE

I t grew easier to move around the more I did it, so it made sense to keep doing it. The next day I went down to the livery stable to arrange for another horse. Liz had her office there, just as mine was above the tavern. Her delivery business was a one-wagon, one-woman operation, but she'd been so successful lately she'd considered hiring an additional person. I did not have that problem.

Before she left that morning, she kissed me while she thought I was still sleeping. Through my eyelashes I watched her stand in the doorway, her figure silhouetted against the gray dawn sky beyond. How had I landed a woman so beautiful? She was slender, with hips just wide enough she'd never be mistaken for a man and breasts that rose deliciously against the front of whatever she wore. She had a lithe way of moving, a natural grace that turned heads wherever she went. I felt a little tug somewhere inside, the way I used to when we first met. Back then it was because I was afraid something might take her away; now I feared something might do the same to me. Mortality is grand.

She descended the rickety steps attached to the outside of the building. I heard one of the town's cats meow as Liz no doubt stopped to pet it. Then she was gone. I rested a little longer, then made myself get out of bed, clean up and face the day. I'd given the world a week and a half to arrange its nefarious plots against me, and now it was time for me to get to work untangling them. I no longer needed the bandage on my head, and could take a deep breath without pain. My hands, when I held them in front of me, remained steady.

After I dressed, I strapped on a sword for the first time since the ambush. I chose the Shadow Slasher III, a little light for my normal tastes, but since I wasn't up to full strength, it seemed like a good choice. I felt a little nudge as the hilt tapped the bruise my Jackblade had left when I fell on it. For some reason this reactivated the anger that had lain dormant since my injury, and a surge of righteous energy shot through me. I burst out the door and down the stairs with the assurance that someone, eventually, was going to get their ass kicked.

"What the hell are you looking so damn happy about?" Mrs. Talbot said as I came around the corner of the building. Our landlady wore a shapeless dress too short for a woman her age, and her dull gray hair fell haphazardly around her plump, drink-veined face. She crouched on the edge of the porch and expertly sharpened a wicked-looking cleaver. "Did that whack on the head make you simple?"

"It just made me appreciate your beauty even more."

She laughed the way a cat spits out hair. "Yeah, you're simple now; that proves it." Then she pulled a leaf from a nearby bush and split it with the cleaver into two paper-thin mirror images. She nodded in satisfaction.

"I should pay you to sharpen my swords," I said, impressed.

"You can't afford me," she retorted, then went back inside. I headed for the livery stable.

I passed Ditch Street (actually Canal Street, but changed in common usage to more accurately reflect its character) and saw the former Lizard's Kiss now completely closed and abandoned. The windows on both floors were shuttered and boarded over, and the welcoming awnings removed. Nothing moved around it. Had I seen it wrong? Had the red-scarved workers been moving things out of the building instead of into it? No, I was certain I'd seen at least one large covered piece of furniture carried *inside* by the sullen-looking laborers. I stood gazing at it for a long time, until someone bumped into me and brought me back to the moment. Yeah, it was odd, but I had enough mysteries to wrangle.

The livery building was located in the middle of town, convenient to both land and river travelers. The stable had room for twelve horses, and the little corral out back could manage additional ones, or any other livestock that needed minding. The big arching sign over the main barn doors read *Pinster Beast Boarding*, and beneath it hung a painted shingle with a horse reclined in a canopied bed. The owner, Hank Pinster, found that incredibly funny and loved pointing it out to first-time customers.

At one corner of the building a smaller door led into a separate, independent office. The much more tasteful shingle over it said *Dumont Confidential Courier Service*. The wagon was gone, which meant Liz was off making a delivery. As Neceda was the only port for this section of Muscodia, lots of things were shipped through it, providing Liz with a steady living. Considering my iffy career, that was a good thing.

Hank met me at the stable door with a sad, rueful shake of his head. He wore heavy boots and a leather blacksmith's apron. Most blacksmiths wouldn't work in the same barn as the horses, but Hank had a way with the animals that kept them from panicking at the noise and burning smells. The ends of his long ragged hair were singed from stray sparks. "Helluva thing to happen to a good horse," he said ruefully. "Helluva thing." He clapped me hard on the shoulder. My ribs reminded me of their existence, and I winced. "Oh, sorry, Mr. LaCrosse. I thought you were well."

"I'm fine," I grunted. "The hospital told me my saddle and bridle and other stuff got dropped off down here."

"'Tack,' Mr. LaCrosse. It's called 'tack.' "

"Guess I'm not very tackful, then."

His expression didn't change. "Well. Yes, the fella who took you to the hospital brought that stuff here on his way out of town, trying to sell it. I told him you were a friend, so he just left it. I've got it stored away. C'mon in here."

I followed him past the stalls toward the little storage area at the back. The stable odor seemed especially strong after the hospital's herb-flavored aroma. Seven horses were currently in residence, including a magnificent midnight-black stallion and an equally expensive white gelding. All regarded me with the same superior loathing every horse except Lola always had for me. Hank was right; she *was* a good horse. I realized suddenly how much I'd miss her.

Hank turned and looked behind us, making sure we were alone. Then he led me into the very last stall, where a thick gray mare stood against the back wall. He closed the gate and mo-tioned me over to the horse. "This one ought to do you fine, Mr. LaCrosse," he said extra loud. "She was raised by a little girl and only ridden to school on bright spring days. Take your time and look her over." As he patted her cheek he leaned closer to me and said softly, "Somebody came by here asking about you."

"Official guy with a big sidekick?" I asked.

Hank shook his head. "No. That big black stud and the white gelding belong to *them*. This was an old man. He had white hair, and wore these weird padded gloves, kind of like the ones I use when I'm heating things in the fire. He seemed like he was either crazy or in a lot of pain."

"What did he want?"

"Wanted to know if you'd come down here to get a new horse yet."

"Are you serious?"

He nodded.

"When was this?"

"Yesterday."

So my mysterious hospital visitor knew I'd been discharged and that I was in the market for a new horse. He could only know that if he knew what happened to my old one. "Was it the same farmer who brought my stuff to you?"

"Nah, totally different fella. That one was little and fat look-ing. I don't remember his name, but I've seen him buying meat at the markets and such. And yes, before you ask, if I see him again I *will* get his name. But the old man . . ." He shivered a little at the memory. "He was just weird. Smelled bad, too, like rotten meat. Gave me the creeps. Upset the horses."

I nodded. "Did the fat little farmer mention where he found me?"

Hank shook his head. "All he said was that he found two corpses and a dead horse in the woods down some ravine. When I saw it was your saddle, I sent my boy Leon to tell Liz."

I nodded. "Thanks for watching out for me, Hank. And just so you know, that official fellow with the fancy horse might ask about me, too."

He frowned. "Why is the government interested in *you*?"

"I honestly don't know. I think it was just a wrong place, wrong time situation."

"Anything I shouldn't tell him?"

"No, I wouldn't want you to get in trouble. Don't lie to him, but don't give him any more information than you have to, okay? And," I added as I pressed some money into his hand, "let me know what he asks about."

"I'll tell him you're pure as the gutter snow."

"But I am," I said with a deadpan wink. Hank chuckled and went to get my saddle.

THE gray mare Hank loaned me for the day was a pale, contemptuous shadow of Lola, in both temperament and simple skill. Her trot was much slower, she fought every tug on the reins and when I pulled her to a stop she insisted on pacing in a tight circle for several moments before acquiescing, like a dog preparing for a nap. She wouldn't even stand still for me to mount her, so by the time we left the stable all my old prejudices against horses had returned.

A preoccupied man bumped into us as we emerged on the street, which made the mare snort and stamp. I yanked the reins tighter. The man, dressed in the grimy clothes of a miner, glared up at me. "Why don't you watch where I'm going?"

"Sorry," I said, and nodded at the horse. "She's a loaner."

"I'm not surprised; no other decent horse would be seen with this nag."

"No, I meant—" But he was already gone, muttering to himself and looking at the ground. I watched him until he disappeared in the crowd; he did nothing suspicious. Mud covered his boots, but they were the wrong style anyway.

I headed up the hill toward the moon goddess hospital. Mother Bennings met me in one of the consulting rooms. Her handsome face creased with concern. "Are you all right? Is there a problem?"

I shook my head. "Mending up nicely. I wanted to ask if the old guy with the gloves had been back."

"Actually, yes," Bennings said. "He came by yesterday, after you were released, and—" Suddenly she stopped, and a sly grin split her face. "I never told you about him."

I smiled. "No."

"You are a sneaky one," she chuckled. "And yes, he's been here again. I talked to him myself."

"Who is he?"

"He wouldn't give his name. But he was an odd gentleman. Seemed to be in some sort of chronic pain connected to his hands. I offered to take a look, but he wouldn't let me. He did say he was glad you were all right."

"Did he have an accent or anything?"

"Nothing obvious. So it's no one you know?"

I shook my head. "It doesn't sound like it."

"You should also know that a young Captain Argoset from

Sevlow asked about you as well. He was much more specific. Wanted to know where you were found, who brought you in, a whole lot of things. Unfortunately, or fortunately as the case may be, I didn't know. He seemed a bit put off by that."

"Yeah. We've met."

"Are you somebody important? Is that why he's here?"

I laughed. "I'm less important than just about anyone you know. I think the dead girl interests him a lot more than I do, only she's not around to answer any questions. What happened to her body, by the way?"

"We cremated it while you were still unconscious. No one claimed it, and it's the wrong time of year to keep corpses very long. That didn't make the captain very happy, either." She paused. "We gave her a full ritual to help her spirit through the veil. No one should have to make that trip alone."

I nodded. "Thanks. If anything else interesting happens, would you let me know?"

"Of course. And don't go out and do anything to reinjure yourself. Everyone here knows how badly you were hurt, so as long as you're walking around, I look like a great healer."

On my way out I paused at the main door. Beside it stood a large, long-necked vase covered in symbols of the moon goddess: three women, one a young girl, one a pregnant mother, the last old and stooped. The vase's practical function was to collect donations from people who could pay for their treatment, since most patients could not. And truthfully, neither could I. Yet I took one of the coins in my pocket and dropped it into the waiting mouth, wincing as it hit bottom with a hollow, metallic thud. Guess there hadn't been a lot of donations lately.

It wasn't payment for me, anyway: it was a token of appreciation for granting Laura Lesperitt her last moment of dignity. I was sure the moon goddess understood.

I went back through town and out the other end on the Tallega road where I'd met Laura. The horse had a bumpy, really uncomfortable gait that made my still-tender ribs ache with every step. I would be sure to demand a refund from Hank when I returned the beast.

It was a bright, clear day, and there was plenty of other traffic. I passed Angelina's tavern and nodded to her as she escorted a stumbling patron out into the sunlight. She waved as the man fell first to his knees, then onto his face in the dirt. People stepped over and around him without a second glance.

I checked each person I passed for dragon boots. It seemed unlikely, but it was a way to pass the time and resharpen my skills after my little vacation. Most of them were farmers or tradesmen, although a few wealthy travelers passed me as well. None had the footwear I sought.

I rode under the shadow of the big gallows oak and drifted in behind a three-cart caravan taking two wagonloads of corn to Tallega and points beyond. The teenage boy driving the empty third wagon, its contents no doubt sold that morning in Neceda, kept glancing suspiciously over his shoulder at me, wondering why I didn't just pass them. I simply smiled and nodded. No one was in a hurry, so despite the dry and fairly warm day, the dust stayed at a minimum, hovering in a thin, knee-high cloud.

Several travelers, still camped in the tall grass off the road, displayed tents and wares from every village within a ten-day ride. A ragged dog tied to a stake barked as we crept past, and my gray mare fought to flee across the prairie away from it. The little brother of the kid driving the empty wagon occasionally peeked at me from the bed. I made faces at him, which made him smile and duck shyly away. Their parents, ahead in the first wagon, were oblivious.

This wasn't necessarily the best approach to the problem at hand. I could've stayed in town and found out who else Argoset interrogated, a perfectly appropriate activity for a sword jockey trying to find his way into a mystery. But I'd been attacked in the woods, and moreover, a girl who'd expected me to help her had been killed there. Argoset's mystery might be in town, but mine started here, beneath these ancient, heavy-limbed trees.

I paused before entering the forest. I looked back and saw the river shimmering in the distance, its broad swath dark green and turgid. The Gusay wound in great coils through this part of the country, only growing straight and rapid when it neared the ocean across the border in Balatan. I counted four boats coming upstream, pulled by mules or horse teams onshore; three flatboats loaded with trade goods rode the central channel in the opposite direction.

I'd first come to Neceda on the Gusay, taking passage on a commercial boat with a dozen Wakle Dow slave girls in the care of the scariest matron I'd ever seen. There were other people on board, I suppose, but somehow all I could recall now were those young, flirty girls destined for a life of luxury and isolation. None were forced into the job; all signed contracts giving up every personal right in return for the lavish lifestyle they desired. I often wondered how it worked out for them.

I was coming here to meet Nightingale James, a con man with one of the more original scams going. Six feet tall and muscled like a work ox, James somehow managed to hang on to a high, girlish voice despite still having his full male package. He represented himself as a eunuch to wealthy old men with easily bored wives. Once ensconced in their households, he would seduce the wives, then blackmail them. He would also report to the husbands that the wives were cheating with some mysterious stranger, and offer to keep an eye on them—for an additional fee, of course.

Unfortunately, he was no man of action, and when the son of one of these wealthy old men caught him in the act with his mother, James found himself on the other end of the blackmail pike. He needed me to chase junior away, which turned out to be easy enough to do. I made a nice pile on the job, and also realized how ideal Neceda was to my business: small, isolated, yet a center of trade and commerce. People could find it easily, but few people noticed anyone else in it. I always meant to thank Nightingale for bringing me here, but I never saw him after that job. The last I heard he'd settled in Mauston, teaching music to actual eunuchs. There's irony for you.

The forest loomed ahead like a great wall of dense green, its supporting latticework of black wooden trunks and limbs occasionally visible through the leaves. A round gap marked the spot the road entered it, and beyond that it really did look like a tunnel, with shafts of sunlight poking through the leaves at irregular intervals.

I had no delusions that I'd find any physical clues left from the attack, like distinctive horseshoe tracks or boot marks. But if I could identify the spot the girl first ran out in front of me, I might be able to locate the farm where she'd stolen her jacket. From there, if I was lucky, I hoped to backtrack to the house she'd escaped from, and where the three men took us and tortured her to death. And if I was *very* lucky, those men would still be there, and it would be time for answers and a little payback.

But I wasn't after revenge. I knew its ultimate futility: I'd seen the results of revenge on a scale most people could barely imagine, and I had no desire to walk that path. I wanted justice. I needed to know that the men who had casually tortured Laura Lesperitt would never be able to hurt anyone again. I understood these human monsters—I'd been perilously close to it myself as a younger man—and knew that they'd only stop hurting people when they also stopped breathing. So I intended to cut off their air. And if I also cut off a few limbs as well, I could live with that.

I moved to the edge of the road and traveled much slower than everyone else as I looked for clues. The air beneath the forest canopy was noticeably cooler. I saw many small trails that emerged from the woods and joined the road. None of them looked well or recently traveled, though. They were game tracks, or simply the onetime passage of someone looking for firewood, meat or toilet privacy.

A youngster of about ten cut loose from the traffic and fell in beside me. A tied bundle of fresh herbs and leaves bounced on the rump of his . . . her? . . . saggy, tired horse. "You look like you lost something, mister. Need a hand?"

I really couldn't tell if this was a boy or girl. I nodded at the plants and asked, "You pick those or buy them in town?"

"Oh, I picked them. That's my job. Mama does the selling."

"Then I reckon you know these woods pretty well, don't you?"

"I know them on that side of the road like I do my own fingernails. Daddy won't let me cross the road into the Black River Hills, though. Says all the herbs and plants we need grow just fine on this side. Too many weird things happen over there."

Naturally, the side she/he couldn't visit was the side Laura had emerged from. "Weird how?"

She/he shook his/her head. Little wooden bug-shooing beads braided into his/her hair slapped her/his shoulders. "He won't say. Just that lots of people go in there and don't come out. And there's people who live in there who're . . ." His/her shoulders shivered. "Weird."

I nodded. "That's the word of the day. Tell me, did you ever see anybody with dragons on their boots poking around out here?"

"Dragons?"

"Yeah. Silver design on the back of the heel, maybe."

Again the beads slapped his/her shoulders. "Sorry. Guess I'm not much help after all. Want to buy some foxglove? Can't get any fresher unless you pick it yourself."

"No thanks, er . . . you."

She/he grinned mischievously. "You can't tell if I'm a boy or a girl, can you?"

"No," I said.

He/she laughed, nudged the horse and rejoined the traffic on the road. I shook my head and turned my attention back to the side of the road where the weird things were.

Suddenly I yanked the reins tight. The horse snorted and tossed her head in protest. I *knew* this was the spot. I saw no tangible trace, but the sun shone through the trees at the same angle as the moonlight that night and made identical shadow patterns. And there, behind the trunk of a huge oak tree that hid it from the road, was a trail wide enough for a rider. A mostly naked girl on foot could've used it easily.

It didn't mean it *was* the same trail, but it was a start. The way she'd been scratched up, she could've just bolted through the untracked forest. But it was all I had.

I took the path down the incline. It followed a natural route through the trees, but maintained essentially a southern direction. According to my knowledge of the Muscodian countryside, this would lead me into the Black River Hills, so called because of the narrow, unusually deep waterway that bisected them before joining up with the Gusay. In addition to spooky stories and tales of weirdness, these hills were perforated with caves, old mines and sundry other hiding places where someone could torture a girl in peace. But we'd been taken someplace with a wooden floor, so I sought an actual dwelling, not a hole in the rock.

I reached a fork in the trail. I paused and studied it. I had nothing at all on which to base a decision, so I pulled a coin from my pocket, flipped it and chose the path to the left. As I nudged the horse forward I glanced up and saw, to the right, a thin trail of smoke rising into the sky. Where there was a chimney there was a house. I considered tossing the duplicitous coin off into the undergrowth, but money, even deceitful money, was too scarce right now. I pocketed it and turned down the right-hand path.

I emerged at the top of a steep but not very tall rise that looked over a tiny clearing. Below stood a small, ramshackle house. Goats milled about in a pen, and a huge pile of firewood lay stacked beside a two-wheeled cart. A scrawny garden provided meager produce. A pair of small children ran around yelling in the front yard, and their high-pitched shrieks made my horse snort in annoyance.

I looked again at the big pile of wood, and the cart beside it. Laura had called the people who provided her stolen jacket "farmers." But it had been dark, she was in a hurry and it would be hard to farm in the middle of the forest. Might they have been woodcutters?

I headed down the slope. The two children, both under age five, froze when they saw me. Their clothes were a handmade mix of milled cloth and animal skin, and their hair was cut short. As with the herb collector, I couldn't say for sure whether they were boys, girls or one of each. Kids these days.

"Hi," I said. "Is your mom or dad around?"

"You don't know my daddy," the smaller one said.

"You're right," I agreed. "But I'd still like to talk to him."

"Are you from the government?" the other asked, in a higher voice that implied femininity. She had a hard time with the last word, and pronounced each syllable distinctly, as if well practiced.

"Me? Nah." I dismounted and crouched so we could talk at her eye level. "I live over in Neceda."

"Daddy says King Ar-chee-bald will try to take everything away from us," the little girl said.

I looked around at the shack they called home, the goats they used for dinner and milk and the wood they sold to get everything else. "I really wouldn't worry about it," I said.

"Well, I would," a woman's voice replied. It was deep and firm. "Now step away from my children."

A stout, broad-shouldered woman in a threadbare dress stood in the doorway holding a spear ready over one shoulder. It was the short kind used to hunt wild boar, and her bare feet were spread in a practiced throwing stance. I said, "Hi. I think we've got a misunderstanding in progress here."

"I'll skewer you if you breathe wrong. Misunderstand *that*?"

I raised my hands. "No, ma'am. I'd just like to ask you if you'd seen a friend of mine, though."

Her eyes narrowed in her weathered face. A strand of limp hair hung between her eyes. "What friend?"

"A girl named Laura. Would've been about ten days ago."

"I don't know any girl named Laura."

"Do you know anyone who wears boots with dragons on them?"

Her brow creased with thought, and with her free hand she tugged at her uneven neckline as if it had suddenly grown tight. Then she motioned me forward. I was very cautious and stopped well out of arm's reach. The spear stayed aimed at the center of my chest, but she held it wrong for such a close jab and I was pretty sure I could dodge it if I had to. Then again, I might end up on a spit over their dinner fire. "You know about the dragon people?" she asked.

I nodded. "Ran into three of them out on the road a while back."

She looked me over carefully. "You're not one, are you?"

"No, ma'am, not me."

"Good. You wouldn't walk out of this yard alive if you were." She looked past me at the kids. "Go play!" she snapped, and they scurried off into the woods like upright squirrels. She returned her attention to me. "You swear you're not one of them?"

"Do I look like one of them?"

"They're sneaky. How do you feel about King Archibald?"

I raised my chin and put on my most sincere face. "I'll leave Muscodia before I'll submit to his tyranny," I said, adding equal parts outrage, courage and the fear that comes from espousing a lost cause. And technically my words were true. Of course, since I wasn't a citizen I felt no patriotic loyalty, and from what I'd heard King Archibald was far too disconnected and flighty to ever do well as a tyrant.

She didn't answer for a long, tense moment. I crossed my arms, which put my sword hand close enough to the hilt that I could draw it quickly if needed. Women, I knew, could be just as vicious as men, and if she attacked me I had no compunction about defending myself.

Finally she said, "My husband will be home soon. He's the one you should talk to. Come on inside and wait for him, why don't you?"

I nodded at the spear. "You going to keep pointing that at me?"

She lowered the weapon until its butt end touched the ground. "No. But this isn't the only sharp thing I've got handy, just so you know."

I bit back every single snide comment and simply said, "Yes, ma'am." Then I followed her inside.

er name was Bella Lou, and her kids were Toy (the girl) and Stick (the boy). "We named them after the first thing my husband saw when he walked outside after they were born," Bella Lou said. "The people who were native to Muscodia before we came along used to do the same thing." I resisted the urge to say the choices could've been much worse. She was not as old as she first appeared, her rough-hewn lifestyle having aged her prematurely. Her husband she simply referred to as "Buddy."

The shack's inside was just like the outside. Everything had the look of being homemade or scavenged, then stuck together with no concern for style or safety. The table and chairs were big, square, solid creations that, because they were too large to go through the door, must have been built in the room. Animal skins, some with heads still attached, hung on the walls and covered the uneven floor. The place should have smelled atrocious, but flowers bloomed in window pots and various herbs dangled from hooks, making it actually rather homey. There was even a pleasant breeze through the windows to offset the summer warmth.

I sat at the crude table, drank tea that could tan leather and listened to Bella Lou tell me everything that was wrong with Muscodia and old King Archibald. She and Buddy were convinced Archibald was preparing a return to the old days of iron-fisted royal dominance in preparation for the eventual succession of his diffident son, Prince Frederick. And never mind that Muscodia's capital, Sevlow, was about as geographically far from Neceda and the Black River Hills as it was possible to get: Bella Lou believed that people like her and Buddy, whose independence posed some vague sort of threat to this new royal order, would be rounded up and enslaved once the coup happened. So they'd retreated to the woods, where they lived basically in hiding from the outside world.

I'd met people like this before, and there was no convincing them with logic. So I just smiled, nodded and drank as much of the corrosive tea as I could manage despite my stomach's increasing protests. I wondered how late Mother Bennings stayed at her office, and how extensive was her collection of antidotes.

"I'm sorry for the mess," Bella Lou said as she put the kettle back on the hearth. I noticed she drank no tea herself.

"It's still neater than my place," I lied. "So tell me about these dragon people."

She sat opposite me. "I thought you knew about them already," she said suspiciously.

"I do; I'd just like to compare notes."

She smiled. She had all her teeth, although a couple appeared destined for the dentist's pliers. "You first."

Well, no way around that; smoothly done, LaCrosse. So I gave her the sum total of what I knew. "There aren't very many of them, they've got a place hidden around here somewhere and they aren't afraid to hurt people to get what they want."

She nodded. "That's them, all right. When they first came here, we tried to be friendly and get to know them. In the woods, you always like to find out who you can trust, because you never know when you might need a hand. But whenever we'd run up on one of them, they'd get all crazy and chase us away."

"How long ago did they come here?"

"About a month ago, I reckon. The first time I saw one, I was out gathering berries up near the tree line. The dirt's all washed away there, and there's places where it's nothing but boulders. That's where he was, at one of those rocky spots. He didn't see me at first. He had a stick, like a fishing pole, about twice as tall as he was, with a rag tied on the end the way you'd make a torch. He even poured something that looked like lamp oil all over it. But he didn't light it; he just started shoving it into the cracks between rocks, as far as it would go, real carefully, like he was . . . I don't know, painting the insides of those crevices and things."

"What did he look like?"

"He was a young guy. Had on nice clothes under a big camouflage cloak. The clothes made me think he was town trash— no offense—but he moved around like he was used to being outside."

"Then what happened?"

"He kept painting cracks for a long time, very methodically, like it was his job or something. He didn't notice me. Finally he stopped, and I decided to say hello. I thought maybe he'd lost something down in the rocks, and I could get Toy or Stick to wiggle down and get it for him. I asked if he needed any help."

"What did he do?"

She chuckled. "He screamed at me and threw a knife. He called me a nosy whore and said he'd kill me if I ever told anyone I'd seen him."

"He threw a *knife* at you?"

"Yeah. He just missed me. It stuck in a tree right by my head. I grabbed it and ran. Luckily I know these woods like I do this tabletop, because he came after me. But once I got out of sight, there was no way he could've found me. He looked for quite a while, though, screaming and cursing at me the whole time."

"Do you still have the knife?"

" 'Course. Want to see it?"

I nodded. She went to a trunk-sized box shoved up against the wall and opened it. Light glinted from the blades of a dozen knives clipped to the inside of the lid, ready for the day the king's soldiers came to arrest them, I supposed. She picked one, pulled it loose and closed the box.

She handed it to me: five inches long, perfectly balanced and sharp on both edges. If you didn't know about knives you'd never pick this one, because it was about as visually impressive as a nice letter opener. But I *did* know, and it told me that if the screaming guy had wanted to hit her, he probably could have. This was a pro's throwing knife.

But what it told me most was that I was on the right track: embossed into the black handle was a dragon emblem identical to the one I saw on the man's boots.

I tapped the design. "Is this why you call them the dragon people?" I asked.

She nodded. "Why do you?"

"One of them has the same thing on his boots." I put the knife on the table. "Can I buy this from you?"

She shook her head. "We don't use money. Money feeds into King Archibald's repression."

Slowly so I wouldn't spook her, I drew my own knife from its hiding place in my boot. It was almost exactly the same size and weight and, since I'd left the filigree along the blade, looked much more expensive. "Can I trade with you, then?"

She took both knives and held them side by side, scrutinizing them like two cucumbers at the market. Then she handed me the dragon knife. "Sure. It's probably bad luck for me to keep it, anyway."

I slipped the new weapon into my boot just as heavy steps thudded on the porch outside. "I got us a couple of wild pigs," a rough male voice called. "Ought to be good for a week, at least. Got 'em strung up to drain."

"Buddy, you know you don't have to gut 'em; I'll do that," Bella Lou called through the door. She smiled and shook her head. "I'm a lucky woman, all right. He spends all day hunting and still has the energy to field-dress 'em and start the blood running out."

The front door opened and Buddy stepped into the room. He was a short, round man with arms the size of my legs, dressed in ragged, homemade clothes patterned to blend with the light and shadow of the forest. He'd removed his boots on the porch, and his broad, pasty-white feet slapped the floor with each step. He wore a big knife on his belt and his hands were bloody. Intense little eyes peered from under the floppy brim of his cap and said he was not pleased to see a stranger. He looked me over for a long, tense moment. Finally he growled, "Who's this, Bella Lou?"

"This is Mr. LaCrosse," she said.

"And why is he in my favorite seat?"

She kept her eyes cast demurely down. "He was asking about the dragon people."

"We don't know any dragon people," he said as he hung his hat on a peg. He had a wild tangle of thin, ginger-colored hair around a sizeable bald spot.

"Your wife just said you did," I pointed out.

His hard little eyes flicked back to Bella Lou. "Yeah, well, she's not too smart sometimes. Ain't that right?"

Bella Lou, eyes still averted, nodded. "Yes, sir."

Buddy asked, "That your gray mare out there?"

I nodded.

"Pitiful excuse for a horse."

"I know."

"Bella Lou, get me some water." He wiped his hands across his belly, leaving red smears on the fabric. As she jumped to get water from a barrel, he stepped close to me and looked down. "You *are* in my favorite chair."

"I'm a guest," I said. Buddy had, in the time it took him to walk across the room, gone from annoying me to truly pissing me off, and I halfway welcomed the chance to make a big deal out of something. "Don't they always get the best seat in the house?"

Buddy tried his best glare on me. "You and your pitiful horse better leave, mister."

"Sure. Just as soon as one of you tells me where I can find the dragon people."

"I said before, we don't know any dragon people."

I smiled my brightest smile. "Then your wife's a liar. Or you are."

His face turned red. "Mister, get on your way or next time I'll just leave you out there for the coyotes," he growled.

I frowned, puzzled at the comment. He looked startled as well, and embarrassed, like he'd blurted out more than he should. Then I got it. "Oho," I said softly, "so *you're* the fellow who found me and brought me into town."

His tough veneer turned out to be as substantial as a sneeze; the fear in his eyes could probably be seen back in Neceda. "I think you better leave, mister," he said with no juice.

I loved it when a tactical advantage just fell out of the sky like that. I nonchalantly tipped my chair back. "I'm not ready to give up my seat just yet. Yeah, my friend at the stable described you. He didn't know your name, but he's seen you at the market in town before. You tried to sell my saddle to him."

Now Bella Lou froze in the act of handing him his mug of rainwater. Her eyes grew big and, as I watched, began to sizzle with fury. "You were at the *market*? In *town*?"

Buddy looked helplessly from me to her, unable to think of anything to say.

Bella did not have that problem. She tossed the water in his face, then threw the mug against the floor at his bare feet. It shattered, the noise sharp and loud. "Completely self-sufficient, you said. Never let anyone even know we're here, you said. And now I find out you've been going to the market in town *regularly*?" By the end her voice had risen to a considerable shriek, and I was glad she wasn't yelling at me.

Buddy took a step back toward the door. "Well, I had to—"

She was right up in his face now, hands on her hips. "You had to *lie* to me? To our *children*? You *had* to do that?" She smacked him across the back of the head. "We live knee-deep in goat shit and dead leaves, and you sneak off to *town*?"

He looked past Bella Lou at me, his expression desperate.

I stood and said, "Bella Lou, before you crack his head like a walnut, I'd sure like him to show me where the dragon people are."

She turned that seething glare on me, and I responded with my blandest smile. She snapped, "Sure, might as well get some *honest* work out of him. I'm going for a walk." She pushed past me and went out the back door. "Shut up!" she bellowed when the goats in the pen started bleating. Her muttering was so loud it carried back to us for several moments until she disappeared into the woods.

I turned back to Buddy, who looked like a convict granted a scaffold reprieve. "She's got strong opinions," I said.

"And a strong right arm," he agreed, rubbing the back of his head.

"Maybe you shouldn't lie to her next time," I said.

"I don't need your damn city advice," he mumbled. Then he scooped his cap from the hook and, with as much dignity as he could muster, jammed it on his head. "Come on, then."

I followed him outside. Two good-sized pig carcasses hung by their feet from a nearby tree, blood draining onto the ground; even I could spot them as plump, farm-raised livestock. Buddy pulled on big muddy boots, took the reins of a scraggly pony from the hitching post and mounted in a single leap. The pony visibly sank under his weight. The various tools and implements hanging from the saddle jingled. I mounted my horse and, after battling with her for a few moments, got her under control. "Buddy," I said, "first I want you to show me where you found me. It's close to where you've seen the dragon people, isn't it?"

He nodded without looking at me.

I knew it had to be. They'd taken us from the road to their lair, tortured Laura until she died, then carried us to the cliff, all sometime between midnight and dawn. These woods were thick and would be slow to travel, especially for three men carrying two bodies and leading a recalcitrant horse. They couldn't have taken us very far.

Buddy led me down trails I never would have spotted on my own. His pony had a much easier time of it than my horse, and more than once I thought of insisting we continue on foot. My nag tossed her head and fought any nudge to her flank as we descended an easy but perilously thin ledge to the bottom of a gully, then followed the dried creek bed. Above us the walls grew higher and steeper, until the place almost qualified as a canyon. I got queasy when it also began to look familiar.

Suddenly my horse stopped and would not continue, no matter what names I called her. She pawed at the ground, her hooves clacking on the stones from the old riverbed. I was considering a good smack with the flat of my sword when the wind changed and I smelled what had halted her.

"It's just up here," Buddy said, his pony unaffected by the odor.

"I know," I said, swung off my saddle and released the reins. The horse backed up a step as if tensing to bolt, but I glared at her and she stopped. She lowered her head and began munching on the grass sprouting between the smooth rocks.

I tried really hard to get a grip on myself. After all, I'd seen plenty of dead horses, plenty of dead *people*, in my life. This was just another crime scene I needed to check for clues. So why did it feel like I was about to see the corpse of my best friend? I parted my lips and breathed through my clenched teeth as I approached the big object lying on the ground just ahead.

The flies were doing their job, and the rest of the forest disposal crew were no slackers, either. But most of her was still there. Huge slashes across Lola's flanks showed where she'd been cut with a knife or a sword, most likely to drive her off the cliff. She was far too smart to just jump on her own. In the patches of bare dirt between the stones I saw prints from coyotes, raccoons, possums and other varmints, as well as the wagon tracks from where Buddy had picked up Laura and me.

Buddy, leading his pony, stopped beside me. He held a cloth over his face. "The fall might not've killed her right away," he said clinically. "Coulda just broke her ribs. Then she'd suffocate, or drown in her own blood if her lungs got poked."

I clenched my fists. "Say anything else, Buddy, and I'll open a fresh jug of Bella Lou on you."

He grumbled petulantly, "Hey, it's just a horse; it's not like it's a person or anything."

"Buddy," I said with supreme self-control, "why'd you pick us up? You don't strike me as the help-out-your-fellow-man type."

"Didn't want anyone to come looking for *you* and find *us*," he said to the ground.

I looked at the cliffs. The sky above them was blue, cloudless and magnificent. Where had those men been standing that night? "How was I laying when you found me?"

"Flat on the ground."

"No, I mean, could you tell which side I'd been thrown off?"

ALEX BLEDSOE

He nodded and pointed. It was almost, but not quite, a straight vertical drop, and I saw the place where I'd hit the base and rolled the rest of the way to the bottom. That little bounce had been what saved me. "The dragon people live somewhere up there?"

Buddy made a noncommittal sound muffled by the scarf.

I yanked it away from his face. "Buddy, I got a bellyful of pissed-off and I'm looking for somewhere to throw it up. It could be on your head just as easily as anywhere, so don't give me a hard time."

He turned white, which could've been just from the stench, and snatched the scarf back. "About half a mile down, there's a cut that leads to a trail. It comes back along the top of the cliff up there. If you follow it, it'll take you to a little shack. Only seen it from a distance, but . . . it's theirs."

I dug a coin from my pocket and gave it to him. He stared at it. "What's this for?"

I nodded at the tools on his pony. "You got a shovel with you?"

"Yeah."

I indicated Lola's carcass. "Bury her."

"The horse?"

"*Yes, the horse!*" I yelled.

He quickly pocketed the money. "Okay, fine. Sure thing. I'll get right on it."

"I'll be back to check," I assured him as I turned to mount Lola's completely inadequate replacement.

F I V E

Buddy had told the truth: the cut hit the canyon at a right angle, provided an easy ascent and led to a trail that ran along the cliff top. Smooth as it was, the damn horse still balked at it, and I'd have made faster progress had I let the nag ride *me*. She picked her way up the cut like a barefoot spinster, then seemed determined to turn down the trail in the opposite direction from the one I wanted. After implying many things about her parentage under my breath, I got her pointed the right way, parallel with the edge of the cliff.

Eventually I reached the spot where I'd been tossed to my presumed death. Far below, Buddy dug lethargically at the grave. He looked up, saw me and waved, then returned to work. I had no delusions he'd do a good job.

The stony ground showed evidence of recent activity, but nothing more definite. I'd also crossed some sort of weather line, because up here the breeze was chilly on my sweat-damp skin. Out of nowhere the horse suddenly snorted and balked again, and a moment later the reason hit me: another out-of-place odor, this one very like lamp oil.

I looked around for the source. The hill rose above me to a forested crest, beyond which I glimpsed the top of higher hills. The soil here was rockier and less accommodating than it was even fifty feet below, and in many places bundles of boulders poked from the ground. I remembered what Bella Lou had told me, dismounted and knelt by the nearest one. The odor was incredibly strong, and when I put my hand down into a crevice— belatedly realizing that it might hold things like rattlesnakes, spiders or the odd displaced scorpion—I felt a slippery coating on the rocks down where the wind couldn't dry them. My fingertips were damp when I pulled them out, and one sniff told me Bella Lou had been right. But why go around painting the insides of nooks and crannies with oil?

I wiped my hands on some leaves, climbed onto the horse and wrestled her back along the trail. She kept a ridiculous distance from the edge, ensuring the left side of my head was thwacked by every low-hanging branch. Eventually the trail turned away from the canyon and continued up the hillside through the forest.

I watched the sky for any sign of smoke. Here the trees were gnarled hawthorn, entwined with each other and studded with big spikes. There would be no traveling off the road in this neighborhood unless you were in armor. It occurred to me that perhaps Buddy had sent me after the mythical wild goose, which if true would earn him an ass-kicking not even Bella Lou could rival. But since I knew where he lived, it made no sense for him to trick me, unless he was sending me into a fatal trap. He seemed neither smart nor devious enough for that.

Then the damn horse began to fight me again. I perversely wished for some of the big, vicious cavalry spurs I'd used as a young man when I fought in the Trego marshes. The horse snorted and tried to turn, an almost impossible move on this narrow part of the trail. I ducked the spiked branches and cursed her to the best of my ex-soldier ability.

Finally I gave up, dismounted and threw the reins over a low branch. I drew my sword, once again resisted the urge to smack the animal and started up the trail. The horse let out a high, piercing whinny that must've carried for miles, and certainly alerted any of these mysterious dragon people that someone was coming.

The trail wound around rocky outcroppings that gradually displaced the stubborn hawthorns. I finally spotted a small stone-walled shack beneath a rock overhang, probably once used as shelter for people trying to mine gold or copper from the Black River Hills. Those veins had played out before I was born, but there was no reason a sturdily built structure couldn't survive and be used for all sorts of disreputable things. As I got nearer, I saw that newer stones had been used to repair the damage from neglect, and the roof sported fresh wooden shingles.

I hid behind a boulder and watched for a long time, checking for any sign of occupation. By the time the shadow from the nearest tree crept far enough to mark twenty minutes, no floorboards had creaked or silhouettes moved across the windows. I counted to three, rushed up the hill and flattened myself against the wall by the door. Once my heart settled down enough for me to again hear the outside world, I confirmed nothing seemed to be moving within. I tried the handle; it was unlocked. I pushed it open and went inside.

My eyes took a long moment to adjust to the dimness. The tiny one-room shack contained only a table with two chairs and an odd box on the floor near the fireplace. Three walls each sported curtainless windows, and the fourth boasted a crude fireplace and hearth. The breeze tickled thick cobwebs by the ceiling, and detritus accumulated in the corners. Nobody lived here, but it didn't mean it was entirely abandoned. *Someone* had gone to the trouble of fixing the ravages of time, after all.

The furniture was simple and cheap, but the box got my attention. While it most resembled the kind of strongbox miners might use to hold their precious findings, it had leather padding along all the edges and big loop handles were attached to either end for a carrying staff to thread through. I could think of nothing small enough to fit in the box that would also need two or more people to lift it. Well, sure, gold, but there was no gold to be had in these mountains. Using my sword, I flipped the single latch and carefully opened the lid. It was empty. The inside, though, was lined entirely with thin sheets of lead. Gold wouldn't need that.

The place gave me the creeps. The wind weaseled through tiny unpatched gaps in the stone and made soft, agonized sounds. The smell contained odors of dust, decayed wood and abandonment. Yet the box was so new its leather still reeked of tanning.

I checked the fireplace. It was summer, but this high the nights might require a little help. The ashes were cold, but they were also fresh. Then my eye fell on a stain on the floor in a shadowed corner. The way the light from the window reflected from it was unmistakable.

It was dried blood.

I looked directly above it. From a beam across the ceiling hung two manacles on very short chains. Someone suspended from it—say a short girl with blond hair—would dangle helplessly well above the floor.

I knelt by the stain. Tiny dark strips were matted into the dried liquid, and when I tapped them they did not crumble like ash. I realized they were small ribbons of human skin that had been peeled or cut from Laura Lesperitt.

Something little and cold went *snap* deep inside my chest. I should've been scared, but I wasn't. Instead I was a hair's breadth from full-on battle rage. I'd claimed I could help her, *volunteered* to help her, and yet in the end I'd done nothing. If she hadn't met me on the road, she might've gotten clean away. Perhaps this blood on the floor should be on my hands.

And then that damn horse let out another loud, self-pitying neigh.

I really wanted to split her equine skull with one blow, but I stuck with my training. I scooted to the wall beside the window and peered around the edge. Another horse, this one dark brown, appeared around the boulder. Its rider was hidden beneath a hooded cloak designed to blend in with the forest greenery below, less useful here among the scraggly mountain flora. Behind him came my horse, led by the reins far more complacently than she'd have let me do it. It made me hate her that much more.

I ducked out of sight and heard the man dismount. He did not walk away from his horse, though. I'd made no effort to hide my tracks, so if he was halfway observant he'd spot my boot prints in the dirt outside the door. I listened more closely, trying to separate stealthy human noises from the sighing wind and my own thundering heart. Was that the sound of a sword being drawn, expertly and quietly, from its scabbard? Did I hear a stealthy foot crunch very slightly on the rough ground outside the door?

The man kicked the door open, and it slammed back against the wall with a loud crash. Sunlight shot through the opening and would've blinded anyone who didn't expect it. He'd removed his cloak and, when he rushed in, he threw it to one side to confuse potential ambushers.

He didn't see me against the wall beside the door. I stepped forward and kicked him hard in the small of the back. It knocked him across the room into the table. He spun around, his sword slashing at the air behind him. Nothing wrong with his reflexes, that's for sure.

I blocked his next backhand with my sword, locked our blades together and stepped too close for either of us to do anything. "This doesn't have to get messy," I said. "I just want some answers."

The man said nothing. He was under thirty, with short black hair and a thin ribbon of beard and mustache. His eyes were wide and dark, with no visible feeling. A young hotshot thug, on the way up.

He tried to muscle his sword past me, but I had them wedged together in a way that took little effort to maintain. Surprise flicked across his face as he realized it.

"What do you say?" I said. "Shall we put these down and talk? There's money in it for you."

His jaw muscles trembled with the effort to wrench his

weapon free, but he made no sound. Then suddenly he quit struggling entirely, and I fell for it. He yanked his sword away and rolled around the edge of the table, putting the furniture between us. The ceiling was so low he couldn't manage a vertical killing blow at my exposed neck, but I barely got my sword up to block his horizontal slice. My parry drove the edge of his blade into the table's wood, where it bit solid. In the moment it took him to twist it loose I'd dropped my own sword, scrambled over the table and hit him hard right between the eyes.

I felt the impact into my shoulder and down my spine, and the sensation of finally having someone to actually *punch* overwhelmed me. As he staggered from the first blow, I grabbed the front of his tunic with my left hand and punched him again, across the jaw. When I released him he stumbled back into the wall but kept to his feet. I jabbed my left fist into his kidneys. He grunted, the first noise he'd made, and fell to one knee. Either I'd lost my touch or this guy was really, really tough. I got my answer when he suddenly drove a punch that felt like an anvil into my stomach.

If he'd connected with my sternum it might've knocked the wind from me, but as it was I stumbled across the room, off-balance but not really hurt. I fell over one of the spindly chairs and when I looked up he was leaping over it, boots aimed at my face. I rolled aside and he hit the floor with a thud that made me glad I wasn't under it.

I picked up the fallen chair and used it to drive him back against the wall. While I tried to pin him with my weight, I punched him again in the face. It had no real effect except to make my hand hurt. "Will you *stop* it?" I yelled, my voice tight from his gut punch. "I just want to *talk* to you!"

He braced against the wall and easily shoved me back. He grabbed the chair away from me and threw it out a window. Blood ran from his nose, the only real sign I'd had that he was a human being. He swung at me, but I dodged it and backed away. He kept after me, breath hissing through his teeth and spraying out bloody spittle.

I skidded in the dregs of tacky blood beneath the manacles. The sudden recollection that it belonged to Laura refreshed my temper, and I ducked under his next swing to drive a punch with all my weight, strength and fury into his side. I felt something solid give way and heard a wet, muffled snap. He made an "*Oof!*" sound and fell to his knees.

I stayed out of arm's reach as he cradled his side and gasped. When he looked at me, his eyes showed his agony. I punched him again in the temple. My knuckles would hate me tomorrow, but for the moment I felt completely righteous. I hit him again, but it was wasted because he was already out from the last one. All this one did was knock him over.

As soon as he hit the floor my own head spun, and I grabbed for the nearest wall. The back of my skull throbbed anew, and pain wrenched at my ribs. If he woke up now, I was a goner, but he didn't move. I waited until my vision cleared, the agony faded and I could again think straight. Guess I wasn't as recovered as I thought.

I checked out his boots. They were expensive, but sported no designs. I quickly went through his pockets, making sure he had no hidden weapons. Then I stumbled over to the remaining chair and heavily sat down. I didn't think I was high enough for the air to be really thin, but the only other option was that I was getting older, and I knew it couldn't be *that*. I gulped big lungfuls and wondered just what I'd do with the unconscious man on the floor. I couldn't take him back to Gary Bunson in town; it wasn't his jurisdiction, and as far as he knew the guy had committed no crime. Hell, *I* was the one trespassing.

Then I remembered the manacles.

I slapped him lightly across the face until he whimpered like a whiny child and opened his eyes. Then I stepped back and let him figure it out for himself.

He tried to move, realized his arms were pinned above his head and that his feet only barely touched the ground. He struggled slowly, his body pivoting on his wrists as his boots scraped the floor. As he awoke more he fought harder, gasping at the pain from his ribs. Then he comprehended, and froze. He dangled from the manacles that once held Laura Lesperitt, and looked slowly around until he saw me seated nonchalantly on the windowsill opposite him.

"Welcome back, tough guy," I said.

He said nothing. The only sound was the beam above him creaking from his weight. Wind blew through the windows and ruffled his hair.

"Don't know if you remember me," I said, "but I lay on the floor here while you and your buddies tortured a girl to death right where you're hanging. Don't bother denying it; I know it was you." I held up the knife I'd gotten from Bella Lou. "One of you had this same design on your boots."

He said nothing, but the hate in his glare was a little diminished by fear.

I turned the knife like I was unfamiliar with how to handle it. "Now the thing is, I want to know some things, and I'm not real picky about how I find them out. Given the way you treated that girl, I'm sure you can appreciate that. But I'm a fair guy, so I'm going to give you a chance here. Who are you, and what did you want to find out from her that was so important?"

He said nothing. His face was red from pain, except for the white around his lips from gritting his teeth.

I shrugged. "Okay, then. I suppose I'll just have to have a little target practice until you become chattier." I grinned and turned the knife so the blade caught the light. "Always meant to learn how to throw one of these," I said, then threw it expertly right at him.

Because I'm an expert, I knew I'd miss him by a mile and stick the knife in the wall behind him. He yelped as it swished past his left underarm, then glared at me as I walked across the room and twisted the knife loose.

"Wow," I said as I returned to my spot across the room, "there must be a trick to this. Let me try again."

This time I deliberately nicked his right side. It was little more than a glorified shaving cut, but it also stung like one and made him howl and writhe. He kicked at me as I walked around him to get the knife, and by the time I returned to face him, blood had soaked the side of his shirt.

"Wow," I said, mock impressed with my own skill. "Would you look at that? Does it hurt?"

He glared.

I shrugged, backed up and threw again. This time it stuck in the big muscle of his thigh. I didn't use enough force to go very deep, so it only remained for a moment before its own weight and his spasm of pain knocked it free. He jerked like a hooked fish and whined through his teeth.

I retrieved the knife and he followed me with wide, frantic eyes. I said apologetically, "I'm sorry, but you really have no one to blame but yourself." I held the knife ready to throw and watched him expectantly. "What were you guys trying to find out from that girl?"

He opened his mouth as if to speak, then mustered his resolve and clamped it shut again.

I sighed, said, "I'll be great at this before much longer," and threw the knife again. This time I aimed higher, closer to his groin. This one finally got his attention. He howled as the point jabbed the soft skin at the crease of his thigh and hip, and thrashed madly until he shook the knife free. It clattered to the floor and he turned wide, panicked eyes on me.

"You son of a *bitch*!" he cried, his voice high.

"Don't talk about my mother," I said patiently. "And what *should* concern you is that I was aiming at your heart. So are you ready to talk?"

"*Yes!*" he snarled.

"What did you want to find out from the girl you peeled the skin off of a week and a half ago?"

He shook his head frantically. "Uh-uh, man, not me. That was Frankie. He's into that. I was just the lookout."

"Good for you. *What* were you trying to find out?"

He looked up at the manacles as if he hoped they'd magically open and free him. When they didn't he sighed, looked down and said, "Lumina. We're trying to find Lumina."

"Who is Lumina?"

I heard the distant *twang*, followed by a much closer *snick*, at about the same time I registered his sudden, wide-eyed look of surprise. An arrowhead appeared just above his navel, poking out through his shirt. He tried to say something; then another *snick-twang* combo preceded the solid *thunk* of a second arrow into his back. This one didn't come out the other side.

By the time the second one struck, I'd flung myself to the floor and scrambled over beneath the window. I drew my sword and held it up so I could use a specially polished part of the blade as a mirror. Outside, a man on horseback untied both my horse and the dead man's, then smacked them with the flat of his sword and sent them off down the trail. He watched the house for another moment, then, apparently happy with his handiwork, spurred his own horse after the others.

Crap, I thought.

I snatched up the dragon knife and rushed out the door, scab-barding my sword as I went. I ran down the trail, but no way was I going to catch a guy on horseback. I skidded to a stop, out of breath and furious. Then I had a terrible idea.

If he left by the same cliff-top trail I'd used, there was a chance I could cut through the woods and head him off. He'd have no reason to hurry once he got out of sight, since he knew I was now on foot. But most of the trees were hawthorns, and they were woven together like the lies a king's chamberlain tells to hide the queen's dalliances. They'd shred me to pieces before I'd gone fifty feet. Still, I'd get no answers standing there wheezing. So I pulled my jacket sleeves down to protect my hands, put up my arms to shield my face, cursed the various fates that brought me to this point and headed into the gauntlet.

It was as bad as I feared. A couple of times I dodged around rocky outcroppings and caught another whiff of lamp oil. Finally I emerged on the trail where it ran closest to the cliff's edge, my arms slashed from protecting my head and my shins cut from pushing their way through the branches. Exhausted, I sat down on a fallen tree beside the path to catch my breath. I tried to read the ground to see if my man had already passed, but it was too rocky, and the traces I saw could easily have been my own from earlier that day. Sweat from the exertion trickled into the various cuts and scratches, and the stinging made me even angrier. I was sure I'd missed him, that my frantic race to intercept the bastard had been for nothing. Then, from up the trail, I heard the distinctive neighing of my own borrowed horse as she came toward me.

I ducked out of sight behind the fallen tree and pulled a branch down over me. The dead man's horse went past first at a leisurely trot, smugly unconcerned with the huge drop to its left. Then my gray mare followed, far more slowly, and actually turned my way as if she could see me. If she'd given me away I'd have pushed her off the cliff with my bare hands, but she went past without a sound.

My man had to be next, so I got ready. I heard him approaching slowly, letting his horse set the pace. He would be alert for pursuit, not ambush. I hoped. Then he was right in front of me.

He wore another one of the camouflage cloaks, but appeared taller and older than the man hanging dead back in the shack. I could see only his chin and its sandy-colored beard. His bow hung from his saddle, beside the quiver of arrows. No way he could nock one quickly.

I waited until he passed, then jumped over the fallen tree and grabbed a handful of the cloak. He was too surprised to resist and I yanked him easily from the saddle onto the rocky trail. He landed with a startled, "*OW!*"

I jumped onto him and pinned him with my weight and the cloak's material. He struggled to get his hands free, and I punched him in the face. He grunted and stopped wriggling, so at least it got his attention. He glared up at me with fury that he knew, for the moment, he had to control.

"Nice shooting back there," I said. "Now why don't you tell me about Lumina?"

"Go to hell," he hissed, and with a sudden burst of energy threw me aside. I rolled toward the edge of the cliff, but flattened myself and clutched the ground before I went over.

The guy jumped to his feet and threw off the cloak. He wore modified leather armor, the kind used as a status symbol by a certain type of criminal. It was covered with sword nicks and little pockmarks made by arrowheads, testifying to the wearer's supposed history of violence. They were easy to fake, of course, but my gut told me he'd come by his honestly.

He drew his sword and attacked. I rolled out of the way just in time and the sword buried itself in the rocky ground. I got to my feet and drew my own sword, wishing now I hadn't punched so many people that day. My grip was pathetic when I parried his next blow, and he damn near knocked the hilt right out of my hand. I responded by kicking at his groin. He turned and caught the blow on his hip, but it still made him grunt because my boots had metal toe caps for just such contingencies. His leg nearly buckled, and I jabbed with my sword, forcing him to awkwardly back away. I feinted, he moved to block it and I jumped inside his guard. I slammed the blade of my own sword into his chest and slid it up until the edge was horizontal against his throat, just biting into the skin.

We'd ended up closer to the cliff than I liked. "Tell me about Lumina," I repeated. "And why you want to know so bad you'd kill some poor girl over it."

He laughed. This close I saw the little patches of white hair that had grown from sword cuts on his scalp. He'd done his time, apparently. "Some 'poor girl'? Pal, you don't know who you're talking about."

A shudder went through me. I recognized his voice from that night: he'd been the torturer defending his professional skill. The dead man at the cabin had called him Frankie. That cold rage came again as I said, "I know she died being peeled alive by *you*."

"Who are you working for, tough guy?" he demanded; suddenly *he* was now interrogating *me*. "You know Marantz doesn't like strange noses poking into his business."

"Then Marantz should've hired better people," I said as if the name meant nothing. But it did; in my business, you got to know all about people like Marantz.

He laughed. "Okay, to tell you the truth, we were—" Then he head-butted me in the forehead. I reflexively slashed with the sword and cut the skin of his throat as I fell back, but not deep enough to do any real damage. I sat heavily on the fallen tree and my sword fell from my limp hand. I shook my head hard, and my vision cleared in time for me to see the man's weapon glint in the sun as he brought it around in a wide, full-power slice at my neck. I leaned back so that it swished over my chest, then jumped up so that in one move I pushed him back and punched him in the jaw. He dropped his sword and, with an annoyed cry of, "Oh, god *damn it!*" fell backward over the edge of the cliff.

Almost.

I grabbed the front of his tunic, dug my boots into the dirt and managed to hold him with just his heels barely on the edge. The drop below was about forty feet, onto the same hard rocks that had so gently cradled me and his other victims. It might not be fatal; it definitely would leave a mark.

He froze, his arms flung wide for balance. All I had to do was open my hand. "Ready to talk now, smart-ass?" I said.

He glared at me. "I got nothing to say to you. You shouldn't have been there that night, and we should've made sure you were dead. Mistakes all around."

"Who is Lumina?" I asked.

He laughed. "The fire dreams are made of, pal."

Dirt crumbled under his feet and he slipped a little. I couldn't hold him balanced like this much longer. "What's Marantz after?"

More rock fell. Somewhere a crow signaled to its brethren. "You are in *so* much trouble. Once Marantz hears about this, you and everyone you know will be mutton on the fire. You get me?"

I had to admire the guy's balls for trying to talk his way off the edge of a cliff. "I get you."

"Now if you let me go, we might be able to work this out. I can talk to Marantz for you. I mean, yeah, you killed Jimmy up at the cabin, but he was a kid and he wasn't too smart, so he's no loss. Marantz won't give a shit."

"*You* killed Jimmy, Frankie. Remember? And does Marantz give a shit about *you*?"

He grinned. "Hey, we're family."

I didn't know if he meant it metaphorically or literally, and really didn't care. The chill was back: the image of Laura's dead face in the moonlight loomed vividly before me. "You tortured a helpless girl to death. You damn near killed me, and you *did* kill the best horse in the world."

"The horse?" he said in real surprise. "You're upset about the *horse*?"

"Not anymore," I said, and let him go.

His last words were something like, "No, wait!" But we were way past negotiating.

I watched him bounce off the side of the cliff about halfway down and land with the kind of limp thud that said he wouldn't be getting up. Still, I sat down and waited to make sure he wasn't faking. When something thick and crimson seeped out from under his head I was pretty sure, but after two crows landed and began pecking at the skin of his hands with no response, I knew he was really dead.

Killing him had felt good, but not smart. He might've said more if I'd kept at him. But hopefully he said enough: *Marantz*. That one name told me an awful lot. With a sigh, I got to my feet and walked down the trail toward the cut.

chapter

S E V E N

I t was dark by the time I got back to Neceda riding my
loaner horse and leading the other two I'd acquired. It
had not been hard to catch them: once they weren't being
herded, they stopped and began grazing on whatever pitiful
scrub they could find at the top of the cut. The two bad guys'
horses were placid and much easier to handle than my gray
curse.

After collecting them, I returned to the shack, but a search of
the hanging man's corpse revealed nothing of interest. The
same was true of the man I'd dropped off the cliff, who his late
friend referred to as "Frankie." His pockets were empty, his
clothes contained nothing of use and his sword had all identify-
ing marks, even the smith's name, filed off. The leather armor
was genuine Muscodian government issue, although that didn't
really mean anything: old soldiers were always selling off their

mementos for spare change or more ale. Still, he'd learned archery marksmanship somewhere, so maybe this was a clue. If so, it was the only one either corpse provided.

Their saddlebags, though, were a treasure trove. Jimmy, the man at the shack, carried a big map of the whole Black River Hills area marked with random "x" symbols. There was no legend to explain their meaning, but there were dozens of them. He also had a knife identical to the one Bella Lou had given me. It looked brand-new; was it a replacement for the one Bella Lou had snatched? Were the dragons the symbols of some bandit gang? I knew most of the outfits that worked the river and surrounding countryside, but it didn't mean a new one might not be trying to move in.

Frankie's bags revealed even more. He had a tool kit that at first glance seemed to be for leather-working, but the dried blood on the instruments told a different story. Now I knew exactly how he'd removed those strips of skin from Laura Lesperitt, and felt even less remorse for letting him take the fast trail to the canyon floor. He also carried a healthy bag of gold, all in small-denomination coins. Most odd was a long strip of bright red cloth, like a head scarf. In fact, it was *exactly* like the scarves I'd glimpsed on those people moving into the former Lizard's Kiss whorehouse.

But the day's big clue was the name Marantz.

In Muscodia, all trails of vice and illegality eventually led to Gordon Marantz, who'd moved here after escaping Trasketania one step ahead of the gallows. He gained the favor of King Archibald's court, and so officialdom looked the other way when he began eliminating his competition along the Gusay from Tacketville to Pema. In no time he controlled all the ale, girls, gambling and protection rackets. Many places worked directly for him while others, like Angelina's, paid him protection. He was smart enough to be hard to find, but easy to run afoul of if you tried to cut into his action. In my years in Muscodia I'd only seen him once, leaving a gambling house late one night surrounded by his goons. In his forties, with black hair worn slicked back from his broad, mean face, he looked like a guy who could still get his hands dirty if the occasion demanded it. I wasn't sorry our professional paths had never crossed.

I looked over the shack a second time, but found nothing I'd missed. I left Jimmy hanging, along with the strange padded box. Then, with the two new horses in tow, I descended the cut and retraced my steps up the canyon as the sun began to set.

We scared a fat buzzard away from Frankie's corpse, then reached the spot where I'd left Buddy on grave digger duty. The little bozo was nowhere to be found. As I expected, he'd dug about half a hole and then vanished, probably sure I'd been ambushed. I wondered if he'd actually been on Frankie's payroll, or if he just knew I was walking into a trap and hadn't bothered to mention it.

All the horses balked at the scent of decay. I hated to leave Lola exposed and undignified, but ultimately had no choice. Maybe Buddy's conscience would get the best of him and he'd return to do the job right. It beat facing his wife; I doubted he wanted both me *and* Bella Lou on his case. Besides, this was nothing but a pile of rotted horse meat; if there were a Summerlands, then Lola's spirit now galloped across its smooth plains toward unending grazing.

I arrived at the livery stable after dark. Liz's office was still closed, but I didn't know if that meant she was at home awaiting me, or had not returned from her day's deliveries. I was too tired and sore to worry about it, and she could certainly take care of herself. I knew the noise I made opening the doors and leading the horses inside would alert Hank, who lived with his family in an add-on at the back of the barn.

Sure enough, his napkin from dinner still tucked into the neck of his tunic, Hank came into the barn accompanied by one of his young sons, Howie. Both stopped dead when they saw me. Hank turned up the lamp he carried until I squinted from the glare.

I was a mess. I was covered in scratches, cuts, dirt and blood, and on top of that was so tired I could barely stand, so I understood why Howie slid slowly behind his father's legs at the sight of me. I dropped from the saddle, leaned on the horse and held the reins out toward Hank.

"Cut yourself shaving?" Hank said drily.

I nodded. "With a hawthorn forest."

"You too good to take a man's horse?" Hank said gruffly, and Howie reluctantly took the reins from me. Hank looked over the two additional horses, his expert eyes missing nothing. Their saddles and other gear were expensive, if trail worn, and the animals were clearly well cared for. "Didn't know you were a horse trader, Mr. LaCrosse," he said, his flat voice masking most of his suspicion.

"They just fell into my lap," I said as I waited for the knots to loosen in my lower back. "Ever seen 'em before?"

"Nope."

"Ever seen any like 'em?"

Hank took the bridle of Frankie's horse and looked her over.

He lifted one foot and inspected the shoe. "Howie, get over here."

The boy dropped the gray horse's reins and moved up beside his father. "Hot or cold shoe?" Hank asked.

The boy's face scrunched up as he studied the foot. "Hot," he said finally.

"How can you tell?" Hank pressed.

"The line from the old shoe," he said, and pointed to something I couldn't see.

"Attaboy," Hank said proudly, and released the horse's foot. "Hell, if I don't teach him, how's he gonna know?"

"True fact," I agreed. "Well, if anybody comes to claim them, don't give them a hard time about it. Just try to get a name for me."

Suspicion swallowed his fatherly pride. "Is somebody likely to be upset about them being here?"

"Not with you," I assured him.

"Uh-huh," he said dubiously. "I don't handle stolen horses, Mr. LaCrosse. People tend to feel pretty strongly about things like that."

"These aren't stolen, Hank. I promise. And I guarantee the previous rightful owners won't show up to get them back."

He thoughtfully chewed his lip for a moment. Gravy stained his chin. Then he said to Howie, "Put the two new ones in the stall up front, and then take the mare out to the corral." To me he said, "If they're here for more than two days, somebody'll have to pay for their keep."

"If they're here more than two days, you can have them." I turned, then stopped and faced him again. "And if you *ever* try to pawn that gray manure pile off on me again, you'll get back a load of horse meat and glue."

The gray mare looked back at us with all the equine innocence in the world. "I swear, nobody else has complained about her," Hank said. "I think you're just bad with horses."

I snorted, then waved toward Liz's office. "Has she come back yet?"

"No, but somebody else came looking for you."

"The guy with the gloves?"

"No, a woman. Said she was a Mother up at the moon priestess hospital. Her name was . . . Banner?"

"Bennings," I corrected. "What did she say?"

"To tell you to come see her as soon as you could."

"What about?

He shook his head. "She didn't say, and I didn't ask. Don't care for them priestesses."

I understood; one of his children had died under a drunken priestess' care before they came to Neceda. "That's exactly how I feel about horses."

I tried the door to Liz's office on my way out, but it was still locked. I had a key, but this late she'd probably just drop off her horses and wagon and return home. I could wait for her in far more comfort there.

The traffic was sparse as I walked up the street. The taverns, whorehouses and gambling establishments glowed with light and life, and their noise filled the air. As I passed Ditch Street, I paused and looked over the Lizard's Kiss building. It was dark and apparently lifeless. Tomorrow I'd have to find out who bought it, what was up with the red scarf brigade and how it tied to Marantz.

Now, though, I wanted a quick drink before going home. As I approached the tavern, a man staggered out, one hand to his head. He leaned against the wall and hunched over, and something dark dripped from between the fingers pressed to his skull.

"Hey," I said, "you all right?"

He looked up. He was in his late teens, and dressed like a Muscodian farmer. He bled from a fresh cut over his right eye, and still had that slightly dazed post-punch demeanor. He stared at me, and it took me a moment to remember how bad *I* looked. "Wow," he said raggedly, "did he kick your ass, too?"

I helped him sit on the ground and lean back against the wall. "Did who kick my ass?"

"Some soldier from Sevlow. He was talking to my girl, and I asked him to stop. Next thing I knew I was staring up at the rafters."

I pulled his fingers away from the cut. The damage wasn't bad, certainly not permanent. "Let me guess. Big guy, little eyes, not a smiler?"

The farm boy nodded. "That's him. When my head stops dancing—"

"You'll go have a drink across town at Long Billy's," I said. "I've seen this guy, and believe me, he was being generous leaving your head attached to your shoulders." I wasn't *that* impressed by Argoset's backup, but if this poor kid had been laid out with one punch, he was really out of his league. Better to overscare than underscare.

I helped him to his feet, pressed a coin into his hand and gave him a shove in the right direction. "Thanks, mister," he said, holding his head with one hand, the money with the other. I sighed at my own idiocy; if I didn't stop with the charity, I'd soon be so broke I'd have to go squat with Buddy and Bella Lou. There was no question of dipping into the money I'd scavenged from Frankie, either; that had way too much blood on it.

I entered Angelina's and found the place packed, with a minstrel duo pounding out tunes onstage. The floor vibrated to the peculiar stomp-dancing popular in Muscodia. I went behind the bar, grabbed the stool I kept stashed there for occasions like this and found enough space at the bar for one elbow.

Angelina did a double take when she saw me. "You need a drink," she said without asking, and put a tankard originally meant for someone else in front of me. When the original customer protested from down the bar she fired back, "Keep your jerkin on!" I nodded gratefully and took a long swallow. There was too much noise for us to talk, but if she'd needed to tell me something, she would've found a way. To my relief, she simply went back to work. No news was definitely good news at the moment.

I turned to survey the usual rabble, including many faces I knew but couldn't put names to, all well into their mugs. Argoset's big right-hand man sat in a booth, a girl on either side of him; he didn't appear to have noticed me, and his boss was not around. I didn't see Gary Bunson anywhere, either, but he had "arrangements" at several other establishments in town, and could be at any of them.

"Mr. LaCrosse!" a female voice cried above the din. I turned to see Callie, Angelina's wayward waitress, staring at me. She carried a tray laden with ale mugs, and balancing it kept her body at an angle that emphasized her assets. She was arguably the pretti-

est girl in Neceda, all the more attractive because she didn't realize it. She was also, alas, dumb as a bag of socks.

"Hey, Callie," I said wearily. "When did you get back?"

"Today. Convinced Angelina to hire my boyfriend." She nodded toward the stage. "That's him, on the right."

I glanced at him. Young, handsome, with a quick smile and a
sparkling eye for anything in a skirt. Typical minstrel. "I thought
you left with a conjurer."

"I did, but his tricks weren't the kind that lasted," she said
wistfully. "Tony, now *he's* a keeper."

"The folks do seem to like him."

"What happened to you?"

I shrugged. I was too tired to explain it so that Callie would
understand. "Fell off my horse."

She nodded sagely, as if this truly explained everything.
"Yeah. Well, take care of yourself, Mr. LaCrosse."

"You, too, Callie."

I finished my drink, dropped a coin in the tip vase and waved
to Angelina. She gave me a nod in response. There was no need
to go up to my office, and the only steps I wanted to climb led to
my bedroom.

The tavern door opened as I reached it, and two men entered. Both were smallish, strong-looking guys with faces tanned
and lined from working outdoors. Their clothes were cheap and
home-mended. And both wore the red scarves.

I stepped aside and watched them. They looked around like
anyone would for a seat, and when they spotted an empty table
threaded through the dancers to claim it. Nothing unusual about
that at all.

I hesitated, wondering if I should stay and try to befriend them. Ale, especially the good stuff Angelina served when I paid her extra for it, tended to loosen even the tightest tongues. But I was just too tired.

I meant to lie down just for a moment. Really. About three hours later Liz's scream awakened me.

Okay, it wasn't really a scream, just a surprised yell when she lit the table lamp and saw me sprawled shirtless and barefoot across the bed. I'd left my other clothes, shredded and bloodied from racing through the hawthorns, in a heap by the door. What I hadn't done was clean the blood off *me*, which I'd intended to do after closing my eyes for just a second.

Her cry woke me with a start and I sat up suddenly, which *did* make her shriek. Then she glared at me with all her considerable righteous fury.

"Shit, Eddie, don't *do* that!" she snapped. "You want to make me pee all over myself? God *damn*. . . ."

I blinked, yawned and said, "Wow. You're late."

"Not for a run to Pema and back," she said. She sat heavily in a chair and ran trembling fingers through her hair. The lamp cast flickering light on her face. "You scared the hell out of me."

"If I'd done that, there'd be nothing left of you."

"Don't try your charm on me when I'm pissed at you. So what happened? Did you get mauled by porcupines?"

I gave her the short and simple version, which still made her eyes widen. When I was done she said, "So you went for a quiet ride in the country and killed two people?"

"Only one," I said wearily. "And he had it coming."

"If you'd brought him back alive, you might've learned

more," she said as she pulled off her boots. They hit the floor with a loud *thop*.

"I learned enough. Fair trade for the satisfaction I got seeing him go splat. I know where to go poke into next."

"Marantz?"

I nodded, which turned into a yawn.

She shook her head. "Eddie, sometimes I wonder that your feeble little brain can move your body around."

She stood, untied her trousers and slid them down her legs. This got my attention, as it always did. Then she unlaced her tunic and pulled it over her head. This left her pretty thoroughly unclothed, a sight that, like a sunset, would never grow less beautiful to me. I was about to comment on it when she fetched a bottle and cloth from the tiny cupboard and sat beside me on the bed. I eyed her warily, my eyes flitting from her brief undergarments to the items in her hand. The bottle came from the moon priestess hospital, to clean the spot on the back of my head if it needed it. It didn't. "What are you planning?"

"We paid for this stuff, we might as well use it." She dampened the cloth with the bottle's contents.

"You have to be naked for that?"

"I'm not naked. And you've already bled all over the sheets; I don't want you ruining my clothes, too."

"I'm a big boy; why don't I just go wash myself up?" I said quickly, and started to rise. I noticed the lamp was now making odd flickering patterns on the wall.

She put a hand firmly on my shoulder. "Just sit still and don't be a baby. The more you fight, the longer this'll take."

She touched a medicine-soaked corner of the rag to a vicious scratch on my arm. It felt like I'd been branded, and I winced in response. Someone screamed outside in the street, a fairly common thing in Neceda. "See?" I said through clenched teeth. "It hurts so bad it makes total strangers holler."

"Uh-huh," she agreed, undeterred. She touched me with the rag again.

"*Ow!*" I griped. "Be careful, will you?"

She laughed, then leaned close and took my nearest earlobe in her teeth. Her other hand traced the long scar on my chest. "For a man who once took a sword hit to the heart, you're pretty whiny."

"Yeah, well, this hurts worse."

Someone else screamed outside. It didn't sound like excitement or surprise, the only good kinds of screams. Flames still flickered and danced on the wall, but they didn't come from the evenly burning lamp. A bright glow from outside now lit the whole room.

"Something's wrong," I said.

chapter

EIGHT

Instantly Liz sat up beside me. "What?" Then she saw the light on the wall, too. "Oh, no."

We rushed to the window. Despite being on the second floor in a town with only one three-story building, we couldn't see the actual source of the orange glow: it was behind us, in the center of town. People rushed down the street toward the commotion, although a few timid souls fled the opposite way. The distinctive odor of burning wood filled the air.

I grabbed fresh clothes from the wardrobe; by the time I got my boots on, Liz was also dressed. I grabbed my short Urban Mercenary brand Bodyguard Special sword from the rack, she slipped a knife inside her belt and we ran down the stairs to join the commotion.

Mrs. Talbot stood on the front porch puffing on a pipe. Her hair was tangled, and she was clad in a sleeping tunic that hung

off one shoulder. Her grandson, a toadish little boy of indeter-
minate age, lurked in the open doorway behind her. "Looks
like a fire," she said needlessly.

"Where?" Liz asked.

Mrs. Talbot pointed with her pipe. "Thataway, I expect."

That was helpful. We joined the flow of morbid curiosity as it
surged toward the fire, and at the corner we jammed up against
the back of the crowd. Over their heads we saw the source of the
flames now leaping high into the sky, visible no doubt for miles.
An instant before I realized what was going on, Liz gasped over
the din, "*It's Hank's stable!*"

The lower part of the building was already engulfed, and
flames lapped eagerly at the sides and roof above, chewing their
way up like hungry worms on a leaf. The horses in the outside
corral reared and screamed, pressed together as far from the
flames as they could get. No one seemed inclined to let them out,
and their panicked whinnies cut through the other noise. The addition where Hank's family lived was so far untouched, but that
wouldn't last. I didn't see them anywhere, but surely they'd had
time and sense enough to get out.

Because of the corral on one side and the street on the other,
the stable was fairly isolated from the other buildings, which kept
the flames from jumping to them. Still, people scrambled around
on top of the other structures, pouring water from buckets
handed from windows or hauled up on ropes. They weren't trying to put out the fire, just wet down and protect their own places.
I wondered if anyone had tried to start a bucket chain down to
the river to actually fight the main fire, but it seemed unlikely;
Neceda thought only of its avaricious little self. And now, judging
from the size of the flames, there would be no point.

"My office," Liz said numbly. "All my records are in there. . . ."

I took her hand and pulled her through the crowd toward the fire. Everyone in town had emerged to see the blaze, but they stopped well short of it. The only people in the open space between the crowd and the building were Gary Bunson and his two deputies, Pete and Russell. They looked confused, terrified and useless.

As we burst through the crowd, Pete lowered his toothpick spear, so old and dry it might shatter if someone sneezed in the vicinity. "Stay back!" he cried, his voice cracking like a teenager's.

"Good grief, Pete, it's me," I said. Russell scampered over to back up his friend, the tips of their fragile lances trembling as they pointed them at us. Luckily Gary also saw us and waved them off before they embarrassed themselves.

"At ease, morons," Gary snapped. He was sweaty and smoke stained. "Liz, there's nothing left of your place, either, I'm afraid."

"Is Hank okay?" Liz asked breathlessly. The wind shifted and engulfed us in smoke.

"Beats the hell out of me. I haven't seen him, and if he's smart he'll stay hid 'til he can get out of Neceda in one piece. The whole town could go up if that fire starts roof-hopping, all because he got careless." He looked at me, taking in the scratches visible on my arms and face. "What happened to you?"

"I was dancing with your ex-wife," I said.

"Which one?" he shot back.

Somewhere inside the stable a horse screeched in terror. A great cloud of sparks surged out on the wind, and we all ducked and covered our heads. People in the crowd behind us screamed. I patted out a small flare on Liz's sleeve. "What about Peg and the kids?" Liz demanded.

"Over there somewhere," Gary said, waving toward the other side of the fire. "All of them, except Hank." He looked away, fully aware of the implications. "Nobody's seen him since this started."

I looked at the stable. Wood and hay; it would go up fast and quick, and anyone trapped inside wouldn't last long. It might be too late already. "We have to see if he's in there," I said.

"*We?*" Gary repeated sharply. "Uh-uh, my job is to keep the peace and I'm doing that just fine right here."

"He's your *friend*, Gary," Liz said.

"So's my ass."

I was about to say something regarding Gary's likely parentage when movement caught my eye. Between two of the buildings across the way, at the mouth of Ditch Street, stood a man with white hair, wearing an enormous pair of gloves. I was so surprised that I stared, momentarily forgetting the crisis.

He was a small, thin man with the kind of hatchet-like face that lent itself to stern disapproval. That made the pain visible in it, even from this distance, somehow more affecting. His snowy mane swept back from a pronounced widow's peak and fell to his shoulders, and he wore the simple tunic and trousers most local people favored. The heavy gloves looked more like some giant child's mittens than something an adult would wear in public.

Shapes suddenly appeared out of the darkness behind him, loping down Ditch Street toward us. The firelight revealed them to be short, thick-bodied men wearing those red head scarves.

I had not seen them emerge from the Lizard's Kiss building; they just appeared as if from out of the ground and stopped well short of the intersection, clustered together like a press-gang.

The white-haired man paid them no mind. He watched the fire with more trepidation than most, and of course I immediately wondered if he might be the arsonist behind it; not for a moment did I agree with Gary that Hank had gotten careless enough to burn down his own barn. Hank was a fourth-generation black-smith and farrier; he wouldn't make such a dumb mistake.

Without taking my eyes off the old man, I nudged Liz. "See that old guy over there?"

She looked and said, "Where?"

"On the street outside the alley by the cobbler's shop."

"Oh, yeah."

"That's our mysterious visitor from the hospital. Go grab him. Gary and I will check for Hank."

Liz nodded and immediately moved into the crowd. I felt a momentary thrill of pride that my girl, *my* girl, could be counted on to handle that sort of job. Plenty of men I'd known couldn't be.

Then I realized Gary was glaring at me. "The hell we will," he said.

"You owe him money," I reminded him as I pushed him to-ward the fire. "If we don't try to find him, people will think *you* set it to get out of the debt."

"Why would they think that?"

"Because that's what I'll tell them."

"I don't care!" Gary wailed, but by then we'd reached the stable doors. Even the metal hinges were smoking as they baked off the grease that lubricated them. I tried the handle, but the bolt had been locked on the inside. I slid my sword between the doors and, using it for leverage, popped a plank free enough to get a hand in and slide the bolt. The heat scalded my knuckles.

We jumped aside to avoid the belch of flame that shot out. "This is crazy," Gary said, pressing a kerchief to his face. The inside of the barn looked like the very mouth to hell. "I'm not going in there."

"Yes, you are," I said, grabbed his arm and pulled him into the stable after me.

he smoke's odor immediately told me more than hay was burning. The place had been deliberately torched, most likely with oil or alcohol, so there was even less time than I initially thought. The blaze was at that liminal point where the stable looked like a line drawing rendered in flame: every edge and straight line glowed, and in moments they would all crumble and collapse. Even above the mingled roars of crowd and fire, I heard the creaking protests of beams about to snap.

"Hank!" we yelled, but our cries were too muffled to really be heard. The heat sucked the air from us and replaced it with foul, acrid smoke. Crouching low and skirting the burning debris, we made our way to the rear of the stable. Gary hid behind me just as Hank's son had done behind his father.

All the horses, including the ones owned by Argoset and his henchman, had been cleared out. Only a young stallion barely out of colthood remained, kicking futilely at the gate of one of the rear stalls. I unlatched the gate and the wide-eyed horse rushed toward the front door. The animal was already badly singed, and so terrified that he didn't even pause before he dashed through a fresh sheet of flame into what he supposed was freedom outside.

"He's not here," Gary said. "Let's get out while we can!"

"We haven't checked the back," I insisted.

"It's on fire! The *front's* on fire! The *sides* are on fire, and look! The ceiling! Guess what? *It's on fire!*"

The heat grew so intense I was sure my beard would combust. I danced around several blazing clumps of hay that filtered down from the loft through widening cracks in the ceiling. We reached the back of the barn where the door led into Hank's house. I pounded on it with my sword hilt, but it was bolted from the other side. That meant someone had been alive to lock it, and I had a moment of relief before I turned and suddenly felt a chill despite the blaze.

Hank Pinster was pinned to the wall by a pitchfork through the torso. His hands, already burned down to blackened talons, uselessly clutched the smoldering handle. His feet barely touched the floor; whoever had killed him had been stronger and taller. The ends of his hair burned slowly toward his skull.

Gary and I looked at each other, neither of us with the extra air to speak. We both knew this meant arson, and murder.

Then the ceiling above Hank gave way, and we barely avoided the surge of flaming wood, hay and debris that burst out from the impact. The hayloft was disintegrating above us, and the whole structure would collapse at any moment.

We dashed for the front doors, but a fresh pile of burning

hay and crossbeams thundered down. Gary's watery eyes opened wide in a panic, and I think he would've made a break for it just like the colt if, at that moment, Argoset's huge lackey hadn't emerged from the smoke and fire *behind* us. He had a rag of some sort wrapped around his head against the smoke, and only his size let me recognize him. He scooped each of us up under one enormous arm like two rowdy children and toted us through the now-open door to Hank's home, out another door and into the street. Even though it was summer, after that inferno the air felt like a blast of ice water. He dumped us unceremoniously before his boss.

Coughing so hard I expected a lung to land in the dirt beside me, I looked up at Argoset in amazement. He wore clothes coated in road dust and held the reins of their two horses. His muscleman unwound the cloth from his face and wiped at the soot streaking his bare, sweaty arms.

"Are you two all right?" Argoset asked, and offered me his hand. "You're really lucky, you know that? Marion had just finished making sure no one was left in there, and then one of Magistrate Bunson's deputies said you'd gone in the front door. He volunteered to go back in and get you."

I looked at the big, implacable face with the unlikely name of Marion. "Thanks," I said. He nodded.

Gary remained on his knees, bent double in a convulsive coughing fit that seemed like it might snap him in half. "Water," he choked out, and Argoset nodded to Marion, who took a canteen from his saddle. He handed it to Gary, who could barely swallow between coughs.

I took the canteen and drank gratefully. Even now the fire was beginning to chew its way into the Pinsters' living quarters.

It progressed more slowly, though; that part of the structure hadn't been doused with whatever had been used on the rest of the building.

Argoset stared up at the stable's burning roof. "It's going up pretty fast."

"Hay and wood," Marion grunted.

Argoset nodded. "Glad you made sure no one was in there."

I kept the reaction off my face—not hard, the way I was coughing—but I couldn't miss the fact that Argoset had twice mentioned that the barn was empty. It would be hard for anyone with working eyesight to have missed Hank pinned to the wall, and Marion was certainly big enough to have killed him in the way we saw. But why would he? And did he know we saw the body before he found us?

I continued to gulp as much night air as my lungs would accept, and returned the canteen to Marion. Gary was still on the ground. Much of the crowd had dissipated now that the initial excitement was over and the hard work of cleaning up would begin. I looked around for Liz, and spotted her at the end of Ditch Street where I'd previously seen the old man.

She wasn't looking my way; instead, she shoved the old man ahead of her up the street away from the crowd. They were talking animatedly almost like old friends as they turned down an alley between Jack Talon's herbalist shop and the Lizard's Kiss.

I opened my mouth to yell after them. A fresh fit of coughing seized me and little white specks danced in my vision. I made a sound like a bleating goat as the cough took over, and when I looked again, Liz and the old man had vanished.

Something inside the barn crashed behind us, and the remaining crowd collectively gasped. Some young wags from a casino began cheering. I turned in time to see the last of the hayloft and roof collapse down into the first floor. Like a wave on the ocean, light and heat surged out and then up, driving us all back before settling into a single column of flame.

Then Liz appeared at my side, so abruptly that I yelped with surprise. This made me cough again, and her arm snaked around my waist. She cocked her hip so she could take some of my weight, which she'd had plenty of practice doing lately. "Two seconds," she said. "That's all it takes for you to get in trouble when my back is turned."

I tried to ask, *What did the old man say?* but only managed the words "old man."

She shook her head. "Didn't find him. Come on; let's get you back home." To Argoset she said, "Did someone have to drag him out? He really *doesn't* have the sense to leave a burning building."

"Marion rescued them," Argoset said with a nod to his subordinate.

Liz turned to the big man. "Thanks, then." He grunted a response.

"Glad we were around to help," Argoset added. "And glad no one else was in there."

As Liz pulled me away, I grabbed Gary's arm and dragged him after us. Argoset raised his hand as if about to stop me, but changed his mind in mid-motion and turned it into a fake-jaunty wave. He locked eyes for a moment with Gary, then resumed watching the fire.

Pete and Russell started to stop us, then looked from Argoset to Gary, uncertain who they worked for at the moment. Gary waved at them to stay put, and they nodded. Pete glanced uncertainly at Marion.

People stepped aside as we staggered through the crowd. The night's implications whirled in my head, and there was no way I could just go home. Once we turned the corner and were out of sight, I said, "I want a drink. A big one."

"First smart thing you've suggested," Gary agreed.

Liz was about to protest, then wearily changed her mind. *Just because "drink" and "think" rhyme,* she once told me, *doesn't mean they always have to go together.* We cut behind the buildings and down the alleys that separated the main street from the few smaller, residential dwellings that backed up to it. These were dangerous passageways at night, but since most everyone was at the fire and I knew Liz and I could handle any bandits we might encounter, I wasn't worried. We gave a wide berth to one body sprawled in the mud; I couldn't tell if the guy was drunk, beaten or dead, but if he'd wandered back here, he probably deserved what he got.

We emerged at Angelina's. She stood outside, a pipe in her hand, watching the orange glow in the sky. A few patrons lounged against the wall with their tankards. She looked tired, and her blouse was sweaty above her corset. When she saw us she smiled at Liz, then frowned at me and Gary.

"First you're cut to pieces; now you're half burned up," she said. With a "hmph" of disdain she added, "And you're keeping this kind of company."

"Kiss my ass, Angelina," Gary said, leaning wearily against the wall.

"What burned down?" she asked Liz and me.

"Hank Pinster's stable," Liz said.

Angelina's eyes opened wide, and her attitude vanished. "Doesn't that mean your office, too?"

"Yeah," she said wearily.

Angelina patted Liz's arm sympathetically. Then her normal disdain returned. "Let me guess—these two geniuses went in to make sure everyone was out."

"Somebody had to," Gary said. He glanced at me; I shrugged. If he wanted to claim credit for something noble, I wasn't going to contradict him.

"Think you can get these two heroes a drink?" Liz asked drily. "Then maybe I can get mine off the street for the night."

"Oh, sure," she replied acidly. "Heroes are our favorite patrons."

We followed her inside. Except for Callie busily washing tankards and the two minstrels sharing a pipe, the place was empty. Tables and booths were still cluttered with signs of occupancy, though, and the crowd would return as soon as the excitement ended.

Gary and I dropped heavily onto bar stools, still coughing and wheezing. Callie did a double take at us and said, "Wow, Mr. LaCrosse. You look worse than you did before." I couldn't argue.

Angelina placed two tankards in front of us, and a cup of wine before Liz. I drank mine gratefully, coughed some more, then turned to Gary and said, "Argoset lied to us."

He nodded. He tried to speak, but choked on the ale.

"About what?" Liz asked.

"Hank was in there," I said, low so only she and Angelina heard.

"He was?" Liz gasped. "Why didn't you bring him out?"

"He was already dead. Somebody thought he was a hay bale and stuck a pitchfork through him."

Angelina shook her head. "Poor Hank. With all those kids, too. And he still owed me money."

"Argoset said no one was in there," Liz said.

"Yeah."

"Maybe that big lummox didn't see him?"

"He was pinned to the wall like a royal decree. Kind of hard to miss."

"Who was hard to miss?" Callie said as she elbowed in beside Angelina.

"Your new boyfriend," I said.

She glanced over at him. Whatever he and his friend had in their pipe, it clearly made them happy, as both were laughing like toddlers. "Yeah, just wish he'd lay off the giggleweed. Makes their second set pretty sloppy."

"This audience probably doesn't notice," I said.

Callie gave me a lopsided smile that, for the first time since I'd known her, carried a hint of shrewdness. "I *hope* they won't always be playing to audiences like this. There's something else on the horizon, a real big-time gig. But I don't want to jinx it by talking about it." Then she took a basket out to the floor and began collecting more discarded tankards so she could wash them before the patrons returned.

We all fell silent and nursed our drinks. In all honesty, though, despite the fact that a nice guy had died, I was far more concerned that Liz told me she hadn't found the old man, even though I'd seen her do it. Bathed in amber light from the tavern's lamps, she looked younger and lovelier than ever. I'd first met her in this tavern, in fact, two bar stools away from where she sat now. Maybe, I reasoned, she was just waiting to tell me once we were off the street. I leaned close and softly asked, "So you didn't find any sign of the old guy with the gloves?"

"Nope," she repeated, straight-faced, no hint of guile. I think my heart broke a little.

"So what are you crusaders going to do next?" Angelina said.

"Nothing," Gary croaked.

I said, "First thing tomorrow, I'm going to—"

Gary grabbed my arm. I'd never seen him look so certain, and at the same time so terrified. "*No*, Eddie. You're not going to do *anything*. Whatever's going on, whoever's behind this, you're already in further than you should be. So am I, and it's going to take all my smarts to get *me* out." Then he coughed some more and put his head down on the bar.

I waited until he got his breath before asking softly, "What *do* you know about it, Gary?"

"Nothing. I don't *want* to know. These decisions come from far over my head, and my orders were to smile, nod and look the other way. So I'm looking."

"Even though Hank's dead," I said.

"Yes," he said with no hesitation. "Because whatever's going on is *that* big, and I'm content to be little." He slapped a coin on the bar, then went coughing into the night.

Angelina picked up the coin. "For Gary, that speech was medal-level bravery. And since he paid for his own drink, he must be really scared." She tucked the coin somewhere out of sight, wiped his spittle from the bar and looked at me. "And since you won't take his advice, what *are* you going to do?"

"Right now he's going home," Liz said. "Finish your drink and let's go."

"She sounds like your mother," Angelina said.

"And in bed she sounds like yours," I said. Angelina's harsh laugh trailed us out the door.

When we reached our building, I was surprised to see Liz's wagon and horses tied up outside it. I'd been so preoccupied by the emergency that I hadn't noticed them before. The animals whinnied and tossed their heads when they saw her, but she ignored them and helped me up the stairs. "Is that your wagon?" I asked needlessly.

"Yeah. Didn't feel like walking all the way from the office."

"That's lucky," I said. Normally both wagon and horses would've been at the livery stable. "You bring home your most important assets just before your office burns down."

"Yeah, isn't it?" she agreed, with no sign of suspicion or guilt. She opened the door and went in ahead of me. While she lit the lamp, I undressed at the door and dropped my smoke-ruined clothes atop my earlier bloodied ones. At this rate I'd need a whole new wardrobe before the week was out.

I fell across the bed yet again, adding soot and sweat to the bloodstains I'd left there earlier. The muscles of my chest hurt when I coughed and the back of my head throbbed anew. My knuckles ached whenever I moved my fingers. Liz poured me a drink of water, handed it to me, then went to the window. The glow had almost vanished, and she had to lean far out to see past the corner. "Looks like they've kept it from jumping to any of the other buildings."

"Good," I said.

She turned and sat on the windowsill, her eyes on me. "That was, by any conventional wisdom, a thoroughly dumb-assed thing to do. I knew you were going in, but I didn't expect you to have to be carried out."

I nodded, and coughed. "Me, neither."

"In the last month you've scared the daylights out of me more than anyone ever has. I'd really rather you not, from now on."

"It wasn't on purpose," I croaked.

"It never is. That's pretty damn little comfort, though."

She crossed the room and knelt beside the bed. It reminded me of the way she'd looked when I woke up at the hospital. "I'm not some giggly girl, Eddie. I fell in love with you with my eyes open. I'm not asking you to change, just . . . remember that your actions affect someone else almost as much as they do you."

I stroked her hair. It was damp with sweat. "I will," I said softly. But all I could see in my mind was her talking to the old man with gloves, and all I heard was her lying about it.

The next morning the ruins of the livery stable were still smoking. So was Liz; just before dawn she awoke me by draping her long bare leg over mine, while her hands brought me to life despite a colossal collection of aches and pains. Certain parts of me stirred before my consciousness, so we were actually in the midst of, ahem, battle before I was fully aware. Her skin smelled of sweat, smoke and something deliciously, uniquely her; I let my hands and mouth devour it with all my remaining gusto. She was no tentative, inexperienced girl, and knew how to get what she wanted while making sure I wasn't shortchanged, either. It was intense, quiet and with the hint of violence along the edges that we both seemed unable to avoid. Neither of us minded.

By the time we finished, sunrise peeked through the window and illuminated air still hazy with diffused smoke. I smiled at the thought that maybe *we* had generated it. Liz drifted back to sleep, but I was restless. I slipped out of bed and looked outside. The streets were empty; well, unless you counted the half-dozen drunks passed out in the well-trampled earth. It had been a dry couple of weeks, or else these poor bastards would've found themselves waking up in six inches of mud. The fire's smell permeated everything.

My muscles and joints were not happy with me. Every movement reminded me of what I'd gone through yesterday and last night, and I choked down the grunts and groans they inspired. I started the fire in the stove and put water on to heat. There was actually a slight chill in the room; this would be the only cool part of the day, vanishing as soon as the sun rose high enough to reach over the buildings.

I turned and stopped, momentarily transfixed by the sight of Liz. Sprawled on her back, one arm over her eyes and a foot dangling off the edge of the bed, she again looked golden, like a treasure. I watched her breasts rise and fall as she breathed, and unbidden, the memory of the time I'd seen her identical twin sister naked returned vividly to me. It was a lifetime ago, of course; Cathy Dumont was dead over a decade now. But she lived on in my memories, and her shade grew incrementally stronger the longer I kept the secret from Liz.

Would I ever work up the nerve to tell her? Did I need to? I was used to keeping secrets, especially my own, but this was the first time I had to decide if something really *qualified* as a secret. I'd never been intimate with Cathy, and had not been present at her death, but as far as Liz and her family knew, Cathy had simply vanished years ago. Did I owe it to them to resolve their memories? Or, given the circumstances surrounding her death—decapitated in a bathtub by a mercenary I subsequently killed—was ignorance better for all concerned?

Liz shifted on the bed, dislodging the sheet and showing me a smooth unbroken line of flesh from ankle to shoulder. As my eyes traveled up her skin, I realized her own were open and regarded me with wry amusement.

"Most people pay when they go to a show," she said sleepily.

"I already paid you this morning."

She smiled and stretched, revealing even more pale skin. "That you did, my friend."

I put some tea in two cups and poured hot water into them. She smiled and blew me a kiss when I handed one to her. Patches of sweat still gleamed on her pale skin and lightly freckled shoulders as she sat on the edge of the bed. She took a sip, sighed contentedly; then her expression grew serious. "I should go see if anything's salvageable at my office. And find somewhere to stable my horses."

That comment brought back every bit of the previous night's doubt and worry, which I'd completely put out of my mind. She stood, picked up the heated kettle and went into the next room. I heard water splashing as she washed up.

I stared down into my own tea, my appetite suddenly gone. "Good thing you brought the wagon home."

"Yeah, if I hadn't been so beat from that run to Pema, I wouldn't have." She leaned out, her wet upper body sparkling in the morning light. "Funny how things happen like that, isn't it?"

I nodded. She resumed washing.

After she left I also washed up. The soap and water cleaned out all the minor cuts I'd accumulated, and there were a lot of them. With Liz gone I was free to curse and wince as much as I wanted. I applied some of the moon priestess salve to the worst of them, although after a good night's sleep they'd scabbed over pretty well on their own.

My knuckles, as expected, were swollen and bruised. I could still make a fist, and grab my sword hilt, but I doubted my grip was up to too many parries.

I got dressed and formulated a plan. Well, sort of a plan. Actually more of a next step. As in the next step a blind man locked in a dark room might take as he looked for a key that wasn't there. The dragon people were connected to Gordon Marantz, which meant he was connected to the death of Laura Lesperitt. That explained why Argoset and the Sevlow big shots might be interested, too. What I didn't know was why, and it seemed Marantz would be the best one to ask about it. So it was time to find him.

Mrs. Talbot sat on the edge of the porch, her sullen grandson huddled against her. Something about that boy always gave me the creeps, like he'd seen too much for a child his age, and understood way more of it than was natural. "Hear about the murder last night?" she said as I left the building.

"I just got up," I said, not giving anything away. "Who was murdered?"

"Found some woman dead in the alley. Cut up like a side of meat, they said."

"Dangerous town."

Her lips smacked disconcertingly when she spoke. "Heard somebody say they set the fire to distract people from it."

"Not everything's connected, Mrs. Talbot."

She nodded. "That's a true thing. But lots of things are, and most of us don't even know about it."

I'd gotten sucked into this discussion before, so I quickly excused myself. I went down the street to Angelina's tavern, and my office. The breakfast crowd filled the counter, and rather than force my way in, I waited for an empty stool. When I finally sat, Callie slapped a plate of ham and eggs in front of me without asking. It wasn't my usual breakfast—I didn't really have a "usual"—but her harried glare warned me against any rebuke. She had the look of someone who'd worked all night and would snap off the head of the first person who crossed her.

I picked at the runny eggs and listened to the two merchants beside me as they discussed local gossip. I knew them by sight, but we'd never really interacted and they paid me no mind.

"They say the blacksmith burned it down because he was about to be arrested for rum smuggling," Kopple the tailor said. He had a scar on his cheek that left a gap in his otherwise full beard. "It went up so fast because he soaked the place with his contraband first."

"Can you blame him?" replied Kopple's companion, the stonemason Walsh. He ate voraciously, heedless of the egg stuck in his long mustache. "The thought of gentle Muscodian justice scares the hell out of me, too."

"Man, this is *Neceda*, not Sevlow," Kopple said. "Everybody's into something here, including the king's men. If the guy wanted to smuggle ale no one would care, not like they would in the capital."

"Nobody except the Big Mace," Walsh pointed out, using Gordon Marantz's nickname among the people who didn't deal with him.

Kopple nodded. "Yeah, that's true. He might care. But if the blacksmith had been doing it for a while, he was probably *working* for him."

"Maybe, but did you see that officer from Sevlow poking around? I hear King Archibald is going to bring back torture chambers to get confessions and eliminate the whole appeals process he copied from Arentia."

"Just like the good old days," Kopple said wryly. "When I was an apprentice, you didn't come to Neceda alone unless you wanted to leave bloodier and poorer than you arrived."

"It's almost that bad now," Walsh said sadly. "My wife's knocked up, and we're thinking about getting out before the baby's born. Did you hear that, besides the fire, they found some woman stabbed to death in an alley?"

"How do you hear all this stuff?" Kopple asked, irritated.

"I pay attention."

"It was probably some whore who tried to cheat someone. That could happen anywhere."

"Yes, but the *way* she was killed. They said she was lying in an inch of her own blood with her belly slit open and everything taken out."

"Hey, I'm trying to eat here!" someone farther down the counter bellowed. My own breakfast suddenly looked less appetizing as well.

"Sorry," Kopple said. "The way things work in the real world still amazes my friend."

Callie suddenly appeared in front of me again. Sweat made her hair stick to her cheeks, and she had circles under her eyes. "You've got someone up in your office," she said wearily. "A woman."

"Why didn't you tell me when I first came in?"

"Hey, as busy as we are, you're lucky I even saw her go up the stairs," she snapped. Then she shot away down the bar to deliver tea to a demanding patron.

I scooped up the last of my eggs on a piece of bread, wiped my face and headed upstairs. Before the fire, Hank had told me Mother Bennings wanted to see me, so that's who I expected. But instead Peg Pinster sat on the bench in my outer office, head down, clad in a long black dress with a mourning shawl around her shoulders. Her wavy brown hair was pulled back in a tight bun. In all the time I'd known her, it was the first occasion I'd seen her with no children nearby.

Despite her brood she was still an attractive woman, with the kind of earthy beauty that looked its best in dishevelment and kept husbands honest. Hank had loved her with a ferocity I'd never understood until I met Liz.

Peg looked up as I entered, then stood. "Mr. LaCrosse," she said formally, and attempted a curtsy.

I scowled." 'Mr.'?"

"I need to talk to you professionally."

I nodded. "Okay, but you don't have to genuflect at me. Come on in."

We went into my inner office. I opened the window—even smoky air was better than stuffy—and indicated she should take the guest chair. I closed the door and sat behind my desk. "I know it's early, but if you'd like a drink—"

She waved a dismissive hand. "No, that's all right, thank you." She slumped to one side, as if it took the last of her strength to simply stay in the chair. I doubted she'd slept at all. "Mr. LaCrosse—"

"What's this 'Mr.' stuff, Peg? I've known you for years."

She forced herself up straight and said with immense dignity, "Because this is business, and business has its own language." I heard the echo of Hank in that statement.

"All right, Mrs. Pinster. What can I do for you?"

"I want you to find my husband and clear his name. He did not set fire to the stable, either accidentally or on purpose."

"I know," I said. I couldn't bring myself to tell her how.

"There's already talk. Nobody's seen him since before the fire, and people mutter about arson after I walk past with the children. The ashes aren't even cold yet."

"Okay. But I need to ask you some questions about last night. And I need you to be honest with me."

"Of course."

"What happened just before the fire started?"

"We were eating a late dinner, just Hank and I. I'd fed the kids earlier and put them to bed. Someone knocked at the door. That happens fairly often; people get into town late and need to put up their horses. So Hank went to the door and answered it."

"Who was it?"

"I don't know. I couldn't see from where I was. Hank talked to them for a minute, then excused himself to go with them. He was gone a long time, and I dozed off. Then Cornelius, our middle son, woke up because he smelled smoke."

"Any idea how much time had passed?"

She shook her head. "I would assume not long. But I can't say for certain. I tried to get into the stable, but the fire was already out of control. I had to take care of the kids; I didn't have time to find Hank." New tears filled her battered eyes. "He was always so *careful*. . . ."

I went around the desk, sat on the edge and took her hand. "Somebody set the fire, Peg. I could smell it when I went in. You couldn't have helped; it spread too fast."

She nodded, and dabbed at her eyes.

"Did Hank seem anxious before the person arrived? Like he was expecting someone?"

She shook her head. "No. In fact, he looked surprised when he opened the door."

"Did he look up, like the person was taller than him?"

She frowned in concentration. "I don't think so. I can't say for sure."

"That's okay. Did you overhear anything that they talked about, or did Hank react in any way that seemed strange?"

"He shook his head a lot, like he was answering questions 'no.'"

"Did he seem to be talking to more than one person?"

"I couldn't tell."

I nodded. This was about to get really uncomfortable for a whole lot of reasons, not least because I knew for certain her husband was dead and she apparently didn't. "Peg, I hate to ask this, but have you and Hank been having any trouble lately? Money problems, or, ah . . . personal issues?"

She shook her head emphatically. "No. I swear to you. The stable was doing fine; we were doing fine. We'd even talked about having another . . ." Her lower lip trembled as she tried to get the word out. ". . . child."

There was no sense in prolonging this. I stood, made sure both the outer and inner doors were closed, then knelt in front of her. I took her hands. "Peg, I have to tell you something. Right now only Liz, Gary Bunson and Angelina downstairs know about it."

She looked up at me with a mix of hope and dread that could easily break a heart much harder than mine.

"Hank's dead," I said, sharp and clear. "He was in the barn when Gary and I went in. He was already dead when we found him. And the fire didn't kill him; he'd been murdered."

She showed absolutely no reaction for a long moment. When she spoke, her voice was normal. "That large man, the one who works for the officer from the capital, said he checked the stable before the fire got so bad. He said no one was in there."

"He told me the same thing. He's either blind or a liar."

She nodded. Again, it was as if I'd reported nothing more important than a new coat of paint. She said, "Then I'd like to hire you to find out who killed my husband, and why. And bring that person to justice."

"So noted." I stood and went back around my desk. "And if you don't mind, I'll help myself to a drink. My throat's still sore from all the smoke."

That was true, but it wasn't why I wanted a drink. While I fished the bottle from its hiding place in the bottom drawer, Peg said, "And I suppose we should discuss your fee."

When I looked up, she was naked to the waist and in the process of undoing her underskirt. Her hair fell loose past her shoulders and made her look young and wild. I jumped to my feet. "Whoa, Peg, what are you doing?"

In the same mechanical, normal-sounding voice she said, "I have no money, Mr. LaCrosse. I'll pay with what I do have."

I turned away and looked out the window, not before realizing that a less scrupulous sword jockey would've hit the jackpot. Peg was round in all the right places, and all those kids had left very few traces on her body. But there was no way, even if I'd been unattached, that I'd jump even a willing widow the very day after her husband died. "Put your clothes on, Peg. You should know me better than that. You don't have to pay me; Hank was my friend."

"Yes, I do. Hank always insisted we pay as we go. Except for his bar tab here, he didn't owe anyone anything."

"All right, you can pay me, but not *that* way." She was silent and still behind me. "I'm serious, Peg. Put your clothes on."

In a small voice she said, "I'd never tell Liz. No one would ever know."

"I'd know. And so would you. I understand Hank's rules, admire him for them actually, but they don't apply here."

Another silent moment passed. Then fabric rustled as she began dressing. When she'd had time to finish, I turned and faced her. She was lacing up the last bit of her dress front. I said, "Most of your livestock got out okay, right?"

"Yes. They're a bit scattered, but except for one colt so badly burned we had to put him down this morning, they're all safe."

"Well, here's how you can pay me, then. I need a new horse."

I should've seen it coming. Anyone else would've.

Hank's eldest son, Bruce, who now looked suddenly much older than his fifteen years, delivered the beast to me at the tavern an hour after I spoke to his mom. Somewhere he'd acquired a beat-up old saddle, as mine had also burned up in the stable. The creature regarded me with the same animosity I felt toward her.

"She's a little contrary," Bruce said. "But since you've borrowed her before, you already know that." He held out a folded piece of vellum. "Here's her papers."

"Thanks," I said with all the considerable cynicism I could muster. I had no one to blame but myself for not being specific. "Tell me, didn't you have any other horses? Maybe a three-legged one with a missing eye or something?"

He looked at me with the same vaguely perplexed expression

my sarcasm always elicited from his late father. "No, this is the only one left. Mom traded the rest for a farm outside of town. She says we're never coming back to Neceda again."

"Well, tell her thank you. And that I'll be in touch."

He started to turn away, then stopped and faced me again. He stood to his full height. "My daddy didn't burn down the stable."

"I know."

"And once I get Mom settled, I'll be finding out who did."

He said it with a real attempt to sound like a grown man. I said, "Before you do, come see me."

"Why?"

I had my sword out and at his throat before he'd finished exhaling the word. My free hand grabbed the back of his hair and held him firm against the blade. Nothing he could do, even kicking me in the balls, could stop me from slitting his throat, and he knew it. His eyes were wide with a child's terror. In the same reasonable tone I said, "Because whoever killed your dad can do this, too. And your mom doesn't deserve to lose anyone else."

He nodded quickly. I released him and he jumped back out of what he assumed was blade's reach. I put my sword away and said, "As the oldest son, you've got a lot on you. Let that occupy you for right now."

He nodded again.

I offered my hand. He tried his best to give me a solid, man-to-man handshake, and it *did* hurt a little because my knuckles were still sore. Then he walked away as rapidly as he could without appearing to flee.

He nearly ran smack into Angelina, heading wearily toward

the tavern. She caught him by the shoulders, smiled ruefully and mussed his hair. This seemed to completely realign his teenage priorities: he continued slowly now, surreptitiously following her with his eyes until he turned the corner.

When she reached me Angelina said without looking back, "Hank's boy was checking out my ass, wasn't he?"

I nodded. "You'll be the standard all his girlfriends have to live up to."

She chuckled. "I've got tattoos older than him." Then she looked at the horse. "New ride?"

"Yeah."

"What's her name?"

"I have no idea." I opened the horse's ownership papers. "You've got to be kidding."

"What?"

"Her name's 'Pansy.' "

Angelina smiled. "Pansy. Eddie and Pansy." She made kissing noises.

"Stop it."

"She doesn't look as friendly as Lola."

"Neither do you. Hey, would you do me a favor?" I handed her a wax-sealed note on which I'd detailed as much of my plans as I knew. It said I was going to find Gordon Marantz in Walpaca, the town commonly thought to be his home base, and hoped to be back in three days at the most. "Give this to Liz. I may be gone for a while."

"Trying to find out what happened to Hank Pinster?"

"Where you from, Angel?" I shot back. It was my standard reply when she asked questions she knew I wouldn't answer.

"Okay, okay. No questions, no lies. Of course I'll give it to her." She tucked it into her belt and looked up at me. "And you be careful. You still owe me rent and a pretty big bar tab."

"I'm always careful," I promised. Then I tossed Pansy's reins over the hitching post.

"Hey, whoa, you're not leaving that nag here," Angelina said. "She'll scare off the respectable horses."

"Relax; I just have a couple of errands to run. She'll be gone before lunch."

"She better be, or my lunch special will be your ass."

ANY connection with Gordon Marantz was cause for alarm, but the link between Marantz's so-called "dragon people" and those weird folk with the red scarves nagged at me as well. Nothing happened in Neceda without a lot of people knowing about it, but that information was often unreliable, filtered through suspicion and self-interest. I needed a solid source for local gossip, and knew just the man.

Sharky Shavers stood on one of his flatboats moored on the Gusay. His shipping business operated out of a small building on Main Street, and the back door led straight down to the water. Like a lot of people who worked in town, he, his wife and four kids lived in the same building as his business. I went down the public walk to the docks and spotted him as he gazed over the side of the boat into the water. He did not look up, engrossed in whatever he observed.

Suddenly a head popped up at his feet. I thought at first it was his oldest son, Kenny, but the face was feminine, if not exactly attractive. Apparently his daughter, Minnow, was now old enough to join in the family business, and in Sharky's world, everyone pitched in with the hard stuff.

"Looks like a branch snagged up there, dragging on the river bottom," Minnow said as she hauled herself onto the boat. Sharky did not offer to help. She flopped on her belly like her namesake, then jumped to her feet. She was about fourteen, and the skimpy, waterlogged shift she wore would be scandalous on her before winter.

"Did you get it out?" Sharky asked.

"Not 'til we discuss my deal."

"You are *not* going off to be one of those weird-ass moon worshippers. That's final."

"What 'going off'? It's right outside town!" Minnow shot back. Their inflections, body language and obstinateness were identical.

"And they do bang-up work on banged-up heads," I said by way of announcing myself.

"Hey, Eddie," Sharky said. "Go put some clothes on," he snapped at his daughter. "And send Terrell down to get that branch out."

Minnow ran her hand coyly along the shift's hem. "Then you *have* noticed I'm not a baby anymore."

"I've noticed you're about to get my foot up your ass for smarting off. Get!" He smacked the back of her head, not hard but firmly, and she scampered past me with a big grin. He sighed and climbed onto the dock. "Three boys, and put together they're not as much trouble as that girl."

"Why not let her go? She might not like it; then you can say you told her so."

"Oh, she'll like it. That's what worries me." He wiped his hands on a rag, then shook mine. "What brings you down here?"

I flipped a gold coin in the air so it caught the sunlight. Sharky's eyes narrowed. "I wondered," I said casually, "what you knew about the new owners of the Lizard's Kiss."

Sharky caught the coin on its next flip. "Bunch of weirdos from deep in the Black River Hills. They all look the same because they've been inbreeding for generations."

"What's with the scarves?"

"Religious symbol. Dragon worshippers."

My eyebrows went up, but only slightly. Had to appear a little surprised. "Dragons?"

"Yeah. These guys believe dragons were real, and that they'll come back one day and burn up everyone who ain't part of their church."

"Why did they buy a whorehouse?" Usually these strange little cults enforced strict, ascetic behavior that certainly didn't encourage promiscuity.

"Don't know, but Joan Diter had to skedaddle in the middle of the night. I saw her load onto a boat and head downstream with barely more than she could carry. And she was no wilting flower, that woman."

The pattern was forming. Marantz certainly had the muscle to run off anyone he wanted, and his thugs had the same red scarves as these backwoods lacktooths and wore dragon emblems. I couldn't imagine Marantz had suddenly found religion, though. Why bring these guys to town, buy a whorehouse and then close it? Why send his men into the hills to look for something by coating rocks with lamp oil? And why torture Laura Lesperitt to death? "Thanks," I said, and patted Sharky's arm.

As I climbed the hill from the riverbank, Minnow rushed to intercept me. She had on a dry dress, but her hair was still wet. "Mr. LaCrosse! Can I talk to you? You know Mother Bennings, don't you?"

"She patched me up, but we're not best friends."

She looked up at me, eager and breathless. "Would you put in a word for me? I really want to learn from her."

"Why? It's not an easy life. There are places where moon priestesses are arrested on sight and turned into prostitutes."

"Really?" She blinked in surprise. "Around here?"

"No. But they do it in Menasha. And in Brule their tongues are cut out if they speak in public." That was a slight exaggeration, since *all* women were forbidden to speak in Brule, but in my experience moon priestesses were harder than most to shut up.

Minnow turned as pale as her dress. "Wow. You're not lying to me just to help my dad, are you? Because he's afraid if I join—"

I put my hand on her shoulder. "Minnow, I'm telling you things I've seen with my own eyes. Your dad probably doesn't know about them, and if he did, he'd keep it to himself just to spare you. He loves you."

I could see her mind working behind her big dark eyes. "Wow," she said again. "Thanks, Mr. LaCrosse." She turned and went back inside much more slowly, lost in thought.

I sighed. One more dream destroyed. Way to go.

THE barber, his hands still smelling of blood from a tooth extraction performed that morning, cut my hair shorter than it had been since I'd graduated to long pants. He was careful around the scab on the back of my head, but it still made my eyes water a couple of times. He also shaved my beard from my chin, leaving my mustache and side-whiskers. He trimmed them down to a fine, spidery line.

One reason I kept my hair long and my beard shaggy was so, in a pinch like this, I could quickly and drastically alter my appearance. I learned the trick a while back, during a particularly awful job on the island of Grand Bruan. When he held up the polished silver plate for me to check myself in, I saw someone I could barely identify; I doubted anyone who'd casually seen me around Neceda would recognize me elsewhere, especially with my new horse. I paid the barber extra, an unspoken agreement for his silence. It would hold, I knew, until someone offered him more.

I turned up Ditch Street on my way out of town and stopped in front of the old Lizard's Kiss building.

It was two stories, slightly larger than Mrs. Talbot's rooming house. The bottom floor was broader than the top, allowing room for a narrow walkway around the entire upper half. During festivals, the girls would hang over the rails to entice new customers. In the back was a walled-in garden, hidden from the street and the neighboring buildings. Upstairs were four rooms, while downstairs held four more, plus the large sitting room where guests could meet the ladies. The décor, on the outside at least, was drab and nondescript. I'd never personally seen the inside, and only knew as much as I did from piecing together stories told at Angelina's.

From the street it looked abandoned: the doors were closed, and all the windows boarded up. The comfortable chairs that once lined the street-level porch had been removed. Still, the dirt had been trampled recently by a lot of feet, and footprints led up the steps to the door.

I added mine to them. I put my ear to the wood and listened. I heard faint hammering sounds and indistinct voices.

Then I felt the porch shift under new weight. Without acknowledging it, I slid my hand toward my sword hilt. I was ready when the voice said, "It's closed."

I turned. One of the red-scarfed men, his clothes streaked with dirt, stood behind me. He had hands the size of skillets that looked like he could twist off a mule's head. His eyes were small and dark. The top of his head came up to my shoulder.

"Sounds like they're renovating," I said genially. "When will it open back up? There used to be a curly-headed redhead here who could swallow—"

"It's closed for good," he said in his guttural backwoods accent. "There's other whorehouses in town."

"Yeah, but this is the Lizard's Kiss. It's a legend."

"It's a closed legend."

I sighed with all the weariness of a disappointed traveler. "Aren't they all? Okay, thanks."

He stepped aside as I went back to my horse, but he kept watching me until I disappeared around the corner. Sharky had them pegged, all right. But why were they here? And what did they have to do with Marantz?

MY route to Walpaca took me past the hospital, and Minnow's questions reminded me that Hank had mentioned Mother Bennings. I detoured up the path to the building, where several of the young apprentices gathered outside the main door. As I got closer I heard some of them sobbing. I dismounted, threw the reins around the post and approached. I realized *all* of them were sobbing. "What's going on?" I asked.

A girl with straight black hair and splotchy cheeks turned to me. "Someone killed Mother Bennings!" she wailed.

My stomach clenched. It had been doing that a lot lately. "What happened?" I asked. But the girl resumed blubbering on her friend's shoulder. None of the others looked like they were in any shape to answer questions, either, so I pushed past them into the building.

I followed the line of crying girls into one of the big consulting rooms. Here the adult staff, all women with gray hair and serious expressions, stood around a table on which a body lay under a sheet. A few had wet cheeks and red eyes, but none were hysterical. I was about to say something when Argoset appeared from a side room, his hand on a matronly healer's shoulder.

He was in uniform again, every hair in place and all his buttons shiny. The woman sniffled and nodded along with whatever he was saying. He stopped dead when he saw me, and it took him a moment to place me; guess the new haircut and shave worked. "Mr. LaCrosse. I'm surprised to see you up and around after last night. And freshly shorn at that."

"I'm spry for my age."

"Indeed. Marion's still recuperating; I'll have to tease him about that." He excused himself from the matron and pulled me aside. "What brings you here?"

"Follow-up visit with Mother Bennings." It wasn't technically a lie, and it sounded reasonable.

"I see. Well, as you've no doubt heard, Mother Bennings is no longer available." He gestured at the body on the table.

I lifted the sheet. Argoset said, "I wouldn't do that if I were you."

I didn't flinch. I'd seen more gory death than he'd had wet dreams, although this one was certainly disturbing. The gentle-spirited priestess had been slit from navel to chin in a single clean slice, cutting through ribs and muscle. A lot of her insides were now draped outside. I looked at her face only long enough to assure myself of her identity. "What happened?" I said.

"We're not sure. Some of your town's leading citizens stumbled over her body just after dawn this morning. Seems they'd been celebrating the demise of the livery stable and found her in an alley."

My mouth went dry, but I kept my face neutral. Liz, Gary and I had passed a body in the alley ourselves last night; had it been kindly, strong-willed Mother Bennings? At least, judging from the wound, I wouldn't be tormented by the thought that we could've helped her. "What did Gary say about it?"

"Like Marion, Magistrate Bunson is suffering the effects of the smoke, so I decided to conduct the preliminary investigation myself. We all work for the same king, after all. So far, I'd have to say it looks like somebody with medical knowledge did it." He gestured around us. "No shortage of suspects for that. Except that it would also take considerable physical strength."

He spoke too softly for the other women to hear us. I nodded, thinking of the way Hank Pinster had also been killed by someone stronger than normal. "Well. Guess I'll need to get a new doctor."

"Yes. Oh, and just to be thorough, since you did know the doctor . . . where did you go after the fire?"

"To Angelina's tavern, then home."

"And your wife will corroborate that?"

"Yes. But if you call her my wife to her face, she might neuter you."

"Do you mind if I see your sword?"

I drew it slowly and presented it to him, hilt in my right hand with the blade across my left palm. He looked at it closely, checking for traces of blood. There were none. "I see you don't carry a dagger."

I did, but it was hidden in my boot and he didn't need to know that. "I try not to let anyone get that close."

He nodded again. "I'm sorry. I like to eliminate as many dangling threads as possible. Makes it easier to see the pattern of the blanket."

"Nice metaphor," I said as I sheathed the weapon.

He shrugged modestly. "If you'll excuse me, I have a lot of distraught women to question."

I nodded, turned and left. The morning had certainly started off on a grim, bloody note, and I hadn't even found Gordon Marantz yet.

chapter

T W E L V E

I read once that if you wait long enough, everything eventually comes to you. I'm not sure I believe it as a universal maxim, but it definitely applied on that day. At mid-afternoon, on my way to Walpaca to find him, I ran smack into Gordon Marantz on his way to Neceda.

I was glad it hadn't happened earlier, because after leaving the hospital I was so furious I might have picked a fight I couldn't possibly win. Counting Laura Lesperitt, Mother Bennings was the third person killed since I'd been ambushed, and although I had no hard evidence the deaths were related, I *knew* they were. Bennings told Hank that she wanted to see me, and now both of them were dead. What had she wanted to tell me that could've been so important that it was worth two lives? Why not just kill *me* instead? On top of that was the agonizing knowledge that, for whatever reason, Liz had lied to me. Was I so blinded by love and lust that I just never noticed she had a treacherous, nefarious side?

And why had shack-trash dragon worshippers moved into an old whorehouse?

And who the *hell* was "Lumina"?

Pondering these questions helped calm me down and get focused back on the job. Which was good, considering how quickly I found what I sought. I barely had time to get off the road and out of sight.

Marantz wasn't alone; guys like him never are. Half a dozen tough-looking men rode around him as bodyguards and look-outs. Behind them walked another batch of the red-scarved folk, although these were far more cosmopolitan than the ones back in town. They seemed to come from all over, lacking the hill people's disconcerting physical similarity.

In the midst of them rode an old man, the only red-scarf not on foot. He was clean shaven, with a leathery complexion set in a permanent scowl of disapproval. His scarf was longer, trailing past his skeletal shoulders almost to his waist. Whoever he was, he looked both important and unpleasant.

Behind this bunch came a wagon packed with what looked like women, all covered from head to ankle with red hooded robes. Only their bare, dirty feet showed. I looked for signs of shackles or manacles, but saw none. Two more of Marantz's thugs brought up the rear.

The caravan passed without seeing me, or at least without caring that I saw them. They moved at the pace set by those on foot, and at least one of the hired swords wasn't happy about it.

"Boss, I know he's your friend, but he's getting on everyone's nerves with that 'flame' crap," a thug with short black hair said as he rode past.

"He's not talking to you; he's talking to them," Marantz said, nodding back at the red-scarf brigade. "Just ignore him."

"I'm trying, but he gives me the creeps."

"Me, too," another man added,

"You big fucking babies," Marantz said with a disparaging grin. "One old man's got you pissing your pants. Maybe I should hire grown men next time."

They passed out of earshot before I could catch any reply, but by then the old man's voice drowned them out anyway. He spoke without looking at anyone, a monologue that could've been a prayer, part of a story or just senility. I sensed he'd been going on like this for most of the trip and would not stop anytime soon.

". . . the flames will consume the unbelievers, turning them to ashes and scattering their souls to wander in the winds. No one but the Lightkeepers will be safe, praise the flame. And then the world will belong to us, to be tended and guarded by the great Lumina and her consort, Solarian. . . ."

Well, hell. Even I recognized that as a clue. So Gramps knew about Lumina. I needed to talk to this guy.

His followers dutifully echoed, "Praise the flame." They were all young, with the pale look of wealth and privilege about them. They were also exclusively male. Each looked exhausted, and I wondered how long they'd been walking. Certainly none seemed suited to real physical exertion.

I could see nothing of the women as the wagon rattled by. It wouldn't be unusual for Marantz to be trafficking in girls brought from outside Muscodia, but normally they'd be on display for all to see, the better to drum up word of mouth. The hooded robes seemed to correspond to the red scarves as some sort of religious clothing. None of those I'd seen in Neceda were women, either; perhaps they were kept separate from the men. I listened for talking, whispers, even singing, but there was nothing. The women rode in silence.

So. Marantz was taking a bunch of citified dragon worshippers to Neceda to join their backwoods brethren in an old whorehouse. That made no sense at all.

I needed to find out what the hell they were doing, why they were involved with Marantz and who or what "Lumina" might be. I couldn't just ask to join their caravan, and if I showed myself Marantz's thugs were as likely to gut me as to chase me off.

I had only one real chance: get to Neceda before they did, disguise myself as a dragon worshipper with that red scarf I'd taken from Frankie and hope both groups would assume I belonged to the other. That's all. Simple. Except that they were on the only road between here and town, and in front of me at that. I'd have to go around them through the woods and cut back to the road ahead of them.

Once they were out of earshot and crossbow range, I turned Pansy toward the woods. "Don't mess with me," I said to her; I always suspected that horses understood everything we said, no matter what other people thought. "This is important, and I need you to go fast. Understand?" I patted her neck, then nudged her firmly with my heels. ·

She didn't go fast. She was as annoying and balky as she'd been in the Black River Hills, but at least luck was with me. Marantz's convoy traveled so slowly we still got ahead of them, worked our way back to the road and reached Neceda first. It was nearly nightfall, so it was unlikely I'd be recognized as long as I avoided my usual haunts.

My luck continued. Strangers from a recently docked passenger riverboat filled the streets, and with that many new faces in town, I'd blend right in. Unless, I thought wryly, I ran into Gary, Argoset, Marion, Sharky, Angelina or Liz. Maybe I had too many friends here.

I tied my horse to a hitching post outside Long Billy's, the tavern that was Angelina's main competition on the opposite side of town, and headed for Ditch Street. The embers of the stable were still glowing, and a small crowd gathered around them, swapping gossip and innuendo. Some were tourists from the riverboat, getting the lowdown from the local wags. I gave them a wide berth in case someone recognized me, but stopped when I heard a voice ask, "So what can you tell me about the fire and how it started?"

I stood at the back of the crowd, head down, well aware that every moment I spent here was one less moment to prepare for Marantz's arrival. The voice made the hairs on my neck stand up, though, and I wanted to know why. Experience had taught me that I ignored such cosmic hints at my own peril.

The man asking the questions was about my age, dark skinned and with the curly black hair of men from the tropics. He carried the distinctive gear of the Society of Scribes, those independent chroniclers of anything and everything. They served no king or queen, and their accounts of the world's history were the only ones that preserved things like the long-ago massacre of Fechinians in Arentia or the poisoning of Lord Frank Fisher in Ulkper, which led to the Dandelion Skirmishes.

They also didn't waste time with trivial events. Why would one care that Hank's stable burned down?

He listened as a young woman described the previous night's events. She got most of it right, although she included the common belief that Hank torched the place himself. When she finished he smiled paternally and said, "Thank you, young lady. Tell me, did you see anything unusual *before* the fire started?"

"Unusual how?"

The scribe pretended to think. "Oh, I dunno . . . maybe something flying overhead?"

"Like a bird or something?"

"Like a bird, yeah."

She shook her head. "No, it was dark, and I was . . ." She paused to giggle. "A little tipsy. A girl can't be serious all the time, you know."

He smiled, his irony entirely for himself. "I surely do. Do you think any of your friends saw anything?"

She looked back at three girls and two boys, all in the first flush of young adulthood, away from home and easy prey to the excesses available in Neceda. They laughed among themselves and one of the boys said, "Naw, we didn't see anything. Come on, Deedee."

"Sorry," Deedee said as her friends pulled her away.

The scribe smiled and nodded, then furiously scribbled on a sheet of vellum attached to a large tablet worn on a shoulder strap. "Okay," he called without looking up, "can anyone else help me out? How about you, sir?"

He stepped close to a man with long gray hair, who jumped at the sudden attention. I couldn't hear his words, but he shook his head and waved his hands in front of his face—hands covered by heavy, mitten-like gloves.

I clenched my fists in frustration. *There* was the man who'd been haunting my steps since I was injured, now less than a dozen feet away. I also really wanted to know why a scribe was here asking questions. But there was no time. This was one more weird thing to comprehend, and it would have to wait its turn. I made haste to the Lizard's Kiss.

The building was completely dark. The front porch was as empty as it had been that morning, and there was no sign of anyone. I put my ear to the door again, but heard nothing. I dropped to my knees and tried peering under it, looking for any sign of light or movement. Perhaps I'd guessed wrong, and Marantz wasn't coming here after all.

I slipped around the side to the garden wall. There was a gate, of course, but I was stealthier than that. I heaved myself atop the seven-foot stone barrier and quickly dropped over, landing with reasonable silence in the dark behind a tall bush. I waited to see if my arrival called out the cavalry. All remained silent, so I moved along the shrubbery until I could peek through a gap.

I'd been right after all. The garden itself was empty, but two torches burned on either side of the slanted doors to the cellar, and a man with a red scarf and a serious-looking curved sword stood guard beside it. He was clearly not a pro: he yawned, bored, not expecting any trouble. He never saw me coming.

After I whacked him, I propped him against the side of the building, sword still in his hands, so he'd appear asleep. I didn't know how long he'd be out, but he'd be found as soon as Marantz and company arrived. At least he couldn't identify me.

I tied Frankie's red scarf around my head in the same fashion as the guard. My clothes weren't as rustic, so I took some mud and smeared it around the cuffs of my sleeves and the bottom of my pants. I was pretty sure I could mimic the accent with no problem. I debated abandoning my sword, but decided if the guard had one, others inside might, too. I carefully lifted the cellar door just enough to slip inside and closed it silently behind me.

The steps were totally dark except for a thin sliver of torch-light seeping in from outside. The sounds of Neceda's nightlife faded almost at once as I descended. I didn't know the Lizard's Kiss stood directly atop bedrock, but the stone walls were hewn, not built, and the uneven steps followed the stone's weak spots.

I counted thirty-five steps to the bottom, where another door stopped me. My eyes had adjusted enough to determine that this door was recently installed in place of an older, no doubt less secure one. An iron "x" covered the front, rendering it impenetrable to forced entry: there was no room for a battering ram, and the metal would defend against ax or sword. But when I tried the handle, it opened inward easily and silently on its new hinges.

Beyond this door, more stairs led to a landing lit by a faint orange glow. I crept down, listening for any sign of life. As I neared the bottom I heard soft, distant voices. The steps ended in a small room, an antechamber outside the arched entrance to a much larger space. The flickering light came from the bigger room.

The antechamber was a coatroom, with pegs driven into the stone and benches for removing boots. I flattened myself against the wall beside the archway and crept forward until I could peer into the other chamber.

A natural cave, some fifty feet long and twelve feet high, stretched away from the opening. The floor had been cleared and reasonably leveled for the installation of six rows of benches with an aisle up the middle. This made seating for around eighty people. At the far end, a raised wooden stage held a podium and a table. A small cage rested on the table; at this distance it appeared to be empty.

A dozen of the red-scarved men gathered at the front of the benches, casually talking among themselves. Some smoked pipes or sipped from wineskins. One tapped idly on a drum. The light came from a single brazier, although others stood unlit along the walls. Either I'd just missed church or they were waiting for Marantz's group to arrive before starting.

That question was answered at once. The outer door above me slammed open, and loud voices announced the caravan's arrival.

I looked around for somewhere to duck out of sight. A small door set in the corner formed some kind of closet, so I jumped inside. It was empty, shallow and barely closed over me. I sucked in my stomach and swore I'd go on a diet as soon as this case was over.

The room quickly filled with Marantz and his men. They sat

on the benches with the heavy thud of worn-out travelers. Two of them were on either side of the door I hid behind, mere inches away. "Man," one of them sighed, "that took forever."

"Pilgrims," the other said with disdain.

"A bunch with that much money, and they spend all their time walking places. *And* they pay for the privilege of doing it."

"They pay to listen to that weird-ass preacher," the first man said quietly. "I don't care what the Big Mace says, that old guy's gonna get out of hand; you watch."

Then, over all this, Marantz bellowed, "*What do you mean he's not here yet?*"

He sounded farther away, like he was inside the ceremonial cave. I couldn't catch the reply. A moment later he stormed into the antechamber and said, "You two!"

The men outside my door jumped to their feet. "What's up?" one of them asked.

"Our guest of honor is wandering the streets of Neceda looking for a good time. Go get him before he finds it."

"What if he doesn't want to come?"

"Then *convince* him!" Marantz roared.

They went up the stairs. Marantz told someone else, "We have about fifteen minutes before old man Tempcott finishes giving thanks for the safe journey and comes down here. You people better have your act together by then."

"We've been waiting for him for months," one of the Black River Hills red-scarves said. "We're more than ready. Thank you for giving us this place to worship."

"Yeah, sure. Thank me by keeping your preacher happy, okay?"

Any moment someone was likely to open the door and find

me, so I turned my back, unbuckled my scabbard and propped it against the back wall. This was not easily done in the cramped space. Then I waited, facing the rear of the closet.

I stayed that way a long time, sweating under my clothes, fighting down every itch and cramp. At last more people descended, and when the sound of movement and noise seemed to indicate the room was full, I backed out of the closet as if I'd been putting something into it.

Every time that trick works, I'm a little surprised, but it's never failed me. I found myself among a collection of weary, dusty young men, all too exhausted to either notice or care where I came from. They collapsed onto the benches or up against the walls, wheezing and gulping water from skins. I leaned back against the door I'd emerged from and slid to the floor, mimicking their tiredness.

The man on the end of the bench to my right looked at me. His face shone with sweat, and the dark circles under his eyes betrayed his weariness. "I can't feel my toes," he said flatly, too tired to sound worried about it.

"Long walk," I said noncommittally.

"I couldn't even concentrate on the teaching most of the time. It was all I could do to keep moving."

"That's why teachers repeat themselves," I said.

He nodded. "You don't sound tired."

"It just doesn't show," I assured him.

"I didn't see you join the group. Where are you from?"

"Arentia," I said honestly, reverting to my proper accent. If he noticed the change, he didn't mention it.

"I didn't know Father Tempcott's message had reached that far."

With all the unctuousness I could summon, I said, "It has if you know where to listen."

He nodded, leaned back and closed his eyes. I did the same, peering through my lashes at the others. They reclined against the walls, squeezed onto the benches or sat cross-legged on the floor, filling the little room to capacity. They were all in their twenties or early thirties, unmistakably scions of privilege, yet they did not banter or carry on the way young rich boys often did. Exhaustion only partly explained it—they each had something about them that spoke of sincere spirituality. Whatever they believed, they took it seriously.

Through the archway, I saw Marantz down by the stage. He seemed to be instructing the backwoods folk on how to arrange things, and they jumped to comply with his orders. He looked harried and exasperated, two things that would not improve his notorious temper. He strode back to the waiting room.

"On your feet, hummingbirds," he snapped to us. His glare passed over me for a moment, but he gave no sign he knew I was out of place. "Your prophet is about to make his entrance."

We collectively stood. Slow, heavy steps approached down the stairs. Two more of Marantz's muscle boys preceded the old man, who appeared in the doorway, propped on a cane, his natural glower enhanced by the dim light. "Praise the flame," the others muttered, and bowed their heads. I copied them.

"Bring the relics," he said to Marantz.

The gangster stiffened, unaccustomed to being treated so cavalierly. But he only said, "Of course," and nodded for his two men to obey.

"No!" the old man rasped. He had a really unpleasant voice, and when he raised it, it was hard not to wince. He pointed at

Marantz with the finger of his free hand. "*You* do it. You need a lesson in humility."

Every muscle in Marantz's body tensed, and his men looked at him as if he might pop and shower them with viscera. But he choked it down, nodded assent and said, "Praise the flame," through his teeth as he went upstairs to follow orders.

The old man looked at us pilgrims with contempt. "As for the rest of you, the ceremony will begin as soon as he returns. You have until then to recover yourselves."

One of the hill people approached the old man and bowed before him. "Father Tempcott," he said, pronouncing the name carefully. "Welcome to your new temple."

"Hmph," Tempcott said. "As a young man, I attended temples of Lumina and Solarian that rose into the sky like the spires of great mountains. Now we are reduced to scuttling about in holes in the ground, like roaches."

"One day, Father Tempcott, all will be restored," the man said hopefully, his eyes still downcast.

"One day, yes, the world will burn," Tempcott agreed. Then he caned past the man and went into the sanctuary.

Just then Marantz reappeared, staggering under the weight of a rectangular metal case three feet long and two feet square on the ends. It looked solid and old and heavy enough to make carrying it alone a daunting proposition. The cords on Marantz's neck stood out with the effort, and we all stepped aside so he could stagger into the sanctuary with it.

More feet shuffled down the steps, and the red-robed women entered, filing past us with their heads down. All but one, that is; she had her hood pushed back far enough to look around, and stole glances at us pilgrims. She was young, probably around sixteen, but there was nothing of the demure religious acolyte about her. Yet she appeared to be neither slave nor captive, although some kinds of captivity don't always show. They entered the sanctuary and lined up along the back wall.

One of Marantz's men stuck his head through the archway. "Okay, boys. Your father is ready for you."

We formed two lines and walked down the aisle between the benches. The other braziers had been lit, and their flames sparkled off the crystals embedded in the stalactites above us. Two drummers pounded a slow, rhythmic pattern that we immediately adopted as our pace. We filed neatly onto the benches, taking up the first four rows. The hill people took up two more behind us.

The metal box rested on the altar. Tempcott made his way slowly up the steps to the platform, then crept to the front, the thunk of his cane echoing in arrhythmic counterpoint to the drums. When he reached the lectern, the drummers rose to a crescendo and then stopped. The attendees said in unison, "Praise the flame."

Tempcott cleared his throat, propped his cane against the podium and grasped it with both hands. As he opened his mouth to speak, he suddenly froze and squinted toward the back of the cave. "I see our final pilgrim has arrived," he said with venomous sarcasm.

We all turned. Marantz and his goons flanked a tall, slender young man fumbling with a red scarf. Marantz helped him tie it in place, a gesture so friendly and kind it seemed completely incongruous. The young man smiled his gratitude. He was well dressed, a little drunk and instantly familiar: Prince Frederick, only son of King Archibald, and heir to the throne of Muscodia.

chapter

FOURTEEN

I studied the reaction of the others, trying to get some context. Did they even know their guest of honor? While there were a few whispered comments about his tardiness, he caused no undue surprise. Either they didn't recognize him or they didn't care. He was merely another one of their flock.

I had never met him before, but his image was familiar from the official family portrait hanging in Gary Bunson's office. Frederick was a tall young man, still thin but with the beginnings of a paunch. His nose and eyes were red even in this light, and a thin sheen of sweat covered his face. Marantz helped him down the aisle to a spot on the first bench evidently kept open for him. He sat with a heavy sigh.

"Forgive me, Father Tempcott," he said with his head bowed. "I was weaker than even I knew I could be."

Tempcott hobbled to the edge of the stage and glared at

him, but there was calculation in it; clearly he knew Frederick was his meal ticket. "You have disappointed me, as well as Lumina and Solarian. You were given a simple task and you failed to see it through."

Frederick nodded. "I know that, Father Tempcott."

"You are the brightest hope for our future, and you seem determined to bury your light under drink and women."

"I'm truly sorry, Father Tempcott. Discipline is unfamiliar to me."

Tempcott knew just how far to push it. Instead of pounding on the boy some more, he moved to the podium and said, "Now that we've gotten all our interruptions out of the way, let's get on with what's important."

Frederick hunkered down into his seat, grateful to no longer be the center of attention. He looked hungover, possibly still a little drunk, but his contrition seemed genuine. Evidently he really *did* care what Tempcott thought of him, which seemed odd given his reputation. The Prince Frederick I'd heard about loved only drink, women and games of chance, in that order.

Tempcott stood silently for a moment, eyes closed, composing himself and restoring the sense of sanctity. When he spoke again, he was in full high priest mode.

"Behold!" he cried, startling us as his voice echoed among the stalactites. "The day of the flame is approaching, and only a few will survive it to walk among the ashes." He looked up at the ceiling as if seeing his vision in the air before him. "Soot will drape the hills, and the river will run black with ash. Nothing green will remain, and the sky will be as dark as the hearts of wicked men."

Then he scowled at us poor wretches. "But you, my friends, may be saved, if you can prove yourselves worthy to Lumina and Solarian. You have completed merely the first challenge to join their service; more and greater challenges lie ahead. Only I can show you the way, for only I am left from those who once prepared the path for their great return. Long ago we were legion, and our truth was feared and honored. Now we are merely tales told to frighten children. But you will be the first of the new flames to set fire to the land."

He placed his hands on the big box Marantz had carried down. "Just as a flame requires fuel, a believer requires divine revelation. This precious relic is our sign, the fuel to our fire of belief, the proof that Lumina and Solarian once lived, and will live again." He unsnapped the lid, reached inside and said again, "Behold!"

It took all his strength to lift the object from the box and raise it over his head. It was nearly three feet long, jagged and blackened with age. Only when the bottom dropped open, revealing even rows of sharp teeth, did it resolve into something I recognized.

A skull.

Not a human skull, clearly. It resembled a crocodile, an animal I'd once seen far too closely when I was a younger man. They lived in the swamps and rivers of the coastal nations, and the big ones could easily take down a horse. They were ambush predators, waiting with just their eyes and noses above the surface of the water until something big enough came to the bank to drink. I had been big enough; luckily I was also faster, though it had been a near thing.

I knew what Tempcott and the others thought the skull was, though. And if I hadn't, the chanting of, "Praise the flame!" would've tipped me off.

A *dragon* skull. The ultimate icon for these backwoods religious fanatics and their new converts.

Tempcott carefully placed it on the table in front of the box, where all could bask in its glory. It settled with a solid thunk. Then he turned to the cage beside the box.

"This holiest of relics proves our great Lumina once burned through the skies. She was no figment, no myth, no child's bedtime tale. But for those who seek her fire now, we ask a sign of her presence among us. And she *answers! Behold!*" He opened the top of the cage and reached inside.

Apparently the cage *wasn't* empty. He lifted out a heavyset black lizard about two feet long. Unlike the lithe reptiles of Muscodia, this one had a short, fat tail and a wide head. Its skin was beaded, not smoothly scaled, and a blue, snake-like tongue flitted in and out of its mouth. It lay limp and heavy in Tempcott's hands.

People gasped and whispered around me. Clearly neither these scions of privilege nor the backwoods believers had ever seen anything like this, but *I* had, in the deserts of Minong. They had immensely strong jaws and, once clamped on, were almost impossible to pry off. Unlike other lizards, their bite was poisonous, and their venom burned like fire or acid according to an archer I knew who'd lost three toes to one.

"Behold the spawn of Lumina and Solarian," Tempcott said as he held the big lizard in his bony hands. Its claws moved slowly, and it turned its flat, square head seeking the source of its annoyance. "Our lack of belief has weakened it, so that the sacred flame is now a mere burning liquid. But if our faith is strong, even that holds no terror for us. See how it will not strike me? It knows I am the greatest of its followers. Who among you will dare the challenge?"

The big lizard suddenly twisted its head and tried to bite Tempcott. We all jumped; Tempcott didn't. The lizard let out a deep, ragged hiss of disappointment.

"It can't harm *me*," Tempcott said. "Rather, it senses *your* fear. Who will show courage instead?"

No one made any move to join Tempcott onstage. They all thought it genuinely might be some sort of baby dragon. Tempcott held the creature aloft again, looking deliberately at Frederick. The prince gazed steadfastly at the floor. Tempcott placed a kiss atop the creature's knobby head and returned it reverently to its cage.

"Until you can face the spawn of Lumina and Solarian, you can never embrace the true flame," he said. For once, there was no disapproval in his words; they sounded sad and tired. But it didn't last. "And to embrace the purest of flames, you must learn to summon the basest."

He clapped his hands, and the drummers began again, this time a faster, more primal rhythm. The red-robed women left their position along the back wall, walked down the central aisle and lined up in front of the stage. When they were neatly in a row, they pushed back the hoods. Their faces were now hidden behind lizard-like masks.

Once we'd had the chance to appreciate this, they dropped their robes to the floor. Except for the barest of loincloths they were naked, and the room's energy level took a sudden spike. Then they began to dance.

They were an eclectic bunch, these women. It was hard to judge age without seeing their faces, but the oldest had gray hair, while the youngest was probably barely old enough to count as a woman. Some had elaborate tattoos; others bore scars and even brandings. There were blondes, brunettes and two redheads. They danced in place with individual, untutored styles, some simply weaving while others did elaborate hand routines. The intent was blatantly sensual, and I have to admit it had its desired effect on me. But what did this have to do with dragons?

The girls undulated up the central aisle. They made no eye contact with any of the men, even though we watched them very attentively. Tempcott totally ignored them, hobbling to the side of the platform where one of Marantz's goons helped him down the steps. I tried to see where he went without being obvious, but too many swaying breasts got in my way.

The women moved down the individual aisles directly in front of us, unashamedly displaying themselves. Most had worked up a sweat, and the room filled with sexual tension. No one made any move toward the women, though. This was some sort of test for the believers, just as the poisonous lizard had been. The young man beside me dug his fingers into his knees so hard he'd have bruises tomorrow, and the man beyond him repeatedly mumbled some sort of prayer.

One of the dancers, a supple thing with a body that could make a dying man kick a hole in a straw-paneled door, dislodged her mask during one especially emphatic combination of hand gestures. It was the girl I'd noticed earlier in the waiting room. She quickly replaced the mask and resumed her dance, but now I was doubly intrigued. She continued looking around as she danced, adding a somehow endearing distractedness to her moves. But try as I might, I couldn't figure out what she was looking for.

Then I realized she was actually doing something else as well: keeping the other women, especially the younger girls, away from Prince Frederick. She did not blatantly dance *for* him, the way a particular blonde was doing for me, but any time another girl seemed inclined to do so, she moved to block her. It was subtle, and certainly the prince was enthralled by all the women.

Finally, though, a discreet approach didn't work. Too many girls wanted to sashay up to Frederick, so she staked out her position in front of him. She presented herself to him with raw but untrained moves that were somehow more erotic than many of the experienced dancers. Frederick smiled, as well he might; she was a natural, smooth skinned and lacking any apparent inhibitions. She jiggled in all the right ways, in all the right places.

I looked around for Marantz. He stood at the side of the cave, nestled in the shadows between two stalagmites; there was no sign of Tempcott. He hadn't gone out the door we'd used, so there was another exit somewhere. Two of Marantz's men flanked the gangster, trying to remain professional despite the flesh on display. Marantz could've cared less about this religious tripe, although he had affixed a red scarf to his head. He also showed no interest in the women, except for the occasional annoyed glance their way. If he disliked this so much, why put up with it? The answer had to somehow connect with Prince Frederick.

Marantz whispered something to one of his men, who nodded before going out the main door and up the stairs. One of the women tried to dance for Marantz, but his glare sent her flitting for another potential audience. He crossed his arms impatiently and watched Prince Frederick like a mother hen.

The drummers changed their tempo, evidently a signal to the

dancers, and the women moved away from us, back down to the front. The drumming stopped, the woman silently donned their robes and returned down the aisle, out the door and up the stone stairs.

Marantz unrolled a small parchment and read stiffly from it. " 'Tonight, you must stoke the flame of Solarian within yourself. Tomorrow you will offer it to Lumina. If your flame is strong, you will be rewarded by her presence among us.' " He sighed and almost rolled his eyes. "Praise the flame."

"Praise the flame," we responded.

"You have quarters waiting for you upstairs," he said in his normal voice. "Breakfast will be one hour before sunrise." We sat expectantly until he added an exasperated, "Praise the flame."

"Praise the flame," we replied again, and stood up. Several men adjusted their visible, ah, *interest* in the girls. Luckily I was better at controlling myself. We filed out toward the stairs. I walked right past Marantz, almost within arm's reach, but he gave no sign I was out of place. Either I'd fooled him or he was waiting to see what I'd do.

As we entered the antechamber the young man beside me said breathlessly, "Wow."

"Impressive ceremony," I agreed with what I hoped was appropriate awe.

"I feel like I really can bring back Lumina," he said. He was in his late teens, unmistakably sheltered and overwhelmed by all the bare flesh.

"Me, too," I agreed.

He leaned close and said with a soft giggle, "I don't know if I can hold off until tomorrow, though."

"Sure you can," I encouraged. I began to understand what

was going on, and what this "flame" they were stoking—or rather, stroking—might be. I would definitely skip that ceremony. "Think about how good it'll feel then."

"I know," he agreed, and giggled again.

As we started up the stairs, I stepped aside into the shadows and let everyone pass me. No one looked my way; they were exhausted from the march and thoroughly distracted by the effect of the dancing girls. I was tired, too, but really didn't want to spend the night with a bunch of horny religious fanatics.

When the cellar door banged shut above me, I went back to the entrance and peered into the cavern. Marantz and his men had not passed me, yet the cave was empty. The braziers still burned, providing plenty of light. I slipped along the wall, hiding in the shadows provided by the uneven rock until I reached the stage.

The big skull had been left on the table beside its box. I listened for any sign of interruption, but heard only the steady drip of water somewhere above me. I climbed onto the stage and examined the precious artifact.

I saw no indication of trauma; the animal this belonged to had not been killed by a blow to the head. I looked for a sign that the skull had been created artificially, glued together from disparate parts, but found none. It had the organic appearance of something meant to look this way.

The idea that this might be a real dragon skull sank its sharp little claws into my imagination. The horn sockets on top were solidly attached like a steer's, and the broken ends of the horns revealed lifelike striations. The teeth curved backward and were all the same size, like a snake's. The upper teeth fit neatly into the gaps between the lower ones. That meant the animal hunted by biting and hanging on, not ripping or tearing. I suppose if it was also flame-charring its dinner while it held it, there would be no need for a fight.

I checked the joint where the jaw fitted to the skull. It moved smoothly, the knobs clearly meant for these sockets. And it was old. The grime and stain would not accumulate on new bone.

There were no signs of workmanship or modification. Fake "monsters" were common in carnivals, but either this was the best I'd ever seen or it was genuine. Yet being a real skull didn't make it a real *dragon* skull. Did it . . . ?

Oh, come on, I scolded myself. *Act like you've been to school before.* Sure, the obvious conclusion that the skull came from a real animal didn't automatically mean it actually belonged to a mythical fire-breathing lizard. There were *lots* of places in the world where strange creatures still lived. It might have been some relative of the crocodile that, divorced from habitat and flesh, struck someone as a perfect prop to prove dragons once really lived.

I lifted it carefully; it was lighter than I expected, like the bones of a bird. Since dragons supposedly flew, that made sense.

I recalled the scribe's strange question about "something flying overhead" before Hank's barn went up in flames. Could he mean . . . ? *No, no, LaCrosse,* I heard the voice of my cranky old tutor say, *dragons are* superstition. This skull fooled these people simply because none of them knew any better. I wondered if Tempcott knew it was a fake, or if he was so far gone it no longer mattered?

I returned it to its original spot, and peered into the cage. The black lizard regarded me with its dull, opaque eyes, its thick blue tongue testing the air.

Behind the stage, I spotted faint light from a small, narrow opening. I found a short tunnel, its entrance mostly hidden by a rock column; the light came from the other end. That had to be where Marantz and Tempcott went.

Once I got through the opening, the tunnel widened enough for three men to walk side by side. My foot hit something that softly clattered, and I knelt to examine it. It was the bottom half of a clay jug, the kind used to transport the cheaper kinds of ale and rum. It was dusty, and a cave spider scurried from it. These containers were easily made, and just as easily broken. More pieces, from jugs of various sizes, littered the floor.

That cleared up one mystery. The Lizard's Kiss had been built over this bedrock with its natural caves so it could front for some of Marantz's smuggling operations. Contraband could be brought in, taken out or stored here until needed. I wondered if Gary and Angelina knew about this and just never thought to mention it to me. In their world, it would be nothing unusual.

I reached the end of the tunnel and was about to peer beyond it when a sword poked me in the back and a voice hissed what could have been my personal litany: "Buddy, you're in the wrong place at the wrong time."

chapter

FIFTEEN

I raised my hands immediately. "Ohmygod, ohmygod, I'm really sorry," I said, and let my voice get high and shaky. "I was just looking for a way upstairs that wasn't so crowded and got turned around. Please don't hurt me." I practically whimpered when I added, "Praise the flame?"

"Right," the voice whispered, deliberately obscuring its identity. "Now start backing up. Slowly."

"Please, I can explain; it's not what it looks like," I whined.

"You're making me cry," the voice croaked drily. "Move."

I did as ordered. When we emerged back into the ceremonial chamber, the sword jabbed me again. "Stop. Turn around. Put your back against the wall. And keep your hands where I can see them, or you'll find your guts warming your feet."

"My guts warming my feet?" I repeated in my normal voice

ALEX BLEDSOE

as I turned. "That's good; can I borrow it?" Then I faced my attacker.

Prince Frederick's distracted dancing girl stood there in her red cloak, my Shadow Slasher III in her right hand. She held it with ease, the tip touching my navel. "You again," I said.

She raised the point to the center of my chest. I tensed; this model Shadow Slasher had a safety catch that you had to press with your thumb; otherwise when the blade was turned upright, spring-loaded spikes shot out of the hilt and made a thorough mess of your sword hand. It was a handy thing if you'd been disarmed by the bad guys, less so when a girl you wanted to question might set it off. "What do you mean, 'again'?" she said.

"I saw you looking around before, and then keeping the other girls away from the prince."

"I don't know what you're talking about."

I nodded toward the gap in her cloak. "I never forget a pair of boobs. Especially when they're attached to a lizard."

"They're all attached to lizards here. So who are you?"

"Just here for the show." I bowed my head solemnly. "Praise the flame."

"Praise my ass. You're too old to be with Marantz's group, and you're too clean to be with the . . ." She unconsciously waved the sword as she sought the word. "Natives."

When the sword momentarily pointed away from me, I jumped forward. I grabbed her wrists, careful to keep the one with my sword pointed down, and spun her back against the wall. I head-butted her, which dazed her enough that she dropped the sword. I grabbed her slender neck and, when she tried to claw my face, slammed her head into the rock hard enough to get her attention. "I'll smash your brains out the next time," I warned. "Understand?"

She stared at me, her face shiny with panic sweat. Her hands clutched my arm. Hell, she was *really* young; maybe my earlier guess of sixteen had been optimistic.

For good measure I lifted her by the neck until she stood on tiptoes. This made the red cloak fall to the floor. Rather than sexy, her nakedness now made her seem achingly vulnerable, a child-woman in a situation way over her head. Still, sympathy was a luxury I had no time for. "If you try anything," I said, "I'll still have time to crush your windpipe, and you'll die before you can leave this room. So mind your manners."

She nodded. Her eyes blazed both intelligence and anger. "Now what?" she hissed.

"Why are you sneaking around down here? Girls aren't allowed." That was a guess, of course, but it seemed reasonable.

"Yeah, well, neither are spies," she snapped. Her bare feet scuffed on the rock floor as she tried to keep the weight off her neck.

I frowned. Suddenly something was familiar about her. "Do I know you from somewhere?"

"Not likely," she snorted. "My tastes don't normally run to crazy jerk-off dragon worshippers."

"And mine don't run to whores in lizard masks, but sometimes we can't be picky. I'm guessing you're not supposed to be here any more than I am. Who are you?"

"Just a girl trying not to get choked to death," she gasped.

"If I let you go, do you promise to behave?"

"I'm not misbehaving; you are."

I smiled. Her defiance was endearing. "Okay," I said, and withdrew my hand. She coughed and leaned on the wall while she caught her breath. I handed her the cloak, and she draped it around her body. I said, "So neither of us is supposed to be here. Your story first."

She wiped spittle from her mouth. "I needed a job. Dancing naked for a bunch of men who won't touch you isn't a bad gig, considering some of the alternatives. If it means I have to pretend to believe in magical dragon gods, hey, no problem. I'm used to pretending."

"The men aren't interested?"

"Oh, they're interested. Part of our job is to keep them that way. But they're saving it all for Lumina. We dance, perform, do whatever their particular quirk requires; then they take their passion and spend it for Lumina. That's what the other women are upstairs doing right now."

This place was getting weirder and weirder. "So if you're happy with your job, why are you poking around down here?"

She shrugged. "I'm curious."

"Nope. Try again."

"Hey, whores in lizard masks can also be curious, you know."

I picked up my sword and held it carefully in front of her. Her eyes opened wide when I raised the blade and the spikes shot out of the hilt. "Shouldn't play with swords you find in closets. Were you hiding in there while everyone else went upstairs?"

She nodded.

I reset the spikes and put the sword tip under her chin. She gasped, but although the fear in her eyes was plain, she did not waver. "So what do you plan to do with me? Take me back in the tunnel and show me your other sword?"

"I *should* just slit your throat and hide you behind one of these stalactites. You'd be less trouble that way. But I'll make a deal with you: I'll keep your secret if you'll keep mine, and help me blend in here."

"Why should I trust you?"

"Because I haven't cut your throat yet. Why should I trust *you*?"

"Because all I have to do is scream and people will come running, and I haven't done *that* yet."

"True. Of course, you wouldn't live to tell them what you were yelling about."

I let her think that over. Her face was strong, with a dimpled chin and full lips, while her eyes were blue behind dark lashes. Where *did* I know her from? Not from Neceda certainly, and she wasn't old enough that I could've encountered her before I settled here. Did she just look like someone I'd once known? Had I crossed paths with her older sister, or even her mother? That thought almost made me laugh, because of the subsequent absurd notion that she might therefore be my own daughter. Man, had I read too many cheap vellum broadsheets in my life.

Finally she bit her lip, cut her eyes at me and said, "All right. You clearly have an advantage you haven't pressed. I'm guessing you're one of the good guys. I'll help you, but you have to help me."

I nodded and lowered the sword. "How?"

"One of the men here, he . . . well, he wants to get me alone. In secret. See, when we excite them, it's supposed to be saved for their gods, but he's not willing to keep things religious. And I'm running out of polite ways to say no."

"It's not Prince Frederick, is it?"

"Good lord, no. His name's Doug Candora."

"You want me to have a talk with him?"

"No, I want you to . . . well . . . take me for yourself. Claim me. Once a girl's taken, none of the others can bother her. If they do, they have to face the test of the baby dragon." She nodded at the cage on the table.

I looked at her dubiously. "Uh-huh. And how exactly do I 'claim' you?"

"All you have to do is just let me stay with you." She lowered her chin and raised her eyes, the very picture of demure supplication. "It won't be a miserable experience, I promise. I know a lot of things, and since you're not technically a follower of Lumina—"

"Stop it. This is a business transaction, not a seduction. I have boots older than you. But it also sounds like a good plan." I took her chin and turned her face toward the light. "How old are you, anyway?"

"Twenty," she said, and twisted free of my hand. "And if this partnership is going to work, you can't touch me."

If she was twenty, then so was I. My tastes hadn't run to girls this young since *I* was that young. I smiled. "I think I can manage to control myself." I offered my hand. "Well, my name's Eddie."

"Nicky," she said as she took it. Her hand was small and, when she placed it in mine, she did so with the practiced grace of someone used to having her hand kissed or bowed over. She noticed it as soon as I did, and abruptly gripped my fingers in a tight man-style shake. "Looking forward to working with you, Eddie," she said.

"So where is this Doug Candora?"

"He's not here yet. Marantz sent him on an errand."

"He's one of Marantz's guys?"

She nodded. "He pretends to be a believer. Knows all the prayers and rituals, but doesn't believe a word of them." She smiled mischievously and added, "Like you. He keeps Marantz up on the flock gossip."

"Okay. I need to finish looking around down here; how will I find you?"

"I'll be in the common room. I'm safe as long as I stay there. We can go to one of the private rooms after that."

I nodded. She started to say something else, thought better of it and swept dramatically out of the cave, her red cloak billowing enough to display her bare feet and calves.

I waited to hear the distant slam of the cellar door. Then I went back down the tunnel. At the far end, a single torch blazed in a sconce and illuminated a second cavern. This one was smaller, and was mostly taken up by a slow-flowing black river that emerged from one low-roofed tunnel and exited down another with a much higher ceiling. Three docks for rowboats stretched out from the narrow, rocky ledge. Two boats remained; Marantz and Tempcott must've departed in the third. There was no way to tell where this river ended up for sure, but to be efficient for smuggling it had to join up with the Gusay at some point. That meant the two ringleaders were probably somewhere in Neceda.

I reminded myself that I was, too. The Lizard's Kiss, or whatever the hell it was now, was smack in the middle of town, yet I'd seldom felt so isolated. A dragon cult, sponsored by a gangster and patronized by royalty, operated underground—literally—in a third-rate river village. The royal might be a genuine convert, but the gangster had to be in it for the money. And why had the gangster ordered the torture and death of a girl in the Black River Hills?

And how did it tie in to Lumina, half of an obscure cult's dragon deities? *The fire dreams are made of*, Frankie had called it. They had one skull for an icon; did Laura Lesperitt know where the other was? Would that be worth her life to these people?

And how did that fit in with the old guy with the gloves? And Liz's apparent betrayal? And Hank Pinster's murder? And Mother Bennings'?

Clearly I didn't have all the pieces yet. And I wouldn't find them huddling upstairs with a pretty young girl.

I'd promised her I'd come back; I didn't say when. I climbed into one of the two remaining boats, untied it and shoved it off. The current caught me and carried me off into the dark.

t least I didn't fall out of the boat.

The softly lapping water and humid darkness put me right to sleep before I'd even gotten out of sight of the little dock. It *had* been a long day, after all. I had no idea how far I'd traveled, and didn't awaken until I emerged from the tunnel. The boat scraped loudly against the shallow bottom at the point the stream entered the Gusay. I grabbed the oars, looked around and had only an instant to orient myself before the current yanked me downstream.

Apparently I slept through some major twists and turns underground, because the hidden tunnel exit was just *up*stream from Neceda, whose lamps and torches loomed out of the night. I got the boat under control and rowed up to an overgrown part of the riverbank. I beached the boat and hid it beneath some brush, hoping I could find both it and the tunnel again when I needed to return. If the one Marantz and Tempcott used was no larger than mine, they could've gone no farther than town. The Gusay was too treacherous for a long rowboat trip in the dark.

According to the stars it wasn't very late, so I'd only slept for a few minutes. The passenger boat was still docked, so the town should be crowded and active, making it easy for me to blend in again. My plan was vague: track down Marantz and Tempcott, then decide what to do based on what they were doing. After that, I'd have to slip back into the Lizard's Kiss, find Nicky and hide her from the guy with more than religion on his mind. It looked like my little catnap might be all the sleep I'd get tonight.

The streets were full, and light blazed from the windows of most public buildings. As I skulked along the streets, avoiding eye contact and darting from shadow to shadow, I thought about where Marantz and Tempcott might go. Neceda wasn't a very big town, and I couldn't imagine the old geezer interested in gambling or women. That left food and drink. I started with Long Billy's, where Pansy was still tied among the other horses. I actually hid from her as I slipped into the tavern, because if any horse would betray me, it was this one.

I seldom came to Long Billy's, mainly because of my loyalty to Angelina. I didn't know much about it except that Billy was the reason Angelina first came to Neceda, and that even though they lived in the same town they hadn't spoken in over five years. Neither ever mentioned the other, and woe to the idiot who asked Angelina about it. I wondered if Billy was similarly touchy. It forced people to make a choice of loyalties, and luckily the town split fifty-fifty, which let both establishments prosper.

Long Billy Hudson sure didn't appear touchy right now, though. He sat on a stool behind the bar, holding forth to a half-dozen men and women young enough to be his children. He earned his name: six and a half feet tall and rail thin, with a round, open face always set in a smile. In five minutes he could convince you that you were his best friend for life.

I sidled up to the group in time to hear the end of the story. "No," the bartender said, "they're there to hold down Old Joe; he doesn't go for that sort of thing, either!"

His audience laughed in appreciation. *Ah, to be so young I hadn't heard that joke a hundred times*, I mused wistfully. At that moment Billy noticed me and scowled. "Eddie LaCrosse? Is that you?"

"It's me," I said. His entourage made room for me, so I leaned my arms on the bar. The girls, much drunker than the boys probably due to some selective pouring, eyed me provocatively. "Got a minute, Billy?"

"For a sword jockey on a case, always."

One of the girls, a blonde who could barely keep her eyes open and her bodice closed, stumbled into me. "Ooh, you're a sword jockey? Really?" She raised her thigh provocatively between my legs.

I put my hands on her shoulders and pushed her gently away. Her skin was silky and firm. "No, honey, I'm just a figment of your imagination. I don't really exist."

She blatantly pressed her hand to my crotch. "Are you sure?" she giggled.

"Hey, sweetie, Eddie doesn't play games," Billy said. He pulled the girl away and firmly but gently pushed her into the welcoming arms of one of the boys. The girl did not seem to miss me.

Then Billy guided me across the floor into his office. It was neat, roomy, and reminded me of my own. I wondered what business a tavern owner like Billy needed it for. He offered me a drink from one of the expensive bottles on his desk. "So what can a lowly bartender do for you?" he asked.

I took the drink and tossed it down. It was smoother than the Biwabik infantry. "I'm looking for some VIPs I know are in town. Wondered if you'd seen them."

He sat on the edge of his desk. "And who might that be?"

"Gordon Marantz."

He nodded, appreciating the scale of the name. "That's a VVIP in my line of work."

"Mine, too."

"Why do you want to find him?"

I smiled. "Billy, if I told you that, I'd have to slice out your tongue to keep you quiet about it."

He shrugged and smiled. "Secrets aren't my specialty."

"But gossip is."

"True. Everyone talks to their bartender. Even you, from what I hear."

I didn't take the bait. "Can you help me?"

"Well, I do owe you for making sure my flatbread supplier didn't get muscled out by that bakery syndicate. Even though you weren't working for me on that, I got the benefits of it. So I *would* help you if I could." He spread his hands in a shrug. "But I haven't seen Gordon Marantz in probably two years. If he's in town, he hasn't come in here."

Many times my job came down to knowing who to trust. Billy had never lied to me, or intentionally misled me. He was slippery, but that wasn't the same as dishonest. So I believed him.

"Somebody was asking about you, though," he added. "Actually two somebodies."

"Who?"

"A Captain Argoset from Sevlow. He was very specific: Wanted to know if you ever took work as killer for hire. And if you'd be willing to kill a woman."

"Who else?"

"An old guy with big gloves on. *He* wanted to know if you'd been seen with a young blond girl." He raised his eyebrows to imply his meaning.

"What did you tell them?"

Billy smiled. "Not a thing. I sent them both to Angelina's. Told them you always took your business there, and seldom darkened my door."

"I *do* have my office there."

"Of course. And that's fine. But . . ." He paused and chewed his lip as he thought. When he spoke again, he was more serious than I'd ever seen him. "I'm not going to say anything bad about Angie, Eddie. Really. Just . . . you're a decent, straight-up guy. I try to be the same. Angie has different priorities."

"Like what?"

His grin returned. "Hey, you're the sword jockey, Eddie. You figure it out."

That mystery, if mystery it was, would have to wait. I left Long Billy's and resumed poking through town, seeking any sign of the gangster and old Tempcott.

Outside the Wheelspinner, one of the gambling houses where you might occasionally actually win, I saw the dark-skinned scribe again. He leaned against the wall and wrote on his vellum until he apparently made an error. With a curse I couldn't hear over the crowd, he tore it from the pad in disgust and threw it to the street.

I stepped beneath the Wheelspinner's awning and bent as if something was wrong with my boots. He began writing again, completed his notes and looked around at the crowded street, pondering his next move. Then he stepped into the crowd and vanished.

As soon as he was out of sight I scooped up his discarded note, getting it just before a horse trampled it into the mud. I held it so light from a hanging lantern shone on it.

Nothing in the sky. No strange sounds. No mention of Lam—

That's where he stopped. Was he misspelling "Lumina"? No way to know without asking, and I didn't have time for that. I crumpled the note and threw it back into the street. I checked every other possible place I could think of for my quarry until, at last, only one was left: Angelina's. Lucky me.

I couldn't just march in and look around, though. I was in disguise, sort of, and while Angelina could be trusted to keep her mouth shut, Callie would certainly give me away with a shout of surprise or a startled, "Mr. LaCrosse, your hair!" Not to mention I'd likely encounter lots of other people I knew. The hitching post was full, and as I approached a pair of drunken tinkers staggered out in mid-song. I caught the door with my fingertips as it swung closed, and risked a look inside.

The place was crowded, but not mobbed. Callie moved among the tables and Angelina was behind the bar. The smell was heavenly, and reminded me that I hadn't eaten since breakfast. I saw no sign of Liz, Gary or any other familiar faces. But at the far end of the room, beside the booth known as "the hole" because its position hid its occupants from sight, Tempcott's cane leaned against the wall. In the next booth sat three tough-looking men, bodyguards nursing their cups of ale and constantly scanning the crowd.

I let the door close and sighed. Any other establishment in town and I could've just sauntered nonchalantly in, taken a seat nearby and eavesdropped, but not here. So I had to be creative.

I went to the rear of the building and entered the kitchen where Rudy the cook nursed his concoctions. Rudy was short, wiry, and never seemed to gain any weight despite working around food. I was taught never to trust a skinny chef, but Rudy had a way with beef that would make a cow proud to be a steak. He looked up and was about to say something when I put my finger to my lips with one hand and held up a silver coin with the other. He took the money at the same time he recognized me, frowning at my new haircut and shave. I took a clean bowl from the rack and ladled some eel soup into it, then tore off a fist-sized chunk of bread. I stood in the shadows by the door and ate with no thought for etiquette until Angelina came back to get some more tankards.

"The hell?" she exclaimed softly when she saw me. "What happened to you?"

"I'm in disguise," I said through a mouthful of eel-flavored bread. "Do you know who's sitting out in the hole?"

"Yeah, I know. Why?"

"The string I'm pulling leads to him."

"Then you better just let it go."

"Sound advice. But I need to know who he's talking to and what about."

She shook her head. "Can't be done. His men are at the only table close enough."

"*You* could do it. Clean a table nearby, take a little too long getting an order."

She stared at me for what felt like one of the longest moments in my life. "That's Gordon Marantz," she said at last.

"I know."

"He's been known to kill tavern owners over a bad bowl of soup."

"That's just one of those stories."

"People don't laugh when they hear it."

"And it'd never happen here," Rudy interjected.

"You'll plug those ears if you know what's smart," Angelina barked at him. To me she said more calmly, "I'm sorry, Eddie, it's too big a chance."

"I understand, but this is important," I said as I put the soup and bread aside. "One of the knots on that string I'm tugging is Hank Pinster."

She scowled, annoyed by being put in this spot. I didn't blame her. Suddenly Callie came into the kitchen, leaned against the wall and, with no warning or explanation, burst into sobs.

Angelina rolled her eyes and stomped over to her. I discreetly slid behind a stack of wooden lettuce boxes. "For *fuck's sake*, Callie!" Angelina said, hands on her hips. "He was a minstrel; they're *like that*! You can't trust them, and you can't depend on them!"

The girl could barely get words out in response. "He . . . said . . . he loved . . . me. . . ."

Angelina, with no warning, slapped the girl hard. Her hair snapped around over her face, and her sobs shut off like a wine cask spigot. Callie took a deep breath, brushed her hair aside and said quite calmly, "Thanks. That should hold me for a while."

"That's the fifth time tonight, Callie. People are going to think I beat you."

"It's the only way to get me out of it once it starts," she said. She fanned her cheek with her hand. "No word from him, then?"

"No, sweetie, no word," Angelina said sadly.

Callie kissed her on the cheek. "Thanks. I'll get back to work." She left the kitchen with the normal bounce in her step. Angelina lightly slammed her forehead against the wall.

"Her boyfriend run off?" I asked when Angelina rejoined me.

"Of course he did. He got what he wanted, which was a few days' work and a few nights' fun," Angelina said wearily. "He could've been honest with her, though. She bought his whole line."

"Good thing she has you," I said wryly.

"Yeah, big sister to the goddam universe. Now back to your problem. I get most of my rum and ale indirectly from Gordon Marantz, and I pay reasonable protection money directly to him, so I'm not risking my ass, in any sense, by attracting his ire. So don't even try to talk me into that again."

She fell silent. "But?" I prompted.

"But if you want to risk *your* danglies, follow me."

She picked up an old bar stool left in the kitchen and led me into a storeroom packed floor-to-ceiling with plates, jugs and tankards. She pointed up. Directly over us was the floor of my office, but the dining room itself had nothing above it. "There's a crawl space up there, over the top of this wall. It leads out between the roof and the ceiling over the whole dining room. It's not really an attic, and if you slip off the rafters you'll fall right through. But you can work your way down over his booth. I don't know if you'll be able to hear anything once you get there, but it's the best I can do."

I nodded, unbuckled my scabbard and placed my sword behind a shelf of plates. I put the wobbly bar stool as solidly as I could against the wall and started to climb onto it. Angelina put her hand on my arm.

"Okay, look," she said, unable to meet my eyes. "There's, ah . . . some other stuff up there, too. I need your word that you'll never mention it." She looked at me with a mixture of guilt and defiance.

I knew Angelina wasn't completely legit, so this didn't surprise me. "Sure," I said without hesitation.

"Thanks. Have fun." She went back through the kitchen to the main room. Rudy kept his attention resolutely on his cooking fire.

I climbed onto the stool. With a grunt I pulled myself up over the top of the wall. Ahead light from the main room's lamps shone up through gaps and cracks in the woven ceiling panels, illuminating the narrow space I had to negotiate. And she wasn't kidding: the beams were ragged and splintery, while the space above them barely let me raise up on my elbows. It smelled like dust and old grease.

I proceeded like an arthritic viper down one of the beams, brushing cobwebs aside as I inched forward. Three long, solid supports ran the length of the room, crossed by four smaller ones. A platform had been built over one of these squares, and it was stacked with small, identical wooden boxes. A well-fed rat sat atop one of them cleaning his front paws. A silverfish scurried over my fingers.

I couldn't resist a peek inside; after all, I'd already given my word I wouldn't talk about it. I lifted the closest box's lid, and found nothing but old, dried beans. When I stuck my fingers beneath them, though, I felt the unmistakable shapes of coins. I pulled one out and held it in a shaft of light. It bore the image not of our own King Archibald, but of revered Queen Malena from Natabetia. Neither Muscodia nor any of the nations around us would honor these, so to be useful they'd have to be melted down and sold for their raw gold. The kitchen's hearth fire got plenty hot enough to do that, I bet.

I put the coin back beneath the beans. I knew Angelina came from somewhere far away, and that she couldn't operate the tavern on what she actually made from it. There were at least a dozen boxes in this stack, and since the gold in that one coin could stock the place for three months, she had no immediate money worries. And yet she constantly nagged people about their overdue bar tabs.

I resumed my progress. Through the ragged gaps, I looked down on tabletops and the heads of diners, and got a view down Callie's cleavage that many men would've paid dearly for. I reached a point where two beams crossed, wriggled my way onto the other one and followed it to the edge. Here I struck a nest of small, harmless spiders and had to close my eyes and mouth to keep them out. My foot slipped from the beam and cracked the woven, clay-daubed ceiling, but my toe didn't poke all the way through and no one below noticed the sudden shower of dust. I squirmed forward until at last I was above the booth where Marantz sat with Tempcott.

A crack let me see down onto the table, although my angle hid their faces. Marantz clutched a tankard beside a plate picked clean of food, while Tempcott's dinner remained mostly untouched. I had to concentrate to pick their voices out of the general din. Luckily Tempcott's was distinctive and harsh, and as usual he was upset.

". . . waiting too long for this to have it yanked out from under me!" He pointed his fork at Marantz. "You *will* live up to your agreement."

Marantz's voice was even, steady, the voice of a man who tried to never sound worried. "Relax, will you? So he's a little late. He had to go up into the hills, after all. We wait, have a little dinner, check out the local girls."

"I have no interest in the girls," Tempcott said with contempt. "And this tavern's poor excuse for food makes me want to retch. I should never have agreed to this excursion. My faithful believe I'm still in the temple, not out in the world with these . . ." He gestured at the room and spat the last word. "*People*. You've made me into a liar and a hypocrite, just like you."

Marantz took a drink, belched and said, "You're not a very pleasant man, did you know that? I don't like getting up early, but I think I'll leave at first light tomorrow just so I don't have to spend any more time with you."

"At least I have no blood on my hands," Tempcott snapped back.

"Don't even *try* to take the moral high road, Tempcott," Marantz laughed. "You need me to bankroll this outfit, just like I need you to get what I want. In the end we'll both get the things we need."

"If your people don't fail."

Marantz's voice grew tight, as if he spoke through clenched teeth. I could imagine just how tired he was of the belligerent old man. "They *won't fail*. If that girl of yours knows where they are, my people will find out."

"That may be complicated," a new voice said.

I jumped so hard I almost fell off the beam and right through the ceiling. I *knew* that voice.

The man from the Tallega road, and that shack.

The one who killed Laura Lesperitt. And wore dragon boots.

SEVENTEEN

y rage boiled up like it used to before a battle, when I first caught sight of whoever I was being paid to kill that week. Back then I learned to summon it at will; now it sprang to life unbidden, with the force of something vicious released after too long in a cage. It took all my resolve to control it as the man responsible for everything stood ten feet below me now and all I could do was perch like a silverfish and listen. If I moved an inch to the right, I'd roll off the beam and crash through the ceiling right on top of him. He'd damn sure never see that coming, and believe me, the temptation was strong. But there was more at stake now than just getting my hands on Laura's killer. I dug my fingers into the wood so hard it bent back my nails.

"Well, you made it," Marantz observed with casual annoyance.

"Hey, had to stop at the house to change clothes when I heard the Big Mace was still in town," dragon boots said. "What made you stick around?"

I risked leaning far enough to the left to peer through one of the ragged holes in the ceiling. There he was: surprisingly slender and wispy, with long brown hair and a dark beard. He looked about thirty years old. There was nothing in his appearance that advertised his vicious nature, but then again, the same thing had been said of me.

He did not wait for Marantz to answer. "Man, the old Lizard's Kiss used to be so neat, with all the satin and velvet everywhere. Now it's like a dungeon. C'mon, Father T., scoot over." The old man grudgingly moved aside, and dragon boots slid into the booth next to him.

"So what do you mean, 'complicated'?" Marantz said coolly.

"I've been on a horse all day; let me get a drink and I'll tell you all about it," dragon boots said cavalierly. Most people would not dare blow Marantz off like that; most people couldn't slip up on me from behind the way he had, either. He whistled through his teeth, and a moment later Callie's breasts appeared below me.

"Well, hey there, Mr. Candora," she said in her professional voice. "What can I get for you?"

"Oh, call me 'Doug,' please," he said.

"As in the hole I'd be getting myself into?" she flirted. "I know all about you. I bet you've got a girl in every tavern in Muscodia."

"Lies, all lies," he replied, and the smile was plain in his voice. Callie made everyone smile. "A tankard of blackberry, please."

"On its way." She turned, making her dress twirl.

How neat. Dragon boots was also Doug Candora, the very man I was supposed to keep away from Nicky. Well, if he was here, he couldn't be bothering her, so at least I was doing *that* right. When Callie had gone, Candora said quietly, "Frankie and Jimmy are dead."

"Dead," Marantz repeated flatly.

"Did they find them?" Tempcott interrupted. "Is that how they died?"

"I don't think so. I found Jimmy hanging in the cabin from Frankie's manacles, and Frankie was at the bottom of a canyon."

There was a pause. I was afraid they'd started whispering, but apparently this news was a big surprise. "What do you think happened?" Marantz said at last, carefully choosing his words.

"Frankie didn't kill Jimmy. He had some knife cuts on him, but nothing like what Frankie would've done. And Frankie wouldn't fall off a cliff, or jump. So somebody else was there."

"What about Laura?" Tempcott said.

"She's being kept somewhere else," Marantz said just a hair too quickly.

"Anyway, the box was still in the cabin, empty," Candora continued. "So it doesn't look like they found them before they were killed."

"Any idea who it was?" Marantz asked.

Candora snorted. "The only three men left alive who knew what we were looking for are sitting at this table, and we'd be idiots to double-cross each other so blatantly. So unless it *was* one of us, I figure it had to be those dirt-sucking idiots who live in the woods and think King Archibald is going to take away all their stuff. Jimmy had a run-in with one of them. It has nothing to do with what we're interested in. I'll go take care of them to-morrow."

Tempcott was not mollified. "But what about the—"

"We send more men up there and keep looking," Marantz snapped. "It's just a setback, and it gets dealt with."

"You *buffoon!*" Tempcott hissed in his most grating voice. "Both of you! You with your smug certainty, and *you*—" He pointed a trembling finger at Candora. "Turning my beliefs into a game, making sacred symbols into *trinkets*—"

"God *damn*, old man, will you lay off about the boots? It's all about building loyalty. Every good organization needs some heraldry. We're Team Solarian; the girls are the Lumina Auxiliary."

"This is not some *club!*"

"Well, they look stylish, and I like 'em. I wear your stupid scarf when I'm around your herd, don't I?"

"I warn you, if someone else *does* know about this—"

"Here you go," Callie said suddenly as she placed the tankard in front of Candora. If she noticed the tension, she had sense enough not to comment on it. "Can I get you other gentlemen anything?"

"No," Tempcott said before the others could speak. "We're done here. Please bring our check."

"Now, now, Mr. Marantz's gold is no good here." I could practically hear the wink that accompanied this.

Marantz and Candora blatantly watched her twirl away. Marantz sighed wistfully. Then, all business, he said to Candora, "All right. Settle up with the people you think killed Frankie and Jimmy. I assume you'll also take care of the search?"

"Yeah. I'll take a couple of more men up there with me."

"You'll forgive me if I'm less than confident," Tempcott said. Then he added, "What happened to your neck?"

"That? Oh." Candora chuckled. "I've been trying to get close to a certain young lady. She insists on keeping me at arm's length, and her nails are sharp. I showed her why that wasn't a nice thing to do." He took a long draught from his tankard. "She won't be trouble to anyone anymore."

I went cold again.

I probably sent a cloud of ceiling dust down on the patrons below, but I didn't care. I scurried backward, dropped to the storeroom floor and grabbed my sword. Angelina looked up from retrieving some clean dishes from the washbasin. "What's wrong?"

"No time," I said, and pushed past her out the back door. I ran around the front of the building and down the main street. Over the thundering of my heart and the breath rushing up from my lungs, I heard a soft, vaguely amused voice in my head: *Oh, Mr. LaCrosse, you think you can help me, don't you? You think you can ride up and save me, like a knight in a children's story.*

Everyone from the riverboat had apparently decided to meet in the street at the same moment, and I shoved people aside with no regard for politeness. I turned up Ditch Street and leaped onto the porch of the former Lizard's Kiss. As always, the building appeared dark and deserted, but now I knew better. I drew back and kicked the door hard; it moved, but didn't open. I kicked it again, and this time it slammed back against the inside wall.

I rushed in and took a moment to orient myself. To my right, the old greeting room had been stripped of all its ornate finery and redecorated with only a long, crude dragon mural that went around all four walls. The image showed two dragons mating, their serpentine bodies twined together, flames shooting from their mouths. The rest of the room was bare except for pillows thrown on the floor for minimum comfort.

A half-dozen people occupied the room. A pair of women, still wrapped in their red cloaks, sat on pillows against the wall. The two drummers from the earlier ceremony froze in mid-pass of a giggleweed pipe. In that pose I abruptly recognized them: the minstrels from Angelina's, including Callie's deadbeat boyfriend, Tony. The other two men were Black River Hills folk. I guess Marantz could imagine no reason anyone would want to break in, so he'd left no guards. His mistake.

I grabbed the nearest backwoods guy, slammed him into the wall and punched him hard in the chest. Completely surprised, he collapsed with a ragged gasp as he tried to catch his breath. The others, frozen and speechless, stared at me.

"Doug Candora was here a little while ago," I said, my own breathing heavy from running. "Where's the girl he came to see?"

They continued to stare. I punched the other hill dweller in his dull-eyed face, and he fell backward onto the pillows. The minstrels dropped their pipe and scrambled back against the wall, huddling like the women.

I glared at the musicians. "Okay, now I'm going to start beating on you two until one of you answers me. That means one of you will take a beating for nothing."

"Hey, man, we just work here," Tony said. His voice was high and jittery.

I grabbed the front of his clothes and yanked him to his feet. He was the kind of handsome that hid all his personality flaws; I wanted to punch him on general principles. "Thanks for volunteering. I'll start with you."

"Up the stairs," one of the women said in a small, sheepish voice. Her expression was young and weary, the face of someone with little hope and fewer choices. "Top floor. The last room on the left. He took her up; she hasn't come down."

The woman beside her, older and more scorpionish, glared her disapproval but said nothing. Both pulled their red cloaks tight around them and huddled together as if they could blend in with the pillows.

"I'm going to take the girl upstairs out of here," I said to the sad-faced one. "Do you want to come, too?"

She looked down and shook her head. Scorpion woman smiled up at me, vicious and triumphant. I didn't have time to argue. The first guy I'd punched got to his knees, still wheezing, but when he saw me he fell back down.

I took the steps two at a time. No one else seemed to be around, and the only light came from sconces on the landings. I found the indicated door and kicked it open. My hip would thank me for all this in the morning.

The room was pitch-black. All the windows were blocked, and the only light came from the feeble candle outside in the hall. I took it from its holder and stepped cautiously through the door.

There was little to hide someone: a narrow single bed, a chamber pot, a small closet with its door open. A man's dusty trail clothes hung in it. In its previous incarnation, this room would've been tapestried, filled with flower petals floating in bowls and lit by scented candles. Now it was a utilitarian cloister.

The bed was disheveled, and I spotted unmistakable dark droplets along the sheets. When I moved the pillow, I found a smear of blood, still warm and just starting to dry. Candora must've come straight to Angelina's from here.

My heart wanted to jump out through my throat and search the room for itself. I made it stay put and called out, "Nicky? It's Eddie." There was no response. I was about to leave when the obvious finally occurred to me and I looked under the bed.

If candlelight hadn't gleamed off her eyes I might not have noticed her curled up in a tight ball. She was still wrapped in the dark red robe, and it made her almost invisible in the shadowy space. I reached out my hand toward her. "Nicky, come on out; it's me."

She said nothing, and for a heart-stopping moment I thought she was dead, but then her bare feet shifted as she tried to make herself even smaller.

"Nicky, it's Eddie. I'm here to get you away."

She did not move, and made a sound like a kitten.

"All right, hang on," I said. I put the candle on the floor, took hold of the edge of the bed frame and lifted. It was magnificently heavy, and I felt its weight in my lower spine and knees. I got it tilted enough to squirm under and brace it with my back, and that allowed me to reach Nicky. I touched her bare ankle.

She screamed and exploded out of the cloak like a trapped animal. She drove us both out into the open, and the bed hit the floor with a sound like a thunderclap. The candle fell over and began to roll, filling the room with disorienting shadows. She was all clawing nails and kicking feet, but she was smaller than me and I finally got my arms around her, pinned her to the floor and used my weight to hold her there. "Nicky, it's Eddie; calm the hell down!"

I retrieved the candle, miraculously still burning, and held it so I could see her face. Her eyes were wide, and her pupils almost covered the irises. Dried blood stained her lips, and a nasty bruise was forming on her left forehead. She again made a noise like a kitten. Saliva dripped from her mouth, and I smelled a rank, sickly-sweet odor on her breath. She'd been poisoned.

"Nicky, can you hear me?" I said, loud and distinct. "Do you know what he gave you?"

She went limp beneath me. I waited to see if it was a trick, but evidently her sense of the world around her no longer included me or anything else real. I didn't know what poison Candora had used, but I had to act fast to save her, whatever it was. I wrapped her in her cloak and carried her out onto the stairs.

When I hit the second floor landing, three men came up the stairs toward me. We all stopped in mid-step. Two were wide-eyed rich pilgrims who'd arrived with Tempcott, while the third was one of Marantz's pros. He drew his knife and said, "Put the girl down."

I was two stairs above him, so I easily kicked the knife from his hand. It clattered down the stairs to the first floor. In the same motion I threw Nicky over my left shoulder and grabbed one of the younger men by the front of his tunic. I shoved him back down the stairs ahead of me, and followed quickly as he took his pal and Marantz's guy tumbling with him.

There was no room for my sword, and I didn't want to stop long enough to get the dragon-embossed knife from my boot. At the bottom of the stairs I stomped on the pro's head as he tried to rise, slamming it into the floor and hopefully taking him out of the game. I was ten feet from reaching the front door when the two backwoods toughs I'd smacked around in the lounge suddenly blocked my path.

Both held wicked-looking, crude knives that would do more

damage coming out than they did going in. "You goin'
nowhere," one of them growled.

I heard outraged voices on the stairs behind me as other pilgrims emerged from their rooms. He might be right.

At that moment a door beside me opened and out stumbled
Prince Frederick, his scarf ridiculously askew. He was barefoot
and shirtless, and past him I saw a bored-looking girl on his
narrow bed. Yawning, he stepped right between me and the
bad guys and said woozily, "Hey, guys, what's with all the slamming and stomping around?"

I never question luck. I grabbed him around the neck and
yanked him against me as a shield. I clutched his throat hard
enough for him to know I could easily crush his windpipe. Suddenly he was wide awake and completely sober.

"Hey, do you know who I—," he started to say.

"Not another word," I snarled. He nodded quickly.

More of the hill people emerged from the sitting room.
Guess they didn't get the fancy rooms upstairs and probably
made do with a common area in the back. They filed in behind
their brethren; that ten feet to the door was getting longer every
minute.

"Any of you toads so much as blinks wrong, and Tempcott'll
need a new walking gold bag," I said as I shoved the prince forward. He was slight and girlish, his bare torso no more muscled than a ten-year-old's. He offered no resistance, but merely
whimpered and raised his hands as if I held a crossbow to his
back. The others stepped aside, grudgingly letting us pass. Any
of them could've leaped forward and knifed me, but I counted
on them knowing how important Frederick was to their leader.

"Open the door!" I snapped. One of the other rich boys

hurried to obey. Nicky's weight made my shoulder ache, and Frederick sweated so much my grip on his throat was beginning to slip. I turned as I went through the door, keeping the bad guys in front of me as I backed out.

And of course, because I'm a total fatalist, I wasn't at all surprised when a voice behind me, from the porch, said, "Well, *this* sure looks interesting."

chapter

EIGHTEEN

I don't have time to banter," I said. "Who are you and whose side are you on here?"

I heard a thump as the interloper slid down off the porch rail, then the soft *shwip* as he drew my sword from its scabbard. Just when I was sure I'd feel my own blade at my throat, the voice said wearily, "I suppose I'm on yours."

I risked a glance, and was more surprised than ever: it was the damn scribe again. He stepped in front of me and faced the doorway full of dragon worshippers. "Okay, listen," he told them. "I'm really not very good in a fight, so I'll probably get this sword stuck in the first guy I stab. The rest of you can take me down pretty easy then, but the question is . . . who's going to be that first guy?"

No one moved. The scribe mock feinted with the sword, and

the others jumped back. He laughed. He had his thumb on the safety catch; he wasn't as much an amateur as he pretended. "You taking the prince, too?" he asked me.

"I'd just as soon not," I said.

The scribe grabbed Frederick by the hair and shoved him through the door back into the house. Then he yanked the door shut. He turned to me and said, "What's wrong with her?"

"Poisoned," I said.

"My horse is in the street; take her to the moon goddess hospital outside town. I'll make sure no one follows and then meet you there." He swung the sword casually. "Wow, a Shadow Slasher III. Nice balance, too, although I always thought they were top-heavy."

I had no time to argue or try to fathom his true intentions. As he said, his horse—a majestic chocolate-colored stallion—waited patiently in the street, and did not balk when I took the reins, tossed Nicky's limp body over his back and leaped into the saddle. He took off with only the slightest nudge from my heels, and people jumped aside as we shot through town.

I repeatedly kicked the door of the main hospital building to get their attention, but not hard enough to break it open. Two heavy doors in one night was all I had in me. Nicky moaned softly, limp in my arms. "Hey! Emergency here!"

The door opened and a kindly gray-haired woman wrapped in a robe held up a lamp. She saw Nicky's pale, sweaty face and immediately stepped aside. "First room to your left," she said. "Put her on the table."

One of the apprentices, a young woman clad in a thin sleeping gown, appeared rubbing her eyes. "What's wrong?"

"This girl's been poisoned," the older woman said. "Get water heated for a bath. Put sea salt and draw-weed in it."

The apprentice understood the urgency and scurried to obey. The older woman followed me into the small examination room, opened the red robe and scowled at Nicky's skimpy loincloth. "Did you buy her for the evening and things got out of hand?" she snapped at me.

"No," I said. "She's not a whore; she's just a girl who got in over her head and fought back."

She looked at me oddly. "Mr. LaCrosse?"

I nodded.

"I didn't recognize you without the bandage around your head. You should reconsider whoever gave you that haircut, though. Here, make yourself useful and light the other lamps." As I followed orders, she lifted the girl's eyelids, sniffed at her shallow breath and checked her pulse at her throat. Exposed this way, askew and covered in unhealthy sweat, Nicky looked even more helpless, as Laura Lesperitt must've looked to Doug Candora. He hadn't hesitated then, either.

"We never officially met, but I'm Mother Mallory," the woman said. "I assisted Mother Bennings on your case, goddess keep her soul. So who is this?"

"Her name's Nicky, and that's really all I know about her."

"Well, we'll do what we can," she said, and turned away from me. I was being dismissed.

I cleared my throat. "I'm not leaving," I said with certainty.

"You can't help."

"I'll try to stay out of the way."

She started to protest again, then nodded. "Pick her up and follow me, then."

We went into the next room, where the apprentice had a large tub filled with water above a low-burning fire. Mother Mallory removed the skimpy loincloth and I placed Nicky, now totally nude, in the bath. The water was already hot. She looked like a deathly ill child, small and pitiful. Her eyelids fluttered and she tried to speak, but made no coherent sound.

"Keep the fire going at this level," Mother Mallory said to the apprentice. I understood the treatment; if Nicky could sweat out enough of the poison, she might survive it, although it could still do permanent damage. If I'd gotten her here sooner, or known what the poison actually was, an antidote might've been provided. Under the circumstances, though, this was her only real chance.

"There's nothing to do but wait," Mother Mallory said sadly. "I suspect, from the smell, that she was given an extract of six-devil tea, but I can't be sure. And if it was more than fifteen or twenty minutes ago, the standard antidote would have no effect." She tenderly stroked Nicky's tangled hair. "It all depends now on how large a dose she ingested, and how strong she is."

The apprentice, her nightgown clinging translucently to her sweaty form, returned with two stools. "If you're going to wait," she said to me, "you might as well sit down."

I took off my jacket and unbuckled my empty scabbard. I placed the stool in the corner where I could see Nicky's face and settled back into the notch of the two walls. I yawned and closed my eyes for just a moment.

I snapped awake when a hand shook me. "Hey."

The scribe looked down at me. He had a kindly, easy smile and eyes that were clear and sharp. The tight curls at his temples were white. He was at least my age, maybe older, and radiated a calm, seen-it-all demeanor. The other scribes I'd met over the years had a scholarly, chilly air befitting their isolation from the world's concerns. This one seemed more grounded. "Sorry. Hate to wake you up, but we need to talk."

I looked around. I couldn't have been out long; Mother Mallory still sat beside the tub, and Nicky hadn't moved, although the apprentice had changed into a less revealing tunic. The room's air was hazy and smelled sickly-sweet, the same odor I'd caught on Nicky's breath. I knew nothing about six-devil tea extract; I wondered if it was toxic in steam, too. I stood, wincing at the door-kicking ache in my leg and hip, and yawned.

"We'll be out in the courtyard," the scribe said. Mother Mallory nodded. I followed him outside, where the summer night air felt cool and dry compared to the sickroom.

"Come on; let's have a smoke and exchange stories," he said, and led me into a courtyard. Neat patches of herbs and flowers showed in the moonlight. The windows of all the other patient rooms were dark.

He reached into the shadowy space beneath a stone bench and withdrew my sword. "No one from the house showed their noses after you left. I stayed and watched until people started yelling inside."

"I bet they did," I said. Marantz and the others would have returned through the tunnel.

He handed me my sword. "The girl that important?"

"No," I sighed, suddenly bone tired. My scabbard was still inside, so I leaned the sword against the nearest wall. "Just that the people who hurt her hate being embarrassed by things like me taking her out the front door."

"Your daughter?"

I shook my head. "Just a friend."

"Name's Harry Lockett, by the way," the scribe said, offering his hand.

"Eddie LaCrosse." His grip was strong. The scribes I'd met in the past had weak grips, betraying their fear that they might injure their writing hand.

He caught my reaction. "I didn't come up through the scribe academy," he said with a laugh. "It was more of a mid-life career change. That's why I don't shake hands like a six-year-old girl."

"And why you know where the safety is on a Shadow Slasher III."

He laughed. "I'm more interested in what *you* know, Mr. LaCrosse. Like why Prince Frederick of Muscodia is living in an old whorehouse in Neceda."

I shrugged. "I was as surprised as you. I suppose he's a dragon worshipper, like the rest of them."

"Then it makes some sort of sense," he said seriously.

"It does?"

"Sure. You know anything about the history of this area?"

"No. I'm not from here."

In a stentorian voice he proclaimed, "Long before men came to what we now call Muscodia, this whole area was the domain of the dragon." This was how scribes recited their stories in royal courts, and even now it made me stand up straight, like I was a little boy back in the throne room with my father.

A window opened somewhere and a sleepy female voice said, "*Shut up!*"

Lockett grinned. "I know, hard to believe, but it's true," he said in a normal voice. "Ever wonder how the Black River Hills got their name?"

"From the Black River?"

He mock sighed in annoyance and began packing a pipe with dark, serrated leaves. "Okay, okay. How did the *river* get its name?"

"I heard because it's so deep in places the water looks black."

"No. There were originally two names, the Black Hills and the Black River. They got combined over time, and their origins were lost. Both came from a time when the river and the hills were black with accumulated ash."

"From dragons breathing fire?"

He grinned. "Now you're catching on." He held the pipe in his teeth, struck a flint over it and sucked until the flame caught. "Want to hear the story?"

I looked back at the door to the hospital. I could do nothing for Nicky; going after Candora right now certainly would not help her. I really wanted to talk to Liz, but that thought sent warning hackles up my back. I felt adrift. So I said, "Sure."

"Once, the whole world belonged to the dragons. They had tribes, territories, politics and wars, just like men. Only their great reptile hearts could not conceive of the idea of compromise. As a result, they killed each other off, until by the advent of the time of men there were only a few widely scattered dragons left." He cut his eyes at me to gauge my reaction; I kept my expression neutral.

"Solarian and his consort, Lumina, were two of these few," he continued. "They once ranged over this whole hemisphere, burning and pillaging as they wished. People at the time didn't understand much about how the world really worked, so they saw these two immense, powerful beings first as harbingers of the gods, then as gods themselves. They built temples, wrote songs, made sacrifices."

"Human?"

"Human and otherwise. When a thirty-foot flying lizard's breathing fire down your pants, you'll try anything once to calm him down. Finally two great men appeared: Gerard Tempcott, great-great-and-so-forth-grandfather of the man you rescued your friend from, and Charlton the Just, the founder of Muscodia. Both saw in the dragons something they wanted to possess. Tempcott the elder believed they could lead mankind into a better world, and Charlton simply wanted to use them as weapons against his enemies."

"That would be useful. Except that I imagine dragons aren't easy to train. Oh, and they *aren't real.*"

"How do you know that for certain?"

"Because I'm not some backwoods yahoo who believes anything he's told. Real animals *can't* breathe fire; they'd burn themselves up. No animal has four legs *and* wings. It's all folklore and mythology."

His eyes narrowed and looked closely at me. "Where did you get your education?"

"The school of hard parries," I fired back.

He smiled. "Hell, you're probably right. I can't argue with any of that, except to say that maybe conventional wisdom could be wrong. Tempcott supposedly brought Solarian's skull here with him; have you seen it?"

"Yeah. It's just some kind of crocodile."

"But it's real? The skull of a real animal?"

"As far as I could tell. But if it's a real animal, then it can't be a dragon, can it?"

Again he paused for a draw. "Do you want the rest of the story?"

I shrugged. "Sure."

"Solarian wasn't interested in a truce or a treaty. Charlton the Just met him for a battle to the death on the plain where Sevlow is today. He couldn't overpower the dragon, so he built a dummy, studded it with hooks and knives and gave it his shield. When Solarian attacked it, he inadvertently slashed and cut himself to pieces on it. Once he was weak enough, Charlton was able to get in close and deliver the fatal blow."

"Clever," I had to admit. "Not exactly sporting, though."

"No. But the winner writes the history, and it's considered a great victory. Solarian, mortally injured, flew back here to the Black River Hills for his death throes. He burned every tree from the mountains. He killed every living thing for a hundred miles around. And he accidentally wounded Lumina. When Solarian finally died, his corpse fell into the river and was never seen again. Lumina, gravely injured and distraught, crawled into a cave and disappeared from history."

"And that's the end?"

"Of the historical record. The rest is just speculation. Some say Lumina died, too; some say she's still there sleeping, awaiting the call of the true believers. And some . . ."

"What?"

He paused for a long, dramatic draw on his pipe. "Some say she still stands guard over the last dragon egg."

Pretty standard bedtime story," I said more sarcastically than necessary, looking up at the stars. A few small clouds scudded sneakily over them. "Think I can get some warm milk, too?"

Lockett put his pipe aside. "Sure, it's easy to mock. But what if it's *not* just a story? There are lots of other myths and tales about dragons, including some where men befriended them, or enslaved them. Can you imagine what a modern army, with all its advanced weaponry, could do if it also had a dragon leading the way?"

"Make a mess?" I offered. I was tired, and this was growing progressively sillier.

"No! Just the opposite. It'd be bloodless coup after bloodless coup."

"How do you figure?"

"Because burns from dragon flames *never heal*, did you know that? They remain just as fresh and agonizing as the day they were inflicted. What soldier is going to want to face that? What king could expect his army or citizens to stand up to it? Just the threat of it will end the war before it starts."

"Sure. *If* dragons were real. And still existed. And could be tamed."

He retrieved his pipe and blew a thoughtful puff of smoke. Then he looked at me sideways. "So if you don't believe in dragons, how'd you get a look at Solarian's skull?"

"I charmed old man Tempcott."

He laughed in genuine surprise. "That a fact?"

I nodded. "What do you know about him?"

"Tempcott? Let's see . . . he first got our notice about a year ago when he showed up out of the blue in Bonduel. There was always a remnant of the old dragon religion there, but it was never more than a few families at best. Then Tempcott arrived waving the skull of Solarian, kicked out the old priest and took over the group. Do you know who the old priest was?"

I shook my head.

"Fellow named Chester Lesperitt."

I kept the reaction off my face.

"Never heard of him?" Crockett pressed.

I shook my head, all innocence.

"Well, Chester was able to keep his group going all those years because he claimed his daughter had once found the cave in the Black River Hills where Lumina slept with her offspring. When Tempcott arrived, all dragonfire about the 'true path' and 'bringing the flame back to the world,' old Lesperitt got brushed aside and left in a huff. But not his daughter. She was captivated like everyone else. Still, she was careful not to give away her secret until she was certain Tempcott was sincere."

Although I knew the answer, I looked blank and said, "So what happened?"

"That's where it gets fuzzy. Six months ago Gordon Marantz suddenly started bankrolling Tempcott and he collected a gang of rich, aimless young men around him, including Muscodia's crown prince. They decided to relocate here, close to the Black River Hills, I assume so Laura Lesperitt could take them to the cave with the sacred relics. Somewhere between Bonduel and here, though, she seems to have vanished."

Or changed her mind about Tempcott, I thought. But I said nothing.

He paused, retrieved his pipe and took a long calming drag. "Then I heard gossip about your little ambush on the Tallega road. I wondered if the girl you tried to save might have been her."

"I never got her name," I said with utter sincerity, and added a little faux wistfulness for color.

He looked at me through a fresh puff of smoke. His expression was inscrutable. Finally he asked, "So what will you do now?"

"Make sure the girl inside is okay."

"And after that?"

"I never think that far ahead."

"Uh-huh," he said knowingly.

"Excuse me, gentlemen," Mother Mallory said softly from the doorway behind us. She nodded at me and said, "She's asking for you."

I looked at Lockett. "Go on," he said with a wave of his pipe. "She needs your help more than I do. I hope she makes it."

"Can we talk more later?" If my chain of association was right, he might help me figure out what to do next.

He shook his head. "I have to hit the road. I stopped here on my own time, and I'm behind schedule as it is. If I don't check in when I'm supposed to, then sad old men in ivory towers get very angry with me."

I offered my hand. "Thanks for helping me out back there."

He nodded as we shook. "Wouldn't surprise me if our paths cross again sometime."

"Nothing surprises me, either."

I followed Mother Mallory to the room. Nicky kicked weakly in the water, and through the steam I saw her eyelids flutter and her lips move. The apprentice stood by, face creased in concern. I knelt beside the basin and said softly, "Nicky? Can you hear me?"

She turned toward me, but her eyes were still glassy and black. "Daddy?" she asked softly.

"No, it's Eddie."

Her face wrenched the same way it had earlier, although with less ferocity, and her eyes filled with tears. "I want my daddy," she said in a faint, trembling voice.

I looked at Mother Mallory. "I'm not her father."

"Well, you are now," she said. "If she lives she won't remember it, and if she dies you'll give her some peace."

Shit. I cleared my throat and, in what I hoped was a suitably paternal tone, said, "I'm here, Nicky."

She turned again, so weak she would've submerged if not for the way the tub supported her, and stared at me. "Daddy?" she asked in a tiny voice.

"You said you wanted to see me."

Again that torturous crying-child face. "Oh, Daddy, I'm so sorry; I never meant to shame you."

Oh, great. A family crisis. "It's okay, sweetheart," I said. "You just concentrate on getting well right now."

"I've been a good girl, you know. No one's touched me, not there. I'm still a virgin."

"I'm sure you are," I said reassuringly. "You're a very good girl."

"But somebody had to do this. I know Ricky's your favorite and you love him the most, but Daddy, he's an idiot. He'll ruin us all."

"You're right. I've come to accept that, thanks to you."

"Oh, Daddy, I love you so much," she said with a child's utter sincerity. She reached for my hand, and I took her slender fingers in my own. "I know everything they say about you is true, but I still love you, and I want to protect you. But you never loved me, just Ricky. And he's . . . he's . . ." She dissolved into quiet little exhausted sobs, and these quickly faded to silence. Her hand slid limply from mine back down into the water. Her breathing was steadier now, without that desperate little rattle.

Mother Mallory put her hand on my shoulder. "Thank you," she said softly. "I think this is a good sign."

"She's hallucinating, you know. I'm *not* her father."

"No, but her mind is working coherently. Except for that one detail, everything else made sense. Maybe you resemble her father in some way."

My knees popped as I stood. "For her sake, I hope not."

She leaned close to me. "And just so you know, she wasn't taken by whoever did this. She is still a virgin."

"You check that?" I asked, too tired to hide my prurient surprise.

Mother Mallory's face turned hard and sad. "If a man hurts a woman, that's usually the reason. And often he doesn't care how torn up he leaves her inside. So yes, we check."

I nodded, properly chagrined. I retrieved my scabbard and went back outside to the courtyard. Lockett was gone, as he said he'd be. I picked up my sword; wrapped around the hilt was a piece of parchment, tied with a black ribbon.

It was a page torn from a bound book, old but still supple; the original volume, wherever it was, had been carefully tended over the years. The page showed an illuminated image of a dragon fighting what appeared to be a cross between a hedgehog and a scarecrow. I recognized it as an illustration of the battle of Charlton the Just against Solarian.

Scrawled across the top were the words *Just so you know what you might be up against. H.L.*

In elaborate, expensive calligraphy was the poetic caption:

No living thing did that regal one leave alive as aloft it flew.
Wide was the dragon's agony seen, its fiendish fury far and
near.

The artwork was done with realistic perspective and colored in what seemed muted naturalism. The sky was blue, with a few fluffy clouds. The meadow showed bright green, while the trees in the background were darker.

That made Solarian himself look somehow more frightening. And make no mistake, this was one scary worm. If the dummy he attacked was the size of the average man, then Solarian was a good forty feet from snout to final scute. As with a lot of reptiles, most of this length was tail. He also did not have the standard four legs and wings; instead, his back legs were long and vaguely bird-like, while his wings grew from his forelegs much like those of a bat. It was this realistic detail that disturbed me the most. Well, that and the thing's head.

It was not shown actually breathing fire, but burnt patches on the field, some still smoking, indicated that capacity. Instead its neck was thrown back and it seemed to be roaring or screaming in agony. Its eyes were set high on its head, and its teeth were all the same length. A long forked tongue lolled from one side of its open maw. Even accepting exaggeration for dramatic effect, there was no denying that Tempcott's crocodile skull would fit easily inside the head as it was drawn.

I shook my head and sighed. It was late, I was tired and hungry and my hip hurt. In the clear light of morning this would all be revealed as the silly-ass idea it was.

At the left edge of the picture, Charlton himself peered heroically out from behind a tree as his dummy did the grunt work. *Smart move,* I thought to myself. *If I ever face a dragon, I'll try the same trick.*

I went back into the sickroom. It was hotter than before, and the air hung heavier and sweeter. Only the apprentice remained, standing beside the tub and gazing sadly down at Nicky.

"Where's Mother Mallory?" I asked softly.

"She's resting in her room. And before you say anything, she's an old woman who's just lost one of her best friends. If we need her, she's ten steps away. But I can watch over your friend just as well as she can."

I settled back onto my stool. "I wasn't going to say anything."

The apprentice smiled crookedly, a flaw that somehow made her more endearing. "Good thing, too," she said, mock tough.

"He can't . . . ," Nicky mumbled, eyes half-closed, completely unaware of her surroundings. ". . . not smart enough . . . not strong like me . . . so what if I'm a girl!" she yelled. The apprentice mopped Nicky's forehead with a sponge and murmured to her soothingly.

"A smart girl is better than a dumb man any day!" she insisted to her phantom inquisitor. Then she faded again. "Ricky listens to the wrong people . . . he drinks too much, smokes giggleweed . . . does what his friends tell him. . . ."

She grew unintelligible, then silent. The apprentice leaned down, lifted one eyelid and sniffed at her breath. She arose with a smile and pushed her thick, sweaty hair back from her face. "I think she's past the danger point. She's sleeping normally now." As if to emphasize this, Nicky emitted a loud, buzzing snore.

The apprentice put her hand to her mouth to stifle her giggle. "Would you mind carrying her to her room? I could call for help, but since you're here . . ."

I pushed up my sleeves, reached into the water and lifted her. She seemed heavier, more solid now, and even snuggled against my chest without waking. I followed the apprentice out into the hall and two doors down, into a room identical to the one I'd occupied. We placed Nicky on a clean, dry bed and drew the sheet up to her chin. Then the apprentice motioned me outside.

"I'll go report to Mother Mallory," she said softly, "but right now what she needs the most is rest. If you don't mind sitting with her, I'll come back and check on her at dawn."

Again I said, "Sure."

She touched my tunic. "Would you like a dry shirt?"

I shook my head. "I'll be all right."

She started to turn away, then abruptly swung back and kissed me on the cheek. "A lot of girls like her get hurt and no one helps them. She's lucky to have you looking out for her." Then she scampered off.

I went back into the room. I closed the door, and except for the starlight through the open window, it was dark. I pulled off my tunic and draped it on the windowsill to dry. I moved the chair near the door, sat and leaned it back. No one could open the door without waking me.

I tried to connect the dots between Lockett's information and what I knew. Marantz's presence now made total sense: by putting up the geld for Tempcott, he had the scions of the region's most influential families and the crown prince of Muscodia under his thumb. Tempcott made sense, too: a true believer willing to do anything, climb into bed with anyone, to further the cause. If Laura Lesperitt had something Tempcott wanted but wouldn't give it up, what could be more natural than that he'd ask his partner to take care of the problem?

But who killed Hank Pinster? And Mother Bennings? And who was the old guy with gloves, and why had Liz lied about him?

God, I wanted to lie down in my own bed, snuggle close to

Liz and inhale that atmosphere of safety and contentment. But for all I knew, Liz was off with the old man with gloves, doing who knew what. Was it her father? Some old (*really* old) lover?

I closed my eyes and was asleep in moments. I dreamed of a huge, befanged mouth bathing me in agonizing flames as Liz laughed.

chapter

TWENTY

Eddie," a voice softly said.

I opened my eyes. Gray pre-dawn light filled the room. Nicky smiled wearily at me. Dark eye circles and the pallor of illness still marked her, but her gaze was clear. The vise around my chest loosened a few turns.

She looked at me for a long time before she croaked, "Where's your shirt?"

"Where's yours?" I replied, and rocked the chair forward until all four legs touched the floor.

She put a hand to her head. "I feel like I've been tossed over a waterfall in a barrel."

I went to the windowsill and pulled on my now-dry tunic. "You were poisoned."

She nodded and stretched, twining her hands together over her head. Her bare feet poked out the bottom of the sheet, toes spread wide. "Doug took me upstairs 'just to talk.' He got mad when I wouldn't put out. I tried to fight him, but he made me drink something he said would make me 'more agreeable.' That's the last I remember."

"You weren't that agreeable. He didn't get what he wanted."

She looked at me steadily for a long time. "Then I'm still . . . I mean, he didn't . . . so . . ."

"Yes," I said.

She sighed with relief, then winced as she sat up, holding the sheet against her. Her hair had dried in a frightening bird's-nest tangle. "I can't wait to see him again. Things will be very different."

"You're not in any condition for revenge," I said firmly. I'd have to get started soon as well, to warn Bella Lou and Buddy that Candora was coming after them. I had no doubt they could protect themselves in a fair fight, but Candora had shown no indication that he played by the rules.

"He's not getting out of my sight again," she said with as much certainty as she could muster. "Not alive, at any rate." She swung her legs over the edge of the bed and tried to stand, but ended up in an undignified pile on the floor. Oblivious to her nudity she snapped, "Don't just stand there; help me up."

I did not move. "I don't think you—"

"Did I ask you to think?" she snarled. She pulled herself to her feet by clinging to the bed, but her legs still wouldn't support her weight and she fell again. Fresh sweat gleamed on her skin.

I lifted her under her arms, sat her back on the edge of the bed and wrapped the blankets around her. "You should be a little more polite to us peasants," I said.

She looked up sharply, her eyes flashing with new fury, but it faded quickly. She took a deep breath and said contritely, "I'm sorry, Eddie. You saved my life, and I start acting like I own you."

"Yes," I agreed. I sat down beside her. "Now, about this revenge thing—"

"He poisoned me, Eddie. I can't just let that pass."

"You'll get your chance, I'm sure. In the meantime, *I'm* going after him now. Mother Mallory will be along shortly to check on you, and I suggest you listen to her. *She* was the one smart enough to save you, not me."

She looked surprised. "Why are you going after him?"

"He did something I can't let pass, either."

"Do you know where he is?"

"No," I lied. "And you need to rest until I get back."

I expected a protest, but she nodded and yawned. "I can barely keep my eyes open anyway."

I helped her lie down and covered her with the sheet. She may have planned to fake me out, but she was so tired she quickly fell asleep for real. When she was again peacefully snoring, I slipped out the door.

In the hall I met Mother Mallory. She said softly, "Since you're leaving I assume the crisis has passed?"

"Seems to," I agreed. "But could you do me a favor? She wants to find the man who poisoned her and teach him a lesson. He's bad news, and I'd just as soon she stay here until he's long gone."

Mother Mallory nodded. "And will you search for him instead?"

"Me? Nah. I never look for trouble."

"But it finds you."

"Like it's got my itinerary," I agreed. "And one more thing. On the day she died, Mother Bennings left word with a friend that she was looking for me. I never had a chance to find out why. Do you know?"

"Yes. She'd put together some new herbs for your head. I think she wanted to give them to you."

I could say nothing for a moment. "Well. I wish I'd had the chance to thank her."

Mother Mallory smiled sadly. "Her loss touched us all."

IT threatened to be another hot summer day, and I needed a bath almost as bad as Nicky had the night before. There would be no time for that, though. I was being generous in my assessment of Candora's professionalism and assumed he was the kind of guy who slept late. Since here I was, on the move at sunrise, I should have no trouble getting out of town ahead of him. Except, of course, that I was on foot, my horse still tied at Long Billy's tavern.

Neceda waited at the bottom of the hill, although the morning mist risen from the Gusay hid it. The fog would disperse once the sun cleared the top of the forest, but for now it was easy to imagine there was no town at all, just an empty little clear space along the river. No burned-down stable, no former whorehouse filled with dragon worshippers. No lying girlfriends.

I stepped off the road and went behind a tree to relieve myself. First, I had to retrieve Pansy, assuming no one had stolen the beast during the night. Then I'd have to feed and water her, hard to do with the stable gone. Then I should probably feed and water myself. I finished peeing, refastened my trousers and stepped back onto the road.

I've had some serious luck in my life, from surviving the massacre that ended my days as a mercenary to having Prince Frederick stumble out just in time to save my ass the night before. But the universe has a way of balancing things, and it's easy to forget that. Which is why I was surprised, even though I shouldn't have been, when I came around the tree and almost walked smack into Gordon Marantz.

His horse whinnied and backed up into the one behind it. At the same moment I recognized Marantz, the man behind him screamed, "*That's him! That's the guy!*"

I held up my hands. "Whoa, guys, I was just on my way to Neceda and got lost in this fog. Am I anywhere close?"

"That's the guy who busted in and kicked me in the head!" the other guy insisted, pointing at me with a frantic waving finger. Well, that was even more luck.

I kept up the innocent act. "Buddy, maybe it's the fog, but you're mista—"

"Shut up," Marantz said calmly, and I realized he had a small crossbow pointed casually in my direction. It wouldn't be accurate for more than a short distance, but in this situation that was plenty. There seemed to be no other bodyguards with him, which was a small blessing at least. Guess Gordon wasn't expecting a fight, although he certainly wasn't thrown off by it. "Who are you?"

I smiled. "Lance Thrower."

"Well, Mr. Thrower, you busted into an establishment owned by me and beat up an employee and one of my guests. Care to tell me why?"

God, I was too tired for this. No useful lie came to mind, so I just shrugged.

Marantz's expression didn't change. "Get his sword, Vinnie."

Vinnie dismounted and strode over to me. A bruise roughly the size of my foot colored one cheek and temple. "You are going to *so* regret this," he hissed, pointing his finger right in my face.

"I already do," I assured him.

He drew my sword, gave me a smug your-ass-is-mine look and turned to Marantz. "Let's take this guy and—"

When he turned the blade upright, the spikes shot from the hilt through his hand. They were two inches long, needle sharp and (because I'm devious that way) coated with dried lemon juice. Vinnie stared at the tips poking through the back of his hand for about five seconds before letting loose with a howl that was probably heard in Sevlow.

I didn't wait for his scream. As soon as I heard the mechanism click, I jumped past him and grabbed a handful of Marantz's clothes. The crossbow bolt shot harmlessly into the trunk of a nearby tree. I yanked him from the saddle and threw him to the ground. Before he knew it I had my knee on his chest and the dragon knife from my boot at his throat.

Vinnie reflexively opened his fingers, but the spikes held the sword in place. Without his grip to control it, though, the weight of the blade made it fall over suddenly, and I heard the crack of a wrist bone. Lockett had been right; the Shadow Slasher III *was* top-heavy, for just that reason. Vinnie howled again.

I saw none of this, though, because I wasn't dumb enough to take my eyes off Marantz. He was completely unruffled. "Now what?" he asked calmly as he looked up at me.

"How about you tell me what you're after here," I said.

He laughed. "You gotta work a lot harder to scare things out of me, bucko."

I put more weight on his sternum and he grunted. "Not that much harder," I said, fighting to stay calm. Rage would do me no good.

"Oh, God," Vinnie sobbed behind us. "My arm . . ."

"It's a business investment," Marantz said, his voice tight. "Tempcott controls Prince Frederick, and I control Tempcott."

"And what're your people looking for in the Black River Hills?"

He laughed again. "You do get around. My people are looking for a long shot. If they find it, then I'll have something any king in the world would give his treasury and firstborn daughter to obtain. If not . . . no harm done."

"Boss . . . ," Vinnie pleaded.

"I'm *occupied*!" Marantz snarled.

"No harm except for Laura Lesperitt," I said. "What *is* it?" I knew, but I wanted to hear him say it, to have his words give it a tangible reality.

Instead he smiled. "The fire dreams are made of."

"Are you suddenly a poet?" Now I grinned. "You think there's no harm telling me about your setup because I'll be dead before I can pass it on, don't you?"

"Pretty sure," he agreed.

I pulled my knife away, slipped it back in my boot and stood. Marantz stared at me, puzzled, but didn't move. I went to Vinnie, took his limp hand and pressed the catch on my sword. The spikes retracted, and he moaned in both relief and fresh pain. He fell flat on his face as I put the sword back in its sheath.

Marantz slowly sat up. "What are you doing?"

"Walking away," I said. "I have no real quarrel with you. You can send your boys after me if you want, and eventually I'm sure they'll get me. But I'll take a few of them down first, and word would get around that you're wasting time and manpower trying to get revenge on someone who had a knife to your throat and didn't slice it."

Amused and bewildered, he said, "You're counting on my sense of *honor*?"

"No, your vanity. You have a lot of pies on your fingers because you don't make silly decisions. No one knows about this little run-in except you, me and Vinnie. *I* won't tell anyone, and I don't have any illusions about how you'll deal with Vinnie. So unless *you* start talking, no one will ever know."

He stood and brushed dirt from his clothes. "Who are you, soldier?"

I shook my head. "The less you know, the safer I am."

He laughed again. He laughed a lot, for a guy with so much blood on his hands. "I can find out any time I want, you know. And every shadow you pass might have a knife with your name on it."

I shrugged. "I could say the same thing to you. Except I already know who you are." With that I turned and walked away into the mist; I couldn't ask for a much more dramatic exit. Marantz's chuckling followed me down the hill.

TWENTY-ONE

It's hard to be nonchalant when you're expecting a crossbow bolt in your back at any moment, but I managed it. Only time would tell if Marantz called my bluff, because bluff it surely was.

I'd gone quite a ways down the hill when wheels rattled in the mist behind me. I stopped and waited as a single-horse wagon came into view. It carried a farmer and his wife on the seat, and four children in the back. They were dressed up and looked very grim. The farmer reined up beside me and looked me over. "You hurt?" he asked with no urgency.

"No, just heading into town. Is this the right way? Hard to tell with this fog."

"We're going into Neceda for the hanging. We could give you a ride."

Hanging? Who the hell was Gary hanging? "Thanks. I'd appreciate it."

"Well, hop in. We don't want to miss it."

I climbed into the back. The four kids, three boys and a girl all under age ten, looked at me with the barest minimum of curiosity. "Who's getting hanged?" I asked as I sat.

"Fella who killed one of the moon priestesses," the farmer said as he snapped the reins on the horse's rump. The wagon jumped forward. "Mother Bennings. She helped out Myrtle here when little Helene was breech. Can't believe someone would just cut her up like that."

"That's why we don't live in the city," Myrtle said. "Too much violence."

I said nothing, but my mind was racing. I couldn't believe that weasely Gary Bunson had actually apprehended Mother Bennings' murderer overnight. "Do you know who it is?"

The farmer shook his head. "Nope. But whoever it is, we want to see his face when the rope snaps tight. She didn't deserve that; she was a good woman."

The sunlight finally rose over the treetops and burned off the mist. Despite his ostensible urgency, the farmer seemed content with his horse's idle walk. Other wagons, lone riders and even three unsupervised children on foot passed us on their way into town. "Break his neck, pay his check!" the kids gleefully called out, a gallows chant children everywhere seemed to know.

I settled into the back corner of the wagon bed, aware that the four children never took their eyes off me. They didn't join in the chant, and all had the same dead eyes as their parents.

Whatever they farmed to eke out a living apparently left no room for childhood joy.

I arranged my sword at my side so the hilt didn't dig into me. The three boys watched, fascinated by the weapon. I stretched out my legs, forcing them to scoot over.

The little girl, Helene, just sat staring at me. I smiled at her and winked. The corners of her mouth turned up ever so slightly.

I closed my eyes in what I thought was a simple blink, and when I opened them again we were rattling into Neceda. Man, the way I kept nodding off it was a miracle I survived the last two days. I sat up, momentarily disoriented, and startled Helene, who'd curled up beside me under my arm. The three boys sat in a huddle at the front of the wagon bed.

We passed the remains of the stable, where a few wisps of smoke still rose from the rubble. People gathered at the far end of town, and a fresh rope hung from the gallows oak. Apparently everyone from the countryside had come to town for the event; word of a hanging typically spread fast. More kids ran loose, and hawkers sold ale, food and little souvenir hangman's ropes. A good execution rivaled the excitement and economic boom of the annual harvest festival, and Neceda responded with new levels of spontaneous greed.

The cart that would bear the prisoner up the street to his demise was parked outside the jail, so we hadn't missed the show. A smaller, rowdier and more inebriated group waited to pelt the condemned man with vegetables and eggs when he emerged. I climbed stiffly out of the wagon, thanked the family and looked around for someone I knew.

Angelina and Callie stood at the back of the more subdued

crowd at the gallows. Both were dressed for work at the tavern, which by law would remain closed until after the execution. Callie bounced in place with excitement, and I spotted two teenage boys discreetly enraptured by the parts that bounced the most. "Ooh, do you think he'll come when his neck breaks?" Callie asked Angelina. "I hear men do that. I wonder if women do?"

"One easy way to find out," Angelina said, as usual looking vaguely bored. Like me, she'd seen enough hangings to be neither impressed nor curious about them. Her eyebrows went up as I approached.

Callie also did a double take. "*Wow*, Mr. LaCrosse. You look worse every time I see you lately." She leaned close and whispered, "Or are you in disguise?"

Angelina ignored Callie, plucked some hay off my tunic and said, "If you came into my tavern like this, I'd throw you out."

"No, you wouldn't. So who are they hanging?"

"Some weird guy who lives out in the woods," Callie said before Angelina could respond. "He cut up one of those nice moon priestesses. They say he might have burned down Mr. Pinster's barn, too. That's his wife over there."

Bella Lou, dressed in an old shawl, huddled protectively over her children. Even at this distance I saw their wide, terrified eyes as they clung to her. She had her back to the wall beneath the high, tiny cell window where, I assumed, Buddy was being held. Two men screamed drunkenly at Bella Lou, and one of them scooped up a handful of dirt from the ground and threw it at her. The others laughed.

"Makes you proud to be a Muscodian," Angelina said flatly.

"She deserves it, I bet," Callie said. "Maybe she even helped."

"That's probably it," Angelina agreed. "Should hang those little babies, too."

As always, Callie missed Angelina's sarcasm. To me she said, "She's been outside the jail all night, screaming that it's all a conspiracy. If it was a conspiracy, they'd have killed him somewhere else and just told us about it. *You* taught me to think like that, Mr. LaCrosse."

I shook my head, gave Callie a quick peck on the cheek and pushed my way to the jail door. Gary's man Russell was on duty outside to make sure the taunting crowd didn't become a lynch mob. They had splattered the wall around the small cell window with tomatoes, eggs and anything else that would stick and stain, and detritus also covered Bella Lou. She did not look my way.

Russell held his shield in front of his face. "No one's allowed inside, sir," he said in a voice that almost cracked from stress.

"Russell, I know the guy you've got locked up in there. I need to talk to Gary about him."

Russell lowered the shield in surprise. "Oh! Sorry, Eddie, I didn't recognize you with the haircut. Did you lose a bet?"

"Funny. Now let me in."

"I can't. I've got strict orders."

"Strict orders from Gary?"

"No, from the guy from the capital, Argoset. Only his assistant, that big guy, can go in."

I leaned close. "You know what I know about your sister."

He went paler than he already was. "Now, come *on*, Eddie; that has nothing to do with this."

"I need in, Russ."

"I *can't*."

I shrugged. "Then *I* can't be responsible for who finds out about Elaine."

Russell sighed. "If I lose my job, I'm moving in with you and Liz." He opened the door behind him, quickly shoved me through and then slammed it shut.

Gary Bunson's office was to the right, across from the two cells. Only one cell door was closed, and the other deputy, Pete, stood in front of it. He frowned when he saw me. I went into Gary's office.

Gary sat behind his desk, his feet propped up. He had his normal wide-eyed, vaguely panicked expression, the one that showed up any time he had to actually do his job. He wore his real uniform, too, down to the medals for longevity on his chest. They were the only ones he was ever likely to win.

And he wasn't alone. Daniel Argoset stood at the window looking out at the crowd. He was also in full gear, resplendent and yet somehow immature, like a very solemn boy dressed in an adult's work clothes. Maybe that's why he pushed so hard to be taken seriously. He looked surprised when he saw me. "Mr. LaCrosse."

I ignored him. I put my hands on the desk and leaned over it. "I need to talk to you," I said to Gary, trying to impress him with my urgency and seriousness. "About this hanging."

He looked at me, then at Argoset, then back to me. "Uh . . . what about it?"

"I don't think you have the right guy."

"I'm pretty sure we do," Argoset said.

I kept my eyes on Gary. "Then let me talk to him."

"Why?" Argoset asked.

"Yeah, why?" Gary repeated. Sweat beaded on his upper lip.

It was clear who was in charge, so I turned to Argoset. "Because it may all be a frame."

Argoset smiled patiently, condescendingly. My fist ached for his teeth. He said, "Mr. LaCrosse, I handled this situation, not Magistrate Bunson. He approached us; we didn't go after him. The man *confessed*."

"Then it won't hurt to let me talk to him."

Argoset's eyes narrowed. "I'm curious why you want to."

"Because he might have done it for reasons other than guilt. Maybe because someone threatened his family if he didn't."

"And who would do that?"

"Ever hear of Gordon Marantz?"

Gary sat up so quickly he nearly fell from his chair, and exclaimed, "What?"

Argoset looked dubious. "Why would Gordon Marantz even care?"

God *damn*, I was tired of talking. "Gary, I really need you to grow a pair right now and let me talk to this guy."

Gary looked from me to Argoset. Argoset said, "It is *your* responsibility, Magistrate Bunson. You know my opinion." He dramatically resumed looking out the window.

Gary sighed, turned deliberately away from me and pointed to the key where it hung from the wall. I took it and went down the hall to the closed cell. Pete looked at me suspiciously and put his hand on his sword hilt. "How'd you get that?" he said, nodding at the key.

Gary called wearily from his office, "It's okay, Pete; he has my permission."

Pete stepped aside; I opened the door and went into the cell. Sure enough, Buddy sat on the straw piled in the corner, his ankle chained to the wall. He had his knees drawn to his chin, and looked up at me with blank, glassy eyes. The window, high on the wall, let the noise of the taunting crowd into the room. Occasionally some produce made it through the bars and splattered on the floor.

"Buddy, you don't have a lot of time left," I said. I crouched beside him. "Tell me what happened, and I'll see if I can't get you out of this."

"I killed that lady healer," he said simply, with no inflection.

I shook him, hard. "Buddy, do you remember me? You helped me find the dragon people?"

He nodded slowly, like his joints were gummed up, and idly pushed some straw with his hand. "Sure, I remember you."

"If someone threatened Bella Lou and the kids to get you to go along with this—"

He shook his head. "Ain't like that. After you left, Bella Lou threw me out 'cause I'd lied to her. I didn't know what to do. I went to that moon goddess hospital outside of town to get a love potion to make her want me again, and instead that woman told me to clean up, get a job and apologize."

For the first time he looked directly at me. His eyes held nothing but despair. "A husband can't apologize to his wife, it's a sign of weakness, you know? So I waited until the healer left work, followed her and begged her. I'm a man, and I *begged* her, a *woman*. And she still said no." He looked down again and moved his manacled foot a little. The chain rattled against the stone floor. "So I got angry."

A big pit opened up inside me, and I felt nauseous. "You're telling me nobody from Gordon Marantz got you to take the blame for killing Mother Bennings? That you really *did* kill her?"

"Gordon who?" he said, and I knew he was telling the truth. Bennings' injuries made sense as well now. They weren't the gleeful work of a sadistic torturer, but the reflexes of a weak, terrified man used to gutting animals.

All my weariness caught up with me and I sat down on the straw beside him. I leaned against the stone wall and closed my eyes. "You're an idiot, Buddy."

He nodded. "I know."

"Your wife and kids are outside just below that window. They've got nowhere else to go, so they're just sitting there, waiting for you to come out and die. People are screaming and throwing things at them."

Tears glinted on his cheeks. "Don't you think I know that?" he said, his voice cracking. "Don't you think I hurt enough?"

I slapped him across the back of his head as hard as I could. It felt good to strike someone that deserved it. "*No*, Buddy, you don't hurt enough. You're a coward, a liar and a failure. The only thing left that you can do for anyone is go get hanged with a little bit of dignity."

He wrapped his arms protectively around his head and whined like a child. "It's because of you, you know! If you hadn't showed up, none of this ever would've happened; Bella Lou would've never found out I was buying food in town and kicked me out." He petulantly threw a handful of straw at me, then flinched as if expecting another slap. "It's your fault! *Your* fault!"

I stood. I seemed to have grown heavier and older in the time I'd been in the cell. Another batch of straw hit my back as I opened the door. I locked it behind me, pushed past Pete and went back into Gary's office. I put the key back on the hook and sat heavily in a chair across from him.

"What did you find out?" Argoset asked, still at the window.

Even speaking took effort. "Looks like you were right. Sorry about barging in and making a fuss."

The crowd outside began another rude chant. "I'll be glad when we get him hung," Gary said.

"Hanged," Argoset and I corrected in unison.

"Whatever. Then this crowd can go back to drinking."

Argoset took his cloak from a peg on the wall. "Magistrate Bunson, if you no longer need me, I'm going to go back to the inn and get something to eat. If you see Marion, tell him to meet me there. I'll return in time for the prisoner's execution." He nodded at me. "Mr. LaCrosse." Then he left.

Gary produced a bottle from his desk and put a tankard in front of me. "You look awful."

"Not a goddam word about the haircut, Gary. I mean it."

"Okay, okay. Where have you been?"

"Hanging with Gordon Marantz."

His eyes opened wide. "No shit? Where?"

I took a long drink of his ale. "The old Lizard's Kiss. And I think I kind of pissed him off, so if you see any strange tough guys around over the next few weeks, I'd appreciate a tip-off."

"Sure."

I swallowed the rest of my drink in one gulp and pushed myself to my feet. "I'm going home," I said, and before anyone could say or do something to change my mind, I went out the door.

chapter TWENTY-TWO

Mrs. Talbot crouched on her porch, pouring some thick, vile concoction over a shivering dog. She held it firmly by the scruff, and it looked as miserable as I felt. She looked up as I approached, my boots scuffing in the dirt. "You look mangier than Filo here," she said. "Maybe I should dip you, too."

I couldn't argue with that. "Not going to the hanging?"

She cackled. "I've seen more hangings than you have titties. Can't imagine this one will be too different."

"Happen to know if Liz is upstairs?"

"Ain't seen her." The dog whined, and she smacked it with her free hand. "Pipe down, ya mutt."

I nodded my thanks and ascended the stairs. I seemed to grow heavier with each step, so that by the time I reached our rooms I was exhausted. I went inside, closed the door and leaned back against it.

I looked around our simple yet somehow comfortable space. Golden morning light made it seem even homier. I found no note, but a last-minute delivery could have called Liz out of town and she might've left word with Angelina, just as I'd done. I was too tired to worry or think about it, just as I was too weary to deal with that damn horse Pansy. If she starved outside Long Billy's, then so be it.

There was no need to rush after Candora; Buddy had done his job for him. So once he got his new people searching for the late, lamented and nonexistent Lumina, he'd come back to town and be easy to find. And before I finally faced him, I needed to be a lot sharper than I felt just then. I hit the mattress, and none of the raucous festivities that followed the execution penetrated my weariness. I was too tired to even dream.

I opened my eyes into the setting sun, winced and cursed. I cleaned up and dressed with great, sluggish effort. Liz was still not home, and that nagged at me, but it also meant I could put off the confrontation about the old man with the gloves. I'd had enough confrontation to hold me for a while, and this one could not end well.

I went to Angelina's tavern and my office. The streets were mostly empty; the party had moved from the gallows oak into the town proper, dispersing among the various establishments. Far ahead, Buddy's silhouetted body dangled from a branch, and a dog barked at it while it swayed in the wind. Someone, I assumed Bella Lou, sat beneath it with her back against the tree. I wondered where the kids were.

I had my hand on the tavern door when I stopped and looked back at the execution tableau. *Just keep going,* my rational self said. *It's not your problem. Don't you have enough things to worry about?* My other hand, in my pocket, tapped my last remaining silver coin.

Bella Lou was asleep against the tree. No one else came near. She was covered with vegetable matter, and flies swirled around her almost as much as they did around her late husband. A crow stood on the ground looking at her, debating whether she, too, was a corpse. It sailed away with a caw as I approached, and Bella Lou opened her eyes.

When she saw someone coming she drew the cloak around her and hunkered down, like an armadillo curling in on itself. "It's okay, Bella Lou," I said. "I'm not going to hurt you."

She recognized my voice, frowned at my new appearance and said, "It's okay if you want to. I'm just waiting for the king's soldiers to come take me away."

I crouched beside her. "They're not coming. The king doesn't care about you. I know you don't believe that, but it's true. Things will go a lot easier when you understand that."

She said nothing.

"Where are Toy and Stick?"

"They're safe. They can take care of themselves."

"Bella Lou, they're *kids*."

She wouldn't meet my eyes. "We've always prepared them for the day when their parents would be taken away from them."

I dug out the bag of money I'd taken from Frankie's saddlebag. I'd finally found a use for it that wouldn't make me nauseous. "Bella Lou, listen to me. I want you to take this, round up your kids and get a room somewhere. This will pay for it for at least a week. I know another woman who just lost her husband, who also has a bunch of kids to raise on her own. That'll give me time to get in touch with her and make some arrangements." I offered her the bag.

"I'm no one's servant."

"No, but do you think you could be someone's friend?"

She said nothing for a long time. The dog returned, sniffing at her feet. I kicked at it, and it scampered off. Above us, the branch creaked as Buddy's corpse slowly turned.

Finally she said, "I haven't had a friend since I met Buddy. He said they could only hurt us."

"He was wrong about a lot of things."

She took the bag. "It may take a while, but I'll pay you back."

"I'm easy to find."

There was nothing else to say. I made the long walk back down the street, ignoring the disapproving looks. It was bad form to consort with the family of the condemned. No one had the bad sense to say anything, though.

Inside the tavern, the regulars at the counter were augmented by people carousing after the hanging. These men and women could barely stand or speak, but they showed no sign of stopping. They were country folk determined to have great stories of summer debauchery to tell around the winter hearth. Callie and two emergency barmaids I didn't know looked exhausted, having worked the hanging rush nonstop. It always amazed me that these young, vapid girls had the physical stamina I'd wished my infantry possessed back when I commanded troops. Angelina handled the bar with her usual cool efficiency.

The stools were all occupied, and I was about to go upstairs and wait in my office when a piece of biscuit bounced off my head. I looked up, and Angelina gestured with the rest of the biscuit toward the kitchen. We went past Rudy into the store-room I'd used to spy on Marantz the day before.

She shut the door, which did little to cut the noise. Her work outfit, as always, emphasized her bare shoulders and exquisite cleavage. For not the first time I wondered what spark was actually missing between her and me, because I knew she'd be a wildcat in bed, and you couldn't ask for a more loyal friend. But its absence was undeniable.

"Guess you weren't able to help your friend," she said. "They strung him up right on schedule."

"Turns out he deserved it."

"Then you probably feel pretty foolish."

I nodded. "And that's not the only reason."

"That haircut will grow out."

"Very funny. No, it's something else." I paused, knowing that if I said it aloud, it would have an independent reality outside my own head. "Liz lied to me."

"Wow," she said evenly. "Are you sure?"

"One hundred percent."

She ran a hand through her luxuriant hair and paced as much as the room allowed. Finally she said, "Eddie, I don't know what to say. It doesn't sound like her at all, but you wouldn't make a mistake about something like that."

"No. Have you seen her today?"

She shook her head. "I gave her your note yesterday at lunch. That was the last time."

She stood quietly for another long moment. I leaned against the wall and watched a spider scuttle under a barrel. Finally she said, "There might be a good reason, you know."

"I know."

"I mean, you'd lie to her if you had a good reason, wouldn't you?"

"No."

"Of course you wouldn't." She looked down, fingered the fringe along her sleeve and said, "She's the best thing that ever happened to you, you know. I was skeptical of her at first, but she convinced me. She was good to you and brought you out of that stupid 'I'm so tough' act, and that was enough for me. If you're right, it means she made a fool of us both."

"If you want to look at it that way."

A firm hand knocked on the door. Callie opened it and presented me with a plate of eggs and biscuits. "Here you go, Mr. LaCrosse. Figured since you'd been asleep all day, you'd want breakfast."

I took it with a smile, and a grateful nod to Angelina. "Thanks. Looks busy out there."

Callie blew a strand of hair from her face. "You might say so. I can't feel my ass from all the pinches and gropes. But the tips'll pay me back for the money that no-account Tony ran off with, so it's all fine with me." She turned to go, then stopped. "Hey, someone went up to your office earlier today. Haven't seen 'em come down, so they may still be there."

I took a bite of the eggs, and at the first taste my appetite roared back full strength. I quickly shoveled more into my mouth, forgetting all the etiquette drilled into me as a boy. Between mouthfuls I said, "Let me guess: some old guy with big weird gloves on?"

"Actually, yeah," she said, and went back into the tavern.

It took a moment for that to sink in. "Holy shit," I said through another bite.

"What?" Angelina asked.

"Tell you later," I said, and handed her the plate.

I rushed up the stairs, opened the door to my outer office and stared at the man curled up asleep on the visitor's bench. It was indeed the man described by Mother Bennings, who I'd glimpsed with Liz the night of the fire. I stood very still; after everything that had happened, I half-expected him to fade into nothingness if I disturbed him.

He was old, all right, and had long white hair gathered in a ponytail. The ribbon holding it had loosened, so strands fell wispily about his face. He needed a shave, and his clothes were wrinkled like he'd slept in them several days running. His hands lay across his stomach and were covered in big gloves like mittens that seemed to be padded on the inside. Even in sleep his face creased into an expression of sadness and pain, and his snoring was mostly little whimpers, like he was about to cry. The room smelled faintly of burnt, rotted meat.

I shut the outer door with enough force to wake him up. He opened his eyes, squinted at me and raised a gloved hand to block the afternoon sun. "Mr. LaCrosse?"

I nodded. "And you are . . . ?"

He sat up and yawned. "Chester Lesperitt. You've met my daughter."

I said nothing.

He waved one gloved hand at my inner office. "Can we talk privately? There are many things I need to tell you, and I'm sure you have many questions."

I escorted him to the inner office, closed and locked the door and sat behind my desk. He went to the window and discreetly peered out, as if watching for anyone spying on us. Satisfied, he sat in the guest chair.

"First, I want to thank you for trying to save my Laura. I wish you had succeeded, of course, but I also appreciate the effort."

I licked my dry lips and, as casually as I could, asked the question whose answer I both anticipated and dreaded. "So how do you know Liz Dumont?"

"Oh, I've known Liz all her life," he said. "Her and her sister Cathy. Haven't seen them in years, but when they were children they came to my church with their parents."

I sighed and rubbed the bridge of my nose. Of course, of *fucking course*. Harry Lockett even told me Lesperitt came from Bonduel, original home of the Dumont sisters. How had that not registered? Maybe Candora's whack to my head had done some permanent damage after all.

"I can't tell you how surprised I was to see her here," he continued.

"So did Liz know Laura?"

He shook his head. "Liz and Cathy left before Laura was born. They really weren't with us that long; it's just that they stood out: beautiful redheaded twin sisters, just on the cusp of womanhood. They attracted a lot of attention."

"No kidding," I agreed. "So why are you here?"

"In Neceda?"

"In my office."

"You were the last person to see Laura alive. She knew something, something more important than you can imagine. Something people were, and are, willing to kill for." He paused. "Did she tell you?"

I shook my head. "She didn't tell anyone. That's why they're still out there looking for Lumina."

He sighed with relief and showed no surprise that I knew the name. "That's good, Mr. LaCrosse. That's very, very good. That just saved your life. You have no idea what they're seeking, no idea."

"A dragon egg?" I said nonchalantly.

His eyes opened wide in surprise. "She *did* tell you."

"No, she didn't. But I'm paid to make connections."

He sighed. "In this case, you're wrong."

"You just said I wasn't."

"No, I just said that it wasn't a dragon egg."

"Then what *is* it?"

He tossed his hair wearily from his face and said, "*Two* dragon eggs."

"Two."

"Yes. Two nascent gods awaiting the moment of their creation."

"They'd be hundreds of years old," I pointed out.

"That doesn't matter. The fire within them, the spark they inherit from their parents, never goes out. The eggs will stay viable until something destroys them, or triggers their hatching."

"What triggers them?"

"No one knows."

"But you believe they're there."

"I *know* they are, Mr. LaCrosse."

I pulled my bottle from my desk, took out the cork with my teeth and drank a long swallow. It tasted better than any drink I'd ever taken. I did not offer any to Lesperitt. "And just how," I asked wearily, "do you know? Have you seen them?"

"Yes," he answered simply. "Laura found them long ago, still beside the skeleton of their mother, Lumina, during a religious pilgrimage. We were waiting for the right time to bring them into the open again, so that they might be tended and worshipped. But when that ass Tempcott showed up, waving his skull and making outrageous claims, Laura believed his lies, believed he was sent by Solarian. But she was smart enough not to give away our secret. Then Marantz got involved, and . . . my girl died."

I looked at the bottle, but still didn't offer it to him. I was a hard-ass, after all.

"When Laura realized what she'd gotten into, it was too late. I discovered Marantz sent her to Neceda ahead of Tempcott, so I came here as well. She escaped from the men trying to force her to reveal the location, and came to me. I was all she had."

He paused, and his eyes grew shiny. "She was such a pretty little thing, and to see what those awful men had done to her . . ."

Well, my ass wasn't *that* hard. I passed him the bottle.

He continued, "We went to the cave, found the eggs and hid them somewhere else. That's how this happened." He held up the gloves. "The eggs were still hot enough to scald, which we didn't know until it was too late. Do you know dragon burns never heal?"

He took one glove off to show me his hand. It looked like he'd stuck his palm flat against a cooking stove sometime within the last day. Laura's hands had looked the same. Worse, the faint odor of rotted, overcooked meat filled the room and threatened to gag me. "You can't imagine how much this hurts. These gloves are the only way I can even function, but they do nothing for the pain. But the eggs were too important to risk falling into

Tempcott's hands. After we moved them, we split up and planned to meet back here in Neceda. But she never arrived until . . ." He looked down and sighed with the weight of the truly lost.

There was no denying the reality of his injuries, and his story held together and explained a lot. Well, except for the part about real dragon eggs. "Okay, so why tell me all this now?"

He wiped his eyes on the backs of the mittens and looked up at me. "Because, Mr. LaCrosse, I had this same conversation with Liz, and she went to find the eggs for herself. And she hasn't come back."

I dragged the little gnome across town to the inn where Argoset and his pet Gargantua kept their rooms. I was probably too rough about it, and at least one person on the street roused himself from his post-hanging merriment to complain that I shouldn't treat an old man that way. I didn't care.

Before this, in my office, Lesperitt provided the rest of his story. When Liz failed to return by yesterday evening, he'd gone to Gary Bunson first thing this morning to report her missing. Gary had brushed him off before he could mention Liz's name, he was so wrapped up in the upcoming hanging. That rang true, all right; anything that required Gary to actually do his job, especially amid the chaos of a public execution, would've sent him skittering under the nearest table like the cockroach he was. Then Lesperitt approached Argoset, who listened politely and promised to look into it. Since Argoset had not mentioned this to me *at all* in Gary's office, either he forgot or he knew more than I first thought he did. He didn't strike me as the forgetful type, so it was time to pile everyone in one place and start kicking until someone talked.

Just before we left my office I asked Lesperitt one last question, the one I really needed answered. "Why? *Why* would Liz even *care* about made-up dragons, after all this time?"

He looked at me with an almost infinite weariness. The backlighting through the window gave him an infuriatingly serene, holy demeanor, and he spoke with the patience of a priest addressing an acolyte. "Have you ever believed in anything, Mr. LaCrosse? Especially when you were young, not yet aware of how ugly the world can be? We do anything to hold on to that spark that says the world is a magical place where gods can be found and touched. Even as old, cynical adults, that hope never fully goes away. *That's* why she went. For the chance, however small, to touch a god she had once believed in."

I did know a thing or two about belief, and about gods that could be touched. But I'd never shared that story with anyone, even Liz. I tried not to dwell on the fact that now I might never have the chance. Instead I said, "Even if dragons once existed, even if they existed *now*, they'd just be animals. Big lizards or snakes or something. Not *gods*."

He smiled at me in what he probably meant to be a compassionate and sad way. It came out patronizing, and restoked the fury he'd momentarily doused with his feel-good mumbo jumbo. I grabbed him by the back of his collar, shoved him ahead of me toward the door and growled, "Yeah, well, keep your gods to yourself, pal. You better hope nothing happens to

Liz, or you might be seeing your daughter sooner than you think." It was a cruel thing to say, but I was in a cruel mood.

A short walk later we went through the lobby of the Saraden's Sword, the only inn ritzy enough for an envoy from Sevlow. Its small tavern was usually reserved for guests only, but a hanging was a special occasion, and the revelers would have simply broken in had they not been freely welcomed.

Slats Pickering, the inn's owner, was halfheartedly trying to keep the drunks under control. He looked up, smiled and said, "Hey, Eddie, what are you—" But something in my face made him abruptly fall silent.

"What room is that guy from the capital in?" I demanded. I must've radiated bad humor, because the patrons gave me plenty of room.

"Seven. The suite. Top of the stairs to the right. He's in there right now."

"And that big guy with him?"

"Eight, right next door."

"The rooms connect?"

"No."

"Seen the big guy today?"

"No. He left this morning and hasn't come back."

I nodded curtly. Some days it was good to be intimidating. I slapped a coin on the counter. "Send someone to get Gary Bunson, and when he gets here send him up to that room."

Pickering nodded. I pushed Lesperitt up the stairs to the indicated door. It was the only room in the place that had a separate sitting room and bedroom, the closest thing to classy accommodations to be found in Neceda. I put my ear to the wood and heard nothing over the noise from downstairs. I started to knock, but decided I'd been polite enough under the circumstances. I drew back and, despite the protest in my hip, kicked the door open.

Argoset, shirtless, looked up sharply from the basin where he was washing his hands. The sudden movement splashed water onto the girl seated in one of the padded chairs. She gasped, "Hey!" and covered her undergarments, all she currently wore, with her hands. Through the bedroom door behind them, the rumpled sheets confirmed what their state of undress implied.

"Is there a reason for this intrusion?" Argoset said, in a voice that could probably reduce cadets and stable pages to tears.

It was less successful on me. I slammed the door behind me and shoved Lesperitt toward one of the other chairs. "Sit down," I said, and he obeyed. I stepped challengingly close to Argoset. "This guy told you my girlfriend disappeared. You did nothing about it, and you didn't mention it to me when I saw you this morning. I'm going to find out why."

I turned to the girl in the chair. I'd recognized her at once. "For a girl so worried about her cherry, you gave it up quick enough, didn't you, Nicky? Or do you prefer 'Your Highness'?"

Nicky's mouth opened to protest, but she thought better of it. Instead she nodded and said calmly, "A worldly man like you would know there are many pleasures for men and women that don't involve *that*, Eddie. How did you recognize me?"

"Your face *is* on some of the money." And that really was true, but I'd been inclined that way by her delirious mutterings about her brother, Ricky. "Ricky and Nicky," were common slang names for Frede*rick* and Vero*nica* in Muscodian gossip, often used in rude rhymes about their supposed decadence.

The clincher had been a fresh look at the official portrait in Gary's office that morning. "Great way to keep an eye on your brother, too, for a girl not concerned with her modesty."

Nicky stood, and her poise was definitely regal. She pulled a robe on over her undergarments. "I seem to have a hard time keeping my clothes on around you, Eddie."

"I've heard that all my life."

She did not smile. She no longer looked like a vulnerable teenager, but like a hard, professional politician. "The fate of Muscodia is far more important to me than to my idiot brother. I can't keep him from behaving like the moron he is, but I can ensure that he does as little damage as possible until he either grows up or debauches himself to death."

"And leaves you next in line for the throne."

She cinched the belt tight. "I thank you for your kindness to me, Eddie, but this is a matter of state and you, as a private citizen and an immigrant, are not involved."

"That's the first wrong thing you've said, Princess." I drew my sword; in the small sitting room it loomed very, very large. "I got involved when Marantz's hatchet man dropped me, this guy's daughter and the best horse in the world off a cliff. And I'm in it until someone either pays for that or drops me off a much higher cliff."

Argoset made a move, probably innocuous, but I slapped his bare stomach with the flat of my sword anyway. "You're not up to it, fancy pants, and I've got no compunctions about gutting you right here. I don't like liars or king's lackeys, and you're both. So why didn't you tell me that this little bozo sent Liz off into the woods?"

Argoset winced and clutched his stomach; the blow would

leave a red mark, but nothing serious. He cast a look at Nicky, who said nothing. "It seems you've forced your way into this issue far enough to become a legitimate part of it," he said to me, and tried to step closer. The point of my sword stopped him. He raised his hands in a gesture of capitulation and stepped back. "All right, fine. But please listen carefully. I'm going to pronounce a few words. They're harmless words. Just a bunch of letters scrambled together. But their meaning is very important. Try to understand what they mean." He spoke softly but with real urgency. "Glaurung. Scatha. Vermithrax. *Solarian.*"

"Lumina," I finished.

"Lumina," he said with a nod.

I almost laughed aloud. These were the names of famous storybook dragons everyone in the world knew from childhood. "So you believe this dragon-egg bullshit, too."

"I believe in my country, Mr. LaCrosse. Muscodia has been the butt of jokes for too long. We have trade routes we don't tax, borders that allow any riffraff to cross, and a king so self-involved he truly thinks he'd be mobbed by grateful citizens if he steps outside his castle."

I looked at Nicky. "I don't mind being called 'riffraff,' but are you going to let him talk about your father like that?"

"Yes, because he's right. I love my father, and as a parent he's the kindest, gentlest man you can imagine. But as a head of state he's an utter failure. And Frederick is just like him, except for all the new vices he keeps inventing for himself."

"And you'd be better?"

She had the dignity of royalty, and the certainty of untested youth. "I wouldn't be perfect, no. But I would be better."

Argoset actually made a fist and held it up to show how serious he was. "If they're real, think about the *power* possessing those eggs would bestow on us. Not only could we prove the existence of gods, for those who need to believe in such things, but we'd also have the ultimate deterrent, a weapon so power-ful that no one would dare attack us for fear of unleashing it." He smacked his fist into his other palm for emphasis, which just made him look silly.

"And if they're not real, which they aren't?" I said.

He shrugged. "Then no harm has been done."

I was cosmically tired of people shrugging things off. My blood began to simmer. "Except that this man's daughter is dead because of it," I said, nodding at Lesperitt. "And I was damn near killed. And Liz . . ." I choked on the words and couldn't fin-ish the sentence. My chest grew tight at the thought.

"None of that had anything to do with us," Nicky said. "That was all Gordon Marantz's doing."

While my eyes were on Nicky, Argoset moved to his left, to-ward the hook where his sword hung along with his jacket. I poked him in the stomach again and he stopped moving. "So Muscodia gets a big stick to wave at the other backwater coun-tries. And you get the princess, for bringing the dragon home instead of slaying it. Not a bad promotion for a career soldier."

"I love her," he said with a nod to Nicky. "And it's mutual."

I chuckled. They had no idea how angry I was. "Nice. Where's your gorilla Marion, anyway?"

Argoset blinked in surprise. "Marion? He has his own room. What does *that* have to do with anything?"

"I'm not sure. I'm digging through this Lumina nonsense because it's personal, but I'm also on retainer to find out why your boy killed Hank Pinster and burned down his stable."

Argoset said nothing. I smacked him in the stomach again and said, "I *know* he did it."

Argoset gasped at the pain. "You knew that man didn't kill the moon priestess, too."

He was quick; I had to give him that. "Touché. But I saw how Hank was murdered. There's no one else within a week's travel strong enough to do it that way."

For a moment I thought I'd have to smack him again; then he blurted in defeat, "It was an accident. Really, I swear."

"What happened?"

"Marion said he was going to ask around, see if anyone had seen Mr. Lesperitt. Usually the local blacksmith knows everyone, even the people who don't live in town."

"Why would you want to find me?" Lesperitt asked in a thin voice.

Argoset turned to him, one eye warily on me. "Because once Marantz killed your daughter, you were the only link to the eggs. Luckily, you came to us." Then he sighed and shook his head. "I took Marion out of prison two years ago to basically stand behind me and provide the, ah . . . scale I might lack. I'm not that intimidating, as I'm sure you've noticed. He went through military training, took his oath to the king, never gave me any indication he was capable of anything like that."

"What was he in prison for?" I asked.

Argoset looked down. "He murdered a man over a woman. Killed him with his bare hands."

My knuckles were white on my sword hilt. "No indication," I repeated. "So when Hank told Marion he didn't know this old man, your boy didn't believe him."

Argoset sighed. "No. He's not . . . the brightest. He . . . well. You can imagine the rest."

My sword's blade began to tremble, making the light twinkle off it. "So a nice guy with a family *died* . . . and everything they had was *destroyed* . . . because your guy's an idiot." I glared at Nicky. "Is this okay with you, Princess? You approve of this sort of thing? Is this the new and improved Muscodia?"

Argoset looked at her, his head down. "It really was an accident," he said.

She tried mightily to let nothing show, but I could tell she hadn't known about this, and it genuinely appalled her. Maybe not as much as it did me, but I felt a little better knowing that she still had a functioning conscience.

I slapped Argoset with the sword again. Anger flashed in his eyes, and I really wanted him to make an issue of it. But he caught himself. "Where is Marion now?" I asked.

Argoset licked his lips and had to force the words out. "Following Miss Dumont," he said, and flinched in anticipation of a blow.

I was too startled to hit him again. The thought of Liz at the mercy of the man who'd pitchforked Hank to the wall sent a chill of fury through me. "*That's* why you didn't tell me this morning," I said.

Argoset took a step back. "Sometimes you have to make tough decisions, Mr. LaCrosse. When I learned Mr. Lesperitt had told your wife the location before he told me, I sent Marion to secure the site. I didn't *want* anyone else to die."

I stepped toward him. "Or anyone to be held accountable for it. You were going to let people think that crazy guy from the woods killed Hank as well as Dr. Bennings. Your man gets off free as a bird."

"I had to do what was necessary for the good of Muscodia," he said, his eyes on my sword. He looked desperately at Nicky. "Veronica, you know me; you know—"

I jabbed at him. I didn't run him through, just gave him a nice slash on his side. He winced and cried out.

"Eddie!" Nicky exclaimed.

I cut him on the other side. I began to feel incredibly calm.

"Eddie, please!" Nicky said.

I slashed him across his stomach. He was in the corner now, his arms wrapped protectively around his belly. I'd seen men do the same thing to hold in their own guts. Would Argoset actually have any if I really sliced him open?

Nicky grabbed my sword arm with both hands. They were small, but I felt real strength in them. "I know he deserves it, Eddie, but he's my responsibility."

I turned to her. She drew back from what she saw in my eyes. "So was Hank Pinster, Princess. And Laura Lesperitt."

Argoset slid to the floor. The shallow cuts bled profusely and hurt more than if I'd sliced off a finger. He looked up at me in a mix of rage, pain and fear. I really enjoyed seeing that.

"If he dies, I'll see you hanged, Mr. LaCrosse," Nicky said in her best regal voice.

That got my attention. I turned to look at her. She was still afraid, but did not back down.

"If you kill an unarmed and injured man in my presence, I'll see that you are executed for it." Her lip trembled, and her face flushed, but she kept her head. "And if you kill me, too, you'll be drawn and quartered, then hanged. We're very thorough about treason."

So she had a conscience *and* a backbone. I don't *think* I would've killed Argoset in cold blood, but I'm glad I'll never have to find out. At that moment the door opened slightly and Gary Bunson said, "Eddie? You in here?"

"Yeah. Come in and shut the door."

He did so, then stayed with his back pressed against it when he saw Argoset bleeding on the floor.

I put my sword away without wiping off the blood. "Gary, I'm going to leave in a minute. I need these people to stay in this room."

He looked at them. He did not recognize Nicky, but he knew Argoset was a big deal, and I clearly had the upper hand over him. "For, ah . . . how long?" he asked in his whiny, uncertain way.

I slammed my fist into the door an inch from his head and glared with every bit of my righteous fury. "*Until I tell you different*," I snarled so softly only he heard.

He nodded rapidly. "Okay, sure thing, no problem. Keep the peace, that's what I do, right?" He managed a weak, sick smile.

"Take care of him," I said to Nicky, and she knelt beside Argoset.

"Did he kill my daughter, too?" Lesperitt asked softly. He hadn't moved during the excitement. "Did he order it done?"

"No. A different man did that." I walked over and stood in front of him. He'd pushed himself deep into the padded chair. I met his eyes. "Where," I asked calmly, "did you send Liz?"

His lips fluttered soundlessly for a moment. Then he told me. In detail so I could find it.

"And you told that man"—I nodded at Argoset—"the same thing?"

He nodded.

"Thanks," I said, and turned to the rest of them. "If any of you follow me," I told him, "I will kill you. Neat, clean and fast. You're not worth any more effort to me."

None of them said anything. I left without another word.

chapter

TWENTY-FOUR

I took Argoset's huge ebony horse from the inn's small private stable; it seemed appropriate. I told the boy who saddled him about Pansy and vastly overpaid him to retrieve her and put her up for a while.

It was almost dark, but I headed straight out of town without even stopping at Angelina's. Liz had been gone overnight; realistically, anything bad that was going to happen had probably already happened and hurrying was pointless, but where she was concerned I was not realistic.

I had only my sword and boot knife as weapons; over the years I'd amassed a large pile of overt and covert death-dealers, including a miniature crossbow that folded down into a tube I could strap to my arm and a garroting wire with a little spring-driven mechanism that automatically tightened it, but I did not stop and gather any of these. Liz was in the middle of the Black

River Hills with Doug Candora and Marion the pitchfork murderer, and I couldn't bear the thought of doing anything else but rushing to her. I no longer even cared that she'd lied to me; I just wanted her safe in my arms again.

The black stud proved equal to the task. I wore no spurs and could only urge him forward with heels and foul language, but neither proved necessary. He made great time down the road, maintaining a full gallop with little apparent effort, not put off by the darkness or the unfamiliar terrain. The stars came out above us as the last light of the day sank into the west.

When I guided him off the road, he took the forest trails with the same sure-footed grace, dodging anything he couldn't leap over. I sank low along his neck and heard branches slash the air above me. We reached Bella Lou and Buddy's place, but it was deserted. All the livestock was gone, along with their wagon and belongings. I'd just seen Bella Lou in town, mourning her loser of a husband; had they been looted out? More likely their paranoia made them prepare their departure so well that when it came time, Bella Lou was able to clear them out single-handed in record time before they set off for Neceda.

As the landscape grew higher and rockier the horse slowed a bit, but never faltered. The sky blazed with stars, and a waning moon provided light enough to see as the trees thinned. I was so preoccupied with thoughts of Liz that we were almost to the tree line before I realized why the horse was so sure-footed: Argoset undoubtedly scouted this whole region on his own fruitless quest for dragon eggs the day the stable burned down, and even if the horse didn't know the specific trail, he remembered the terrain.

Still, the only thing that really filled my thoughts was Liz. I'd lost people I'd loved before, but it was nothing like this. Even the death of Liz's sister Cathy, who I probably *should* have loved, or the long-ago murder of Janet as I was forced to watch, faded next to this new agony of anticipation. The thought of never again hearing Liz laugh, feeling her turn in her sleep beside me, seeing her sweaty face in the lamplight as we made love, twisted my stomach. I *couldn't* be too late, not this time. I had to see her again; I had to save her. Or I'd have to die.

We'd once had that very conversation, lying naked beneath these same stars along another river, after I'd accompanied her on a delivery. We'd made camp, eaten dinner, taken a swim and ended up thrashing on the mossy bank until we were both satisfied. Then we'd washed off the mud and collapsed onto a blanket, wet and sated and content.

"Who do you think will die first?" she'd asked, not seriously.

"I get more sharp things shoved at me," I pointed out.

"Yeah, but you're used to that. I could be robbed and killed at any moment, too."

"I'm older."

"Oh, just barely. Seriously, though. Who do you think it'll be?"

"Me," I said with certainty.

She rolled on her side and looked at me. Her hair was longer than normal then, and her bangs hid one eye. "Really? Why do you think so?"

I brushed them back so I could see her face. "Because I refuse to live without you. So I'll have to make sure I die first."

"What makes you think I could live without you?"

Because you couldn't possibly love me as much as I do you, I wanted to say. *Because you filled a gap I'd learned to live with, and if it opened up again, I couldn't survive it.* That was the real reason.

But that thought, verbalized, would've kept us both laughing for an hour. So I just said, "If you could call that 'living,'" and we both giggled. Then we made out some more.

I was so lost in this reverie that the low, dark shapes moving through the shadows didn't register until I found myself in the middle of them. My horse whinnied nervously and I discerned the red scarves, gray in the moonlight, of two dozen Black River Hills people.

I slowed my horse to a walk as they formed up around me. So this was who Candora got to help him search. It made sense; there were a lot of them, and they were used to the terrain. They emerged from the hawthorns like badgers, low to the ground and without a scratch on them. The big, crude knives they carried would do considerably more than scratch, I knew. The blades reflected the moonlight raggedly, befitting their owners.

"You best stop," one said, and pointed his weapon at me.

I did, pulling the reins and murmuring, "Whoa." The big black stud tossed his head but didn't panic.

Torches flared to life around me. Too bad they hadn't used torches when searching; *that* I would've spotted. But the flickering orange light did nothing to make them any friendlier. If anything, their mean little faces seemed more devilish.

"Fellas," I said genially. "There seems to be some misunderstanding here. I don't want any trouble; I'm just passing through."

"I know you," one said. He had bruises around both eyes, which made him look even more like some low animal that had learned to walk upright. "You punched me in the face."

"Yeah," I said with a weary sigh. So much for playing innocent. Steps scuffed on the rocks behind me as well, and I knew I was surrounded. Time to be clever again.

I swung my leg over the saddle and slid to the ground. I did not draw my sword; I still had some hopes I could talk my way out. I spread my hands in a wide, let's-be-friends gesture. "Hey, be reasonable. I'm sorry I had to punch you, but things happen. Would money make you feel better?"

Black eyes shook his head, slow and serious.

"Good, because I'm flat broke." No one laughed. They moved slowly in, not rushing but simply sliding forward, their boots scraping on the rocks. Those big knives dangled loosely in their hands, and I could see spots that could be either rust, or blood they hadn't bothered to clean off. The torches guttered loudly in the wind.

I took a step toward black eyes. A fence of knives appeared before me.

Okay. Decision made.

I dropped to my knees and stared up at the stars, eyes wide, mouth open. "Oh, my God," I said softly. *"Lumina."*

About half of them followed my gaze, including most of the ones directly in front of me. Yes, it was the old "look behind you!" trick, but if you do it with enough conviction, it'll always work.

I leaped up, drew my sword and struck all in one motion. My wide swing cut through the calf muscles of half a dozen of the red-scarves, including black eyes. They fell with a mass howl, and I dashed past them, turned and prepared for the rest of them to rush me.

Only three of them did, though. The first one swung wide and overhand. I dodged, kicked his feet out from under him, and he fell face-first onto the ground, his head smacking the stone like a cantaloupe. His knife clattered off into the dark. The second one ran at me, knife extended straight out. Again I sidestepped and slashed off his knife hand halfway up his forearm. I spun to face the third, who threw the big knife at me and gave me a nasty cut atop my left shoulder. When he saw he'd missed anything vital, he turned and ran.

The rest of them stood over their moaning, bleeding comrades. Some knelt to help, but most just stared at me with those blank, dead eyes.

I waited to see if any of them would make a move, and also listened madly for anyone behind me. It would be just like Candora to suddenly appear and cave in my skull again.

Finally I said, "Is that it? Are we done?"

"Why you here?" one man said. It wasn't a challenge, more a whine of someone out of his depth seeking to understand. "Why you all here?"

"I'm just here to find my girlfriend," I said. "You'll have to ask everyone else."

"We live back in here," he continued. "This is our home, and nobody don't fuck with us."

"Suits me, pal. Just send my horse over here and I'll be on my way."

One of them slapped my horse, and he trotted across the skirmish line to me. "You ain't gonna find Lumina, you know," their spokesman said. "Only a believer find her."

I swung into the saddle. "Then it's a good thing I'm not looking for her, isn't it?" I headed up the slope into the dark before any of them had a change of heart.

chapter

TWENTY-FIVE

inally I neared my destination. Lesperitt's directions had been explicit, and even at night I was able to follow them with no trouble. The landmarks he'd used—rock formations, places where the trees grew in certain ways—stood out as plain in the moonlight as they did during the day. It helped that I knew the area a bit, but the easy directions meant that both Liz and Marion would've had no trouble, either. Those poor red-scarf bastards had no idea how close they'd really been.

The horse was speckled with foam, and I should've been conscientious and let him drink at one of the streams we crossed down below in the woods. Up here there was no water, only wind, dust and summer heat even at night.

One last bend awaited before the final straight stretch of trail ahead. But something suddenly caused the stallion to balk. He whinnied, fought to turn and eventually stopped dead, emphatically refusing to go any farther. I saw no reason for his abrupt terror, but knew enough to take it seriously. If a good animal gets spooked, there's always a reason.

I dismounted and tied him to one of the stunted, scrubby trees that marked the top of the tree line. The silence was eerie. I continued on foot, checking the ground as I walked. The harsh moonlit shadows actually helped show that another horse had been up the trail recently, but had gotten similarly frightened not much farther on. Manure showed me where it, too, had been tied.

My ribs tightened around my lungs. A set of small boot prints that might've belonged to Liz continued past this spot, and another set, much larger, obliterated them in places.

The trail rose still higher, although the slope was slight and the climb easy. The constant wind blew the path clean down to solid rock and defeated my efforts at tracking. Moonlight bounced off the whitish yellow stone, and somewhere an owl announced its presence, the call echoing among the rocks. I could see for miles in three directions, the fourth blocked by the rise toward the little mount's peak.

At last I climbed the final bit of hill toward the spot Lesperitt had described. I drew my sword and approached. I considered announcing my presence, but past experience taught me that was almost never a good idea. The place I sought was in a flat spot on the bare slope, with no place for Marion, Candora or anyone else to hide in ambush even in the dark. Except, that is, within the place itself.

After all this urgency, it was anticlimactic. The great split in the rock was about fifteen feet long and five feet wide, gaping straight down into the ground. Again I looked for footprints, but the rocky surface was too hard to show anything. I'd make a wider circle and look for another trail if I found no additional clues.

I crouched at the edge. The rock around the hole's lip was covered in something black, like soot. I rubbed some on my fingers and sniffed; it *was* soot. Beneath the scorch I caught the tang of the same oily substance I'd seen the dragon people applying to crevices before. Had it been intended as a marker? Something that would catch fire and burn the ground if a dragon happened by and hiccupped? An impressively practical idea, if dragons actually existed, which they didn't. Although it did explain why the red-scarves had not used their torches while they searched.

I leaned over the edge and peered down into the darkness. The moonlight made the shadows within impenetrable. I imitated a crow, the only birdcall I could do, and nudged some loose gravel into the opening. If someone lurked below, hopefully they'd think the insomniac bird had poked too near the edge. The gravel bounced off some rocks and quickly fell silent. Bottom wasn't too far away.

"Liz?" I called quietly. "You down there?" I heard nothing.

I put my sword away and started to climb down. Then I noticed something else. On the opposite side of the opening, four parallel scratches raked across the stone, leaving white streaks where they cut through the dust and ash. I held out my hand and spread my fingers; it was roughly the same size. It certainly looked like a claw mark of some kind, but it was all wrong for a mountain lion or bear. Just below this, on a rock inside the crevice, was another identical mark, as if something had clawed its way up from the cave below.

I got a chill that had nothing to do with the wind.

Then I shook it off. It was the middle of the damn night, after all, and the spot's isolation would spook anyone. Some random animal used the hole as a den; no big deal. Probably returned to it, found it covered in soot and human scent and ran away.

I carefully lowered one foot and felt my way down. The drop was only about five feet. I landed noisily at the bottom and dropped to a crouch, although my descent seemed to have attracted no notice. A low tunnel headed off directly ahead into the bedrock, and moonlight illuminated its uneven passage for only a few dim feet. The place smelled of char, and something else I couldn't identify.

The space was far too tight for my sword, so I drew the knife from my boot. I entered the tunnel and closed my eyes, both to listen and to help my vision adjust more quickly to the near-total darkness. There was no sound beyond the wind that whistled down and around the opening. I felt no draft from the tunnel itself, which implied it had no other openings.

I opened my eyes. The tunnel was uneven and jagged, the result of two huge slabs of bedrock separating. No wind or water had come through to smooth the edges. Ahead, the passageway narrowed into utter blackness, except for a strange, dim blue glow. Caves were filled with growths and insects that generated their own light, but this appeared as a flickering line, like a brazier seen edge-on. As it was the only item of interest, I moved slowly toward it, knife held out ahead of me.

"Liz?" I tried again. No response.

The tunnel floor was pitted with holes and uneven spots. The last thing I wanted was a turned ankle down here, so I went carefully. I heard no voices or other movement, just the blue light flickering far down the tunnel.

The place also *smelled* weird. Beneath the burnt odor was one I couldn't quite place; I'd smelled gas in caves before, and this was similar, but not identical. I began to get a little light-headed from it, though, and had to stop and lean against the wall.

I glanced down. An odd, bowl-shaped object with irregular edges lay barely visible at my feet. I nudged it, and despite its size it was incredibly light. It was as big as my two cupped hands, with a rough leathery texture on the outside. The inside was smooth as a river stone. I ran my finger along the uneven lip, and a piece broke off.

It sure *looked* like an eggshell. But what bird was big enough to lay it? And yes, I avoided the obvious conclusion because it was, after all, impossible. But I admit I was thoroughly creeped out. I was also sweating like crazy, and realized the tunnel had grown incredibly warm, far more than it should have. Caves were always cooler than the outside.

My head spun from the weird fumes, and I had to clutch the wall to stay on my feet. "Liz?" I tried one last time, to no avail. I put down the eggish bowl and turned back toward the entrance.

I stopped in mid-motion, though; the blue light in the distance had begun to move closer, swaying in the darkness like a lantern carried in a man's hand. It was hard to focus my watery eyes, but an ominous black shape seemed to loom *behind* the approaching light.

I didn't run—I wasn't capable of it at that moment—but I did rush as fast as my wobbly legs would go and, with more difficulty than I anticipated, crawled out. I sprawled on the ground, not caring that I'd gotten the black residue all over me. My heart thundered like a waterfall. I lay there gasping, nauseous, and before I knew it I began to vomit. My recent dinner came up with alarming completeness.

My disconnected rational mind tried to puzzle through this. What the hell was *in* that cave, anyway? I knew some cave gasses were poisonous, but I'd never smelled anything like this one. And had I imagined the blue light coming toward me, or had I really seen it, along with the dark shape behind it? I rolled away from the puddle of bile and gulped mouthfuls of clean mountain air.

I would have to go back down. If Liz was in the cave, she might be just beyond that blue light, passed out in the darkness. I refused to admit any worse possibility. I'd wrap a wet rag around my mouth and nose, and crouch low to stay out of the strongest fumes. Yeah, that was a plan. But I'd need the canteen from Argoset's saddle.

I stumbled down the hill toward the horse. As I approached he tugged on the reins and whinnied; the smell from the cave still clung to me. I took off my jacket and threw it aside, then made soothing noises. He tossed his head skeptically and clopped his hooves on the hard ground, but didn't try to run off. I opened the blessedly full canteen, washed the sick taste from my mouth and cleaned the smell from my mustache and beard. Then I let the horse drink from my cupped hands.

My head still pounded, but my stomach no longer wanted to leap out of my belly and run off into the night. The wind suddenly blew hard and cool, and I poured more water on my face to take advantage of it. The sensation drove the last of the quease from me.

I tore a piece long enough to rap around my head from the ornamental sash along the bottom of Argoset's saddle blanket.

I returned to the hole, and when I peered down, I thought I saw something or someone duck back into the shadows. I caught a fresh surge of that weird gas smell. I dropped to my stomach and waited, peering over the edge into the pit, but neither heard nor saw anything else. The odor quickly faded.

I hadn't imagined it; the thing had been dark, and roughly the size of a man's head. And it had been quick. Both Candora and Marion had dark hair. A mountain lion could also be dark, had reflexes like that and in such a tight space would be as lethal as either man. I imagined it crouched just out of sight, claws spread, muscles trembling in readiness. And if it was one of those two men, they'd also be waiting there in the darkness, with knife or sword or brute strength at the ready. They were both younger than me, and Marion was definitely stronger. I had no choice, though—I'd have to tackle whoever or whatever it was.

I was about to pour water on the strip of cloth and tie it around my head when a high, unmistakable scream reached me on the wind.

Liz. A terrified Liz. And *nothing* terrified Liz.

There was no way to accurately gauge direction, and for a moment I simply spun in place, unable to decide which way to go. It hadn't come from the hole, so given what I knew about the area, it seemed most likely she was in the old miner's hut. It wasn't far away, if my sense of direction wasn't too fuddled.

I ran to my horse. He gave me no trouble about heading rapidly down the hill or plowing through the scrub. We crossed the trail that led to the hut and made great time, until I reined to a stop just below the final stretch. I tied the horse again and rushed up the trail on foot as quickly and quietly as I could.

When I was within sight, I ducked behind the same boulder

as before. A lamp flickered inside the little hovel, its deceptively homey glow drawing the few insects that lived this high. The wind made it hard to hear distinctly, but I thought I briefly caught a woman's muffled whimpering, as if through a gag. I carefully peeked over the rock and saw three horses tied outside the little building. I could see nothing inside the windows, until Doug Candora appeared in one. He wore a sleeveless tunic, and was wiping something red from his hands with a cloth.

Suddenly I couldn't breathe.

Long ago I'd watched someone I loved murdered, and nearly died myself trying to save her. I still heard her screams in my sleep, but not as often since Liz came along. If I was too late to even fight to save Liz . . .

Candora tossed the bloody rag out the window. He stretched, as if he'd been working diligently on something. Splatters of red covered his tunic.

I drew my sword. There would be no stealth now.

chapter

TWENTY-SIX

Once again I kicked open the door.

I'd seen a lot of carnage in my life, and inflicted a fair bit as well. But what I saw brought me up short, and if I hadn't been sick earlier it would've definitely made me so. As it was, my stomach wrenched and tried very hard to find something else to expel.

The distinctive odors of blood, offal and terror filled the little room. Marion, all six and a half feet of him, was tied down naked to the big, crude table. The single lamp hung from a hook above him. He was missing body parts, and not all of them external: his belly and chest were expertly sliced open, and there were spaces among the organs where there shouldn't be. Blood soaked the floor under the table, and red footprints marked where his killer had circled him during the procedure. The ropes holding his wrists and ankles to the table legs had nearly cut down to the bone from his futile struggles. Judging from the look on the eyeless mess of his face, he'd been alive through most of the mutilation.

The sight was so chilling that a full second passed before I looked around for Liz. She hung from the manacles, her feet just off the floor. She was also naked, and her body was bruised, scraped and dirty. She'd almost chewed through the cloth gag tied around her head, and blood trailed down her arms from where the manacles bit into her wrists. Painful as it was, it appeared to be the worst of her injuries; she had not been tortured, at least not the way Marion had been. She looked unconscious, and her breathing was raspy and labored. I'd heard prisoners make the same noise after being restrained in one position too long; soon she'd be unable to breathe at all as her exhausted muscles simply couldn't expand her lungs.

Absorbing this took another second. Then I realized that there was no sign of Candora. There literally was nowhere for him to hide in the little hut, and I'd come through the only door. Had he jumped out a window? Bloody footprints showed me where he'd paced several times between Liz and Marion, but none of them headed toward the door. He instantly became a low priority, though, as I scabbarded my sword, rushed to Liz and lifted her so the weight came off her arms. I looked around for something she could stand on and intended to say, *Hang on, honey; I'll get you down.*

Instead at the first touch, Liz sprang to life and kicked me in the chest.

I stumbled backward into the wall. Candora appeared, having hidden his slender form behind Liz's hanging one, the one place in the room where I couldn't see him. He was in mid-thrust with a knife aimed at the spot I'd just occupied; Liz had saved my life.

Liz tried to kick him as well, but he wasn't as off-guard as me. He brushed the blow aside and, apparently as an afterthought, slashed her across the top of one thigh. She arched her back and screamed through the gag; I knew that *had* to hurt. Candora sighed as if all this annoyed him no end, then rushed me.

I kicked him in one knee with my metal-capped boot, at the same time turned inside his stab and ended up with my back against his chest, his knife hand pinned under my arm. I spun and slammed him into the wall three times while simultaneously bending his thumb back from his knife hilt. I saw it was identical to the one I now carried in my boot; Team Solarian, indeed. Candora was tough; he held on until I felt the bone snap.

He bellowed in pain and thrashed like a decapitated snake, but the slight build I'd observed at Angelina's was no joke or disguise: he really wasn't very strong. No wonder he had to dope Nicky. I punched him in the chest, knocking the wind from him. Then I hit him with both a left and a right to the jaw. He dropped to the ground like a bag of salt.

I returned to Liz, who was now sobbing. Blood ran freely down her leg, but the cut wasn't deep, just hugely painful. I grabbed a chair and pulled it under her feet so that she could stand and take the weight off her arms. She whimpered and whined as her long-tormented muscles refused to work properly. I stood on the chair as well and tried to undo the manacles, but they were the kind that locked with a key. I turned toward Candora, and to my surprise he was on his feet, dangling a key ring from his good hand. "Looking for these?" he taunted. Then he ran out the door.

I was no more than three steps behind him, but it was enough. He simply stepped aside once he was through the door and easily tripped me as I chased after him. I skidded painfully on the rocky ground. By the time I recovered he'd gone back inside. I did the same, knowing what I'd find. I was right.

Candora stood beside Liz, his knife held in his uninjured hand, the tip just under the crease of her left breast. He'd kicked the chair aside so she again hung by her wrists, and the cuts from her manacles had opened anew. The knife's point had already broken the skin, and fresh blood trickled down her stomach. From that angle it would take no strength to kill her; the knife would easily pass between her ribs and reach her heart. His other arm was wrapped around her waist, and she was too weak to struggle anymore. It enraged me to see him touching her that way, but I said nothing. Keeping things off my face was one of the first fighting skills I'd learned.

"It's amazing what a small little world this is," Candora said. "Last I saw, you were at the bottom of a cliff. Now here you are, and you seem attached to this young lady." He turned the knife in his fingers, which dug the tip into the wound. Liz writhed and cried out; the sound cut me the same way his knife did her. "Well, she's not so young. And I have no idea if she's a lady. But I do know you're fond of her." His mocking tone vanished. "And you broke my goddam thumb. And maybe my kneecap. So drop your sword, *now*."

I unbuckled the scabbard. It hit the wooden floor with a loud clank.

Again he twirled the knife, not really driving it deeper but just gouging the wound. Liz was drenched with fresh sweat, and sobbed into the gag. I licked my dry lips. I said, "I know where the eggs are. Let her go and I'll tell you."

He laughed. "Hell, old man, *I* know where they are. Where do you think I found these two? Passed out down in that hole, nearly dead from the fumes. If I hadn't seen their horses they'd still be there. You should thank me for rescuing them."

I nodded at Marion. "Interesting definition of 'rescue.'"

"Eh, he had it coming. We got him out of jail and paid him a nice pile to suck up to that Argoset clown. And then what does he do? Tried to convince me to turn the eggs over to the king. Can you believe it? He went in a spy and came out as a patriot."

"So you dissected him just for that?"

"No, I dissected him for the sake of your girlfriend here. Someone has to go back in there and get those eggs. I'm not dumb enough to do it, or to set this muscle-monkey loose to do it. But I figured if I got her scared enough, she'd march in there without a second thought if it meant she'd avoid my hobby table."

Liz's eyes were fixed on me. I felt her pain, fear and humiliation; I did not acknowledge it. "Idiot, there *are* no eggs," I snapped impatiently. "Dragons *don't exist.* This is all just Tempcott's *bullshit.*"

"Doesn't matter, old man," he said blithely. "It all boils down to this. That night she got away from me, that girl Laura hid *something* in that cave. I want it. And you"—he pointed at me with the knife, now soaked in Liz's blood; a trickle dripped to the floor—"are going to go get it for me. Or else I'll see what your lady friend's lungs look like."

I smiled. "You really think I'll leave you alone with her again?"

"I know you will." He touched the knife to her belly and traced a diagonal line across it in her own blood. "If I cut her this way, her guts will hit the floor before you can even shout. If I cut her here . . ."—he traced a similar line along the inside crease of her right thigh—". . . she'll bleed to death in three minutes. I can do either, or both, before you can possibly get your hands on me." He held up his wounded right hand, the thumb already swollen and purplish. "Lucky for you I'm ambidextrous, isn't it?"

He had me; until I could get between him and Liz, I could chance nothing. And I doubted he'd make the mistake of letting me get there. Still, his delight in his own cruel prowess might be a weakness. "Why not let her go fetch the eggs, then, and keep *me* as the hostage? Don't you want to work on me like you did Marion? Finish what you started that night at the cliff?"

"Please," he snorted. "For one thing, the fact that I found her passed out and had to drag her ass back here says she wasn't up to it then, and hanging around with me all day"—he slapped her bare behind with mocking familiarity—"hasn't exactly toughened her up. No, since you were kind enough to drop by, I think we'll send the *real* tough guy to do it."

I nodded at the table. "He was a tough guy, too."

"He was just a *big* guy. I had him crying like a baby within ten minutes. I have the feeling you're a lot hardier than that. Call it a hunch." This time he violently pinched her nearest nipple, and she moaned in pain. "With your trail whore hanging around with me while you're gone, you'll certainly be better motivated."

I saw from his eyes that appealing to his vanity wouldn't work. What else might get to him? "All right. Say I go in there and actually find whatever it is that's hidden there. You know it's not really dragon eggs, don't you?"

"Of course I know that. Do you think I'm some gullible stable boy? But something's down there, and until I know what it *really* is, I don't know what it's worth."

"What if I find nothing? What if Laura Lesperitt just conned us all? Are you still going to let her go?"

"I never said I'd let her go."

"Then you better say it now."

He mockingly thought it over, bobbing his head like a flighty girl. "Maybe."

Play it carefully, LaCrosse, I told myself. "You know, things like 'maybe' don't motivate me. I work better with promises."

"Oh, well then, sure. I'll let her go. You bring me back those eggs or whatever they are, and I'll turn her loose. Maybe minus a few souvenirs, but not dead."

Again I saw the utter coldness in his eyes, and the relish he had for his job. Still, he wouldn't kill her until I returned, because without her he had no leverage over me. A lot could happen to her, though, that didn't qualify as "killing." And as for me, I definitely didn't want to end up taking Marion's place on that table. I decided to push him a little harder. "No. You don't *touch* her again until I get back. Do we have a deal?"

"You've got nothing to deal with."

"Suppose you're wrong about my attachment to her? Maybe I know her, but I'm still willing to walk away from her if there's a big enough profit in it. What's to keep me from taking whatever is in that cave and simply selling it directly to Marantz? And in the process letting him know what a screwup you are?"

Ah-ha. I'd found something that rattled him, if only a little.

The idea that he'd misread me bothered him. "If that's true, why do you care if I carve her up?"

"Maybe she's just a good lay, and I'd hate to see it spoiled. But whatever my reason, I'm making that part of the bargain. You don't touch her again until I come back. Deal?"

He shrugged. "Yeah, sure, why not?" He held up his hands, the knife loose in his fingertips. He was still within striking distance, though; I couldn't chance it. "She'll stay just like she is, until you get back. But I'm only giving you until sunrise. If the sun peeks over the horizon through that window, I'm going to debone her like a chicken. After I bone her, of course." He winced and gingerly held up his injured hand. "And I'm taking her thumbs first."

I nodded. I bent to retrieve my sword, but Candora said, "Uh-uh. You don't need that. Nothing up here but buzzards, crows and mountain goats."

"Sorry," I said. "Habit."

"You *can* take the box," he said, and nodded toward the leather-padded crate I'd found before.

I lifted it with a grunt; the lead casing inside made it spectacularly heavy for its size. I met Liz's pain-glazed, terrified eyes and hoped she understood what I was trying to convey. *I have a plan. Be ready. Be strong.* Then I went out the door. I heard her yell something like my name, muffled through the gag. It took all my strength to keep walking away down the hill.

chapter

TWENTY-SEVEN

I had no real plan, of course, except to retrieve the broken eggshell I'd found before and use it to stall for more time. If I could get physically between Liz and Candora, I could finish this in a blink. But he was too smart to make that very easy.

Trusting Candora to keep his word while Liz dangled like a side of beef did not reassure me, either. The sight of her so vulnerable and helpless, her eyes filled with pleading, cut me deeper than any sword ever could and brought back memories of every person I'd tried and failed to save. Most vivid was the first one, Janet, who was the worst of all unless I messed this up and lost Liz, too. But these memories had no place in my head now. I had to move fast, and hope to hell another, better idea came to me soon.

I rode back to the crevice. The horse, slowed by the weight

of the box, would approach no closer than before, and I didn't have time to fight with him. I took the canteen and strip of sash cloth back up the hill, soaked the cloth with water and tied it over my mouth and nose. I had no idea if it would work or not, but it was the best I could do.

I left the box at the edge of the hole and climbed down again. Either the gas was weaker now or the cloth did its job, because I could barely smell the rank odor from before. The wavering line of blue light had also vanished. The moon's position now sent light deeper into the tunnel, so I could see better and farther than before.

I found the eggshell where I'd dropped it. I was supposed to bring back evidence of two eggs, though. Even old Lesperitt had said there were two. Maybe Laura and her father had bought or created this fake as part of some elaborate con that got out of hand, and farther down I'd find the other one. I continued on, still staying low to avoid the fumes. This far in, there was not even moonlight, so I dropped to my hands and knees, feeling for more pieces of fake eggshell.

Finally I hit a dead end; the cave was not very long at all. My fingers felt the edge of a ragged piece of cloth. I carefully tugged on it, and it slowly came toward me. It was coated with something that made it stiff and unyielding, and I felt weight on it. I changed my grip and gently pulled the top of the blanket off the object it had been swaddling.

I stopped. My position thoroughly blocked any stray moonlight from the entrance, yet a faint reddish light came from the thing's surface. I bent closer. It was egg shaped, and about eight inches long. Far from shining with reflected light, it *glowed* from within, faint but unmistakable. The surface was a swirl of multicolored patterns similar to lamp oil on a puddle's surface and identical to the shards in my pocket. I also felt distinct heat from it.

I nudged it with my knife. It rocked back and forth; it was no empty shell, but had weight and volume. Then it shivered as something inside it moved on its own. The red glow momentarily intensified.

I suddenly grew weak in a way that had nothing to do with the fumes. I sat back against the cave wall and stared at the glowing thing resting on its fireproofed nesting blanket. My heart battered against my ribs and sweat popped out all over me. I'd had one other moment like this in my life, when my entire sense of the universe had to change to accommodate the reality of an incarnated goddess, and I hated it. I was too old to keep having epiphanies.

Yet here was another one. No matter what I'd previously thought, regardless of what common sense dictated, it appeared that Candora and Argoset and Marantz and Tempcott and Laura Lesperitt had all been right. Dragons *were* real, and this was, in fact, an actual dragon's egg, lain dormant for centuries. Its possession by either Marantz or King Archibald could alter the balance of power in this whole region, maybe throughout the world.

Wait. There was only a single egg on the blanket. Then the other one I'd found, the broken one, must have . . .

I shook my head. *That* was crazy. I'd taken a blow to the skull, sure, but it wasn't hard enough to make me buy all this. I was a cynical ex-soldier and a well-educated, well-traveled guy. I knew better. Dragons might have existed once, but *this* egg was a fake, and a clever one, created by Laura Lesperitt and her father for who knew what reason and abandoned when Laura was killed and Lesperitt went into hiding. Maybe they'd planned to con Marantz, or even King Archibald, with it. Chemicals could mimic the effects of heat, light and movement, and a good potter could probably turn out fake eggs all day. An animal, probably a coyote or a bobcat, had broken the other one and eaten the contents, or perhaps the broken shell was part of the scam. No living egg could survive untended and intact for as long as everyone insisted this one had.

Regardless of its true nature, though, I needed it now to rescue Liz. I reached for the egg and felt the heat on my fingertips several inches away. It didn't seem unduly hot, and the blanket was undamaged, but I couldn't bring myself to take the chance. *Burns from dragon flames* never heal, Harry Lockett had said. Lesperitt's hands were burned, certainly, but that could've been faked, too, or just the result of an unrelated accident. Hell, if he was crazy enough, he might've burned himself deliberately just to help with the ruse. Laura might've done the same.

Yet I withdrew my hand. I'd been cut up a lot, and burned a few times, and let me tell you, burns are worse, even the small ones. A burn that never healed would be torment indeed. I couldn't bring myself to take the chance.

For every moment I hesitated, Liz hung helpless for Candora's pleasure. Perhaps I could bluff my way through with the broken shell, and claim that someone else, either Laura and her dad or Liz and Marion, had broken both eggs and this was all that was left. Not that I expected to free Liz without killing Candora, but he was a pro and I'd have to put him off-balance to stand a chance. The one thing I *couldn't* do was give the bad guys access to what might be a real dragon's egg.

The egg shifted again. It made a wet sound, like something sliding around in the liquid interior. It spooked me, and I turned toward the entrance. Then I froze.

I heard a sound like a sail rippling in the wind, followed by the noise of nails scraping on rock. Something obstructed the tunnel opening. Backlit by the moon, it was a roughly triangular silhouette that reached from floor to ceiling, and held before it that same blue-flaming brazier. The cave suddenly filled with the nauseating gas stink.

The blue light was low to the ground, and swayed back and forth as much as the narrow tunnel allowed. I heard a sound like heavy cloth or leather rustling. Something snorted, and for a moment the blue light flared enough for me to plainly see what now blocked the only exit.

"Oh, shit," I whispered.

TWENTY-EIGHT

So there I was, a middle-aged sword jockey face-to-face with a genuine fire-breathing dragon.

At least it wasn't a big one, no more than eight feet from nose to tail tip. At its widest its body was as big around as my thigh. Its neck arched so that its head hung about a foot off the floor, where it swung slowly back and forth, inadvertently mimicking the action of a man swinging a lantern. Its legs were long, but in its resting position they folded up close to its body. The tail provided a counterbalance to the neck so that, except for the feet and the knuckles of its two huge, opaque wings, nothing touched the ground. Those wings were what really blocked the light, and the way they were folded brought the tips together over its back and created the triangular shape.

The blue flame glowed inside its mouth, flickering behind its small, even teeth. When it breathed even slightly, the light flared and the gas smell grew stronger.

Still, small or not, it sure as hell had me cornered. I stayed very still, wondering if it even knew I was there. Perhaps it was one of those animals that could only see movement, and if I remained immobile it would eventually go away.

Almost as soon as I had that thought, the long neck slowly straightened, extending down the tunnel toward me. It halted and snorted again, illuminating me with a puff of its eerie blue flame that popped almost in my face. The stench was unbelievable. The dragon's serpent-like head was roughly the size of my foot, with a mouth that split almost the whole length of its skull. I wondered if, like a snake, it could dislocate its jaw and swallow things much larger than its head.

It clearly saw me, and just as clearly wasn't pleased to find me here. It opened its mouth wide, and I saw down its throat, where the flame seemed to originate from two jets where other animals might have saliva ducts or poison glands. I gritted my teeth against the expected jet of flame. I'd contemplated many ways of dying, but being cooked alive by a mythical monster had honestly never been one of them.

It belched another warning puff, and the whole cave lit up blue like the landscape during a thunderstorm. Then its head withdrew, and it took a step back. It couldn't be afraid of me, yet it was clearly hesitating. I realized why: I was beside the other egg, and if it attacked me, the egg might be damaged or destroyed. At least I hoped that was what was going on, because I suddenly had an idea that depended on me being right about that. For my plan to succeed, I also had to be right about the way Doug Candora's mind worked, and what he'd do under given circumstances. That was asking a lot, of *my* brain particularly.

But the advantage to my plan was that, for the most part, all I had to do was wait. Since there was no way to get around this animal, it seemed an especially good plan.

I sat on the stone floor and settled back against the wall. My metal-capped boot scraped loudly on the stone, and the dragon's head retracted like a startled snake and resumed its arched-neck position near the floor. Another surge of the noxious gas filled the tunnel, but no jets of fire spurted from its mouth. Whatever sparked it to flame must be voluntary.

The creature ruffled its wings in what seemed to be a display of some kind. Trying to intimidate me? Warn me off? Attract me as a mate? It spread its feet wide and let its belly settle to the floor. The long neck leaned to one side until it draped over a rock protruding from the wall. Then it remained motionless except for the fire in its mouth, its black eyes fixed on me.

It seemed content to wait me out, which was exactly what I wanted. Now all I had to do was sit patiently as well, and hope that I was right about the dragon, and Candora, and that Liz could withstand her ordeal a while longer. Yeah, that's all I had to do.

Well, that and survive the toxic air that grew more foul with every moment. I'd been smart enough to bring the canteen, so using slow movements I poured water into my hand and wetted down the cloth around my mouth and nose. I doubted that it would do more than delay the inevitable suffocation, but even a few moments might make the difference.

My eyes slowly adjusted to the dimness and I could study the creature in much more detail. Its skin was shiny, with smooth, close scales like those of a snake. In color it was mostly black, although there were iridescent stripes along its sides. The belly scales were broader, also like a snake's, and lighter in color. The wings reminded me of bats more than birds, as their skin seemed to stretch between elongated "finger" bones. A single clawed digit protruded from the wing's main joint, and with the wings folded this knuckle rested on the ground to help with balance. The wingtips rose to the cave roof and had to bend slightly to fit.

I was most amazed by how *fast* the thing had grown; even if it had hatched immediately after Laura and her father hid the eggs, it had tripled in size in a very short time. I didn't know enough about dragon lore to know if this was typical, or how big it might ultimately get. If Tempcott's relic was genuine, it could ultimately quadruple in size.

Like most reptiles, it sat very still and watched me with a steady, unblinking gaze. I could hear the rippling flame inside its mouth surge with each breath.

Time passed slowly, and staying conscious became my overriding goal. I found it harder to keep my thoughts straight, and my head thundered from lack of clean air. The sight of Liz, stripped and battered by that asshole Candora, would not go away, nor the sick feeling I had gotten as I turned and left her there, dangling and displayed. Had she understood that it was all a plan to save her? Or was she so delirious from her torture that she thought I really was leaving, that I didn't love her?

What kind of man *did* that to the woman he loved, anyway? I knew what kind: the same kind who let his childhood sweetheart be raped and murdered in front of him because he wasn't strong enough to defend her, that's who. And that guy was me, just as much now as when I was a sixteen. If I couldn't save Janet then, how could I save Liz now? And suddenly Janet was there, standing beside the dragon, her body torn and violated, looking at me as she'd done then, as Liz had done this very night, with eyes that pleaded and begged, saying, *Why can't you save me, Eddie? If you loved me enough, you could save me.* The soft flesh she'd entrusted to me was now being obscenely used by strangers mere yards away, and hands touched her and threatened to carve her up and *did* carve her up right in front of me.

And there was me, young and supposedly strong, screaming and straining, fighting the blows and ropes and sword thrusts that bit into me, and there was me turning and walking out of the hut leaving her hanging naked and bleeding, and her eyes, following me above the gag, following me helplessly until the light faded from them and I knew that my failure was the last thing she'd ever see. . . .

"Hey!" a voice cried. "You in the hole!"

TWENTY-NINE

The words cut through my reverie, and suddenly I was back in the moment. I jumped in surprise, and my sudden movement made the dragon huff a little, sending a small pop of blue flame from its mouth. The burst of heat assured me I was wide awake. I got slowly to my feet, aware that the animal watched every move and could incinerate me instantly.

Behind the dragon, the moonlight had turned into the gray half illumination of pre-dawn. I must've been wandering through my own head for hours. In all that time the dragon had not appreciably moved until I spooked it. Now it was entirely focused on me.

My hands shook, and I was chilled despite the heat. Everything depended on how well I pulled off this next bit. And even then a lot of things could go wrong. I pulled the cloth down from my face.

"Hey," I said. My voice was dry and croaky from disuse, exactly as it needed to be. "Is someone there?"

The dragon snorted again. The puff of blue flame was larger, and got much closer to me before consuming itself with a pop. I winced at the heat.

"You know who's here, asshole," Candora said. "I've got somebody else here, too. She's been running behind my horse, so she's a little beat. Had to drag her in places when she couldn't keep up."

The dragon very slowly turned its head so that one eye watched me, the other on the tunnel entrance. In profile its skull was eerily familiar; it was a smaller, less-formed version of the one Tempcott displayed. The horns of this dragon's ancestor were only nascent knobs.

My mouth really *was* too dry to speak. Did I honestly think this was a good plan? "You gotta help me; my leg's broken," I called pitifully.

"Give it a rest," Candora said. "I'm not falling for that."

The dragon pulled one foot out from beneath its body and shifted its weight onto it. Its claws sounded like daggers scratching across the rock.

"I'm not kidding. Please, I'm bleeding; the bone's sticking out." I used my nervousness to make my voice quiver.

The dragon turned toward me again. The egg's red glow reflected from the surface of its eyes.

"Tough. Drag your fat ass up here anyway, or I start throwing your girl down piece by piece."

"I've got the eggs," I said, as pathetically as I could.

The dragon's neck drew back and arched, like a snake

preparing to strike. At me. For a long moment the only sound was the wind and the soft crackling of the dragon's fire.

"You do not," Candora said at last, like a disbelieving child.

"Uh-huh," I said in the same manner. "They're really here, just like Laura said. But I can't move. Please, help me out of here. I did what you wanted." If I sounded any more pitiable, I'd have to change into short pants and a ruffled shirt.

Slowly the dragon's lower jaw fell open. The blue fire danced as it waited for the breath that would send it to envelop me. It didn't come.

More silence. "You actually have the eggs?" Candora said at last, unable to hide the excitement in his voice.

"Yes," I said with desperation. "Right here in front of me. Two of them."

"Okay, then . . . what do they look like?"

I closed my eyes and sighed with relief; he'd taken the bait. Now I had to set the hook. I turned to the egg on the blanket, and suddenly the dragon spread its wings as much as the tunnel allowed, blocking most of the light. I had to swallow hard before speaking. "I dunno, they're, like, a couple of feet long, they have shells that are all multicolored, and they're hot, like something inside them is burning. You can see something moving inside one of them." I added more whine. "Please, man, I'm dying in here."

Still more silence, but not so long this time. "Crawl out where I can see you." The voice was stronger and clearer, telling me he stood right at the edge.

"I can't *crawl*; my leg bone's poking out and I've been bleeding for hours."

"You better manage." He was trying to sound firm, but the excitement in his voice gave him away.

"All right," I said, just loud enough for him to hear. "I'm . . ." I had to risk a scream, or at least a cry of pain. It echoed through the short tunnel and sounded truly wretched. The dragon did not seem to notice, remaining poised with its mouth open and wings spread.

"Oh, God, I can't move; it hurts," I said, letting my voice tremble. "Please, get me out of here; I don't want to die like this. . . ."

"All right, hold on; shut the hell up. You sound like a damn schoolgirl. I'm sending your honey down; she can drag your wimp ass out."

Every muscle I had was gathered for action now.

"Oh, hell, not you, too," I heard him say in disgust. "Come on; get up. Your boyfriend's down there; don't you want to see him?" There was a pause. "Do you hear me? I'm not kidding, I'll cut your damn tits off if you don't get—"

Suddenly he yelled, and past the dragon I saw him fall into the hole. *Yes!* Liz had understood and played it perfectly, pretending to be too weak to move until she could catch him off-guard.

Candora rolled nimbly to his feet. "You bitch, I'll—"

He never finished the sentence. The dragon, startled by his loud and sudden appearance, forgot me and rushed from the shadows toward him. It hissed like a dozen pots of boiling water and rattled its wings like canvas in a windstorm. When Candora saw it, his eyes opened wide and he went for his sword, but his broken thumb interfered. Then it didn't matter, because the dragon engulfed his whole upper body in a ball of blue flame. His hair and clothing combusted at once, and his skin made a meaty sizzling sound that I'll never forget. His scream, high and girlish, died in a wet gurgle as the fire scorched down his throat, melting all the tissue it touched.

I had no time to gloat or enjoy. I whipped the knife from my boot, ran down the short tunnel and threw myself on the dragon's back. My weight knocked it flat, and its wings tangled beneath and around me. Its feet clawed at the ground, scratching like spear tips against the stone. If it threw me off, I'd be just as toasted as Candora.

I pinned its neck just behind its head, the way you would a poisonous snake. Its wiry, squirming form was impossible to hold for long, but luckily I didn't have to. I slipped my knife under its neck and, with all my strength, ripped it up through flesh and muscle and bone, severing its head.

The head rolled away into the light, where its mouth continued to work as if it could still spew fire. The body thrashed for a moment, then went limp. Past it, Candora lay smoldering, his legs moving weakly. From the waist up he was blackened, and the smell of his cooked flesh mixed with that of the dragon's flames. I gagged and tried to breathe only through my mouth.

I climbed off the dragon, my heart pounding. I wanted fresh air more than anything. I crawled over the carcass and up the soot-covered rock. Candora made a sound I'll hear in my nightmares and reached one knobby, burnt extremity toward me.

The sun had not yet risen above the horizon, but the clouds were ablaze with its promise. Liz lay facedown on the ground just beyond the hole. She was still naked, her wrists tied in front, and except for the wind blowing her hair she didn't move. I knelt beside her and turned her over. Bruises distorted her face, and her eyes were closed. *"Liz!"* I cried, and this time I didn't have to fake the panic.

Her eyes opened. I wanted to cry. Her lips were dry and cracked, and the corners of her lips were flayed where the gag had rubbed them raw. "Can we have a better plan next time?" she croaked.

"Promise," I said, and kissed her all over her face. I tasted tears, not sure if they were hers or mine.

"I feel terrible," she said when I let her speak again.

I spotted my jacket on the ground where I'd thrown it earlier. I retrieved it and wrapped it around her. "We'll get you to the moon priestesses; they'll fix you up. Is anything broken?"

She slowly, laboriously shook her head. "I don't think I can walk, though."

"That's okay; I'll carry you."

She managed a small smile. "All the way back to town?"

I felt like I could at that moment. "If I have to."

She reached one hand up to my face, moving slowly because of her injuries. "Not yet. I have to know, Eddie."

"Know what?"

Something grew young and sad and hopeful in her eyes. "Were there really dragon eggs down there?"

I nodded.

"You're not just telling me that because you think I'm about to die, are you?"

"No. Because you're not about to die. There were eggs down there. One hatched."

I'd never seen a look of such sad eloquence. "What?"

"It hatched. There was a dragon down there. I had to kill it."

Tears welled in her eyes. "A real dragon?" she said in a small voice.

I nodded.

"And it's dead?"

"I had to, sweetie," and felt myself unaccountably wanting to cry, too. "It would've killed me, and maybe you, too."

Her lower lip trembled. "Can I see it?"

The second-to-last thing I wanted to do was climb back down in that hole and drag the dragon carcass out. The very last thing I wanted to do was cause Liz any more pain or distress. So I did climb down in the hole, tossed the surprisingly light headless dragon over my shoulder and was about to climb out again when a thin voice, barely audible, said, "Don't leave me."

At least I think that's what it said. Candora was moving, his arms—if you could still call them that—reaching imploringly for me. His face was completely gone, with only a gaping orifice through which his distorted voice emanated.

I didn't say anything. He couldn't see me, or probably even hear me. At best he felt my movements through the ground; maybe he just hoped someone was still there.

"Don't leave me," he repeated.

Burns from dragon flames never heal.

I remembered Laura Lesperitt, and Nicky. I remembered Liz hanging in the shack.

I turned away and climbed out of the hole.

The sun had now officially risen, blasting us with its golden light. The morning wind stirred, and crows announced their interest in the cooked meat down in the hole. Liz sat up now, clutching the jacket around her. She coughed and trembled, but when she saw what I carried a look of such heartbreak filled her face that I could say nothing. I gently stretched the headless carcass out before her; in death it appeared far more delicate and fragile, and in the sun its black scales shone with the same rainbow pattern as the eggs.

I stood over it. Liz just stared with a look I could not identify.

"There's another egg in the cave," I said quietly. "It's still in one piece, and I think it's about to hatch. I need to go smash it before it does."

She didn't look up, but reached one hand out to gently touch the creature's shiny skin.

"Did you hear me?" I asked gently.

She nodded without looking. "This is no time for the fire dreams are made of," she said, and in those words I heard the little girl who'd once believed in the divinity of dragons. "No time for gods you can touch."

I went back down in the hole, retrieved Candora's sword and used it to smash the last remaining dragon's egg. The smell was awful, and the mostly formed creature that spewed forth writhed for a few agonizing moments before I mercifully cut it in half. Then I drove his own sword through Candora's heart, an act of mercy that most of me argued against. But I was too weary to be a total bastard.

I speared the severed dragon's head on my knife and brought it up with me. I placed it beside the rest of the corpse. The eyes were still open, still black, and the teeth gleamed white. Liz sat just as I'd left her, one hand on the dragon.

"She's a female," Liz said between gulping breaths. "You can tell by the coloring."

"Lumina," I said.

She nodded. "Lumina." Then she sobbed the way people do when they've lost something precious. And I guess she had.

chapter THIRTY

I collected all the horses—mine plus Liz's, Candora's and Marion's—and after retrieving my sword burned down the old miner's hut. The crows, vultures and rats attracted to Candora's handiwork squawked and ran madly from the smoke. The ground was too rocky to give Marion a proper burial, and I doubted what was left of him would survive the trip back to Neceda intact. A pyre is a good way for a warrior to go, anyway. Even one who cried like a baby as he was eviscerated; even one who killed Hank Pinster. Candora had definitely balanced the scales for that crime.

Liz was in really rough shape and couldn't ride on her own. I searched the hut before I torched it, but her clothes were gone. Rather than try to get back to town right away, I made for Bella Lou and Buddy's place. It would give us shelter and

Liz a place to rest, and maybe I could find some discarded clothes for her as well.

As we approached, though, I saw smoke rising from the chimney. When we reached the clearing, Bella Lou and the two kids emerged to greet us. Bella Lou looked sad, and tired, but when she saw Liz's condition she went right to work. The children cleared a bed, Liz drank some medicinal tea and she was hard asleep within minutes. Bella Lou then treated her injuries with some homemade remedies. At no point did Bella Lou ask me what had happened.

Later, after I'd cleaned up a bit as well, Bella joined me on the porch. She packed and lit a long pipe, and together we watched the trees wave in the wind. The kids played quietly in the yard.

"So you came back," I said.

"Yeah." She handed me Frankie's money bag. "It's all there. We don't do charity. We'd always planned to leave if the government came after us, but this wasn't the government's doing. It was Buddy's."

I nodded. "He really *did* kill someone. A friend of mine, actually."

"I know. He came and told me about it first. Cried like one of the children. I made him go to town and confess."

"You did?"

"Yes. And I know you tried to help him. Thank you."

"I owed him one. But if you knew he was guilty, why were you outside his cell yelling about conspiracies?"

Her expression didn't change. "I wanted him to die knowing his beliefs went on. He was a weak, spineless little man, but I loved him. It was the last thing I could give him."

The little girl Toy brought me a cup of tea. She curtsied after

I took it. I thanked her and kissed her hand just the way a prince would. She grinned and ran away before I could see her blush. To Bella Lou I said, "Yep. Beliefs are important."

Now she smiled, wry and very sad. "Only if they're true."

"If it's any consolation, there should be no more dragon people bothering you." I nodded at the horses, indicating Candora's and Marion's. "And those two? You can have them."

She shook her head and blew a puff from the pipe. "Like I said, we don't take charity. We'll be fine."

"Charity, hell. The guys those two belonged to are dead. I don't want the bad luck."

She thought for a moment. "I can understand that," she said at last. "Thanks."

LIZ slept most of the day, and did not stir until sundown. I dozed on the porch, and when I woke every injury I'd accumulated made sure I knew it was around. The red-scarf's knife cut on my shoulder was particularly painful. Bella Lou cleaned and bandaged it for me, and while I slept she also mended and got the bloodstain out of my coat. Buddy had been an idiot not to treat her better.

We all ate some vague stew that Bella Lou conjured up. I didn't recognize the meat in it; I assumed it was best not to ask.

Liz still needed genuine medical attention, especially for the cut on her thigh. She borrowed some of Bella Lou's clothes and we headed back to Neceda. She was still in no condition to ride on her own, so I tied her horse behind mine and she rode huddled in front of me, as Laura Lesperitt had done. The ride through the darkening forest was blessedly smooth and uneventful, and she quickly fell asleep.

That peacefulness vanished as we emerged onto the plain. In the distance, something big was once again burning in Neceda, spewing flames tall enough to be reflected in the Gusay. I couldn't make out what it might be from this distance.

It was full dark as we entered town, and the streets were empty since everyone had once again congregated to watch something burn up. The crowd gathered at the corner of Ditch Street. Being on horseback let us see over the other on-lookers.

Someone let out a cheer as a cloud of sparks billowed forth, and the noise woke Liz. She squinted against the light and asked sleepily, "What's burning now?"

"The Lizard's Kiss," I said.

Like the stable before, it was already a lost cause. Since all the doors and windows had been reinforced and sealed, the fire had gone straight up through the relatively flimsy roof, and the walls acted as a chimney that sent flames shooting into the night sky. The fire also worked its way around the jambs and sills, gnawing into the night air. The front door was open, and a dozen red-scarved men and crimson-cloaked women stood in the street staring up at the flames. The rich boys looked most confused, while the few hill people Candora hadn't recruited seemed resigned to their bad luck. Neceda's normal population gave them plenty of room.

On his knees at the bottom of the stairs was old Tempcott, pounding the dirt and wailing, "Why, Lumina? *Why?*" Prince Frederick, unrecognized and aimless without guidance, stood beside him like a lost puppy.

"Lumina . . . ," Liz repeated softly. "Do you think . . . ?"

The lone dragon hatchling *had* left the cave the previous

night, but it could not have set a fire that only flared to life now . . . could it? "No. Just a coincidence."

A man marched through the crowd, dragging one of the red-cloaked girls after him. People laughed mockingly as they passed. As they got nearer I recognized flatboat captain Sharky Shavers, and beneath the cloak was his daughter, Minnow.

". . . not hanging around with them goddamned *freaks*!" Sharky said in mid-bellow as he passed without noticing us. His eyes were downcast in shame and aggravation.

Minnow tried to simultaneously pull her wrist free and keep the cloak closed to protect her modesty. "I am not a *child*, Daddy! I need something to believe in!"

"You'll believe in my foot up your ass if you ever do anything like . . ." His voice faded into the crowd.

After a moment Liz said with certainty, "We're never having children."

"Agreed," I said, and kissed the top of her head.

There was another commotion up the street. Callie stood over someone crouched on the ground, hands covering his head. She beat at him anyway with what looked like a broom handle. "You lying sack of *donkey shit*!" she yelled. "This was your 'big-time gig'? You dishonest lump of *cat turd*!"

Tony the minstrel risked a look up at her. "Baby, please, I can explain—"

"Explain how come you're a ball of *chicken piss*?" she screamed, and smacked him again. His partner watched nearby, but was smart enough not to come between Callie and the object of her ire.

"And," Liz added, "we're never breaking up, because I don't have the energy to go through all that drama."

"Agreed," I repeated.

There was little else to see, and nothing to do, so I took Liz on to the moon goddess hospital. She'd befriended most of the staff during my convalescence, and they descended on her like a benevolent swarm of tittering hens. They quickly took her from me, cleaned and dressed her wounds, then placed her in a quiet room for rest. Mother Mallory took me firmly aside and told me to go home and clean up so Liz wouldn't wake and see me looking so awful.

"And please," she added, "take a bath. Whatever you've been rolling in almost makes my eyes water."

I still carried the scent from the cave, so I had to agree with her. Another set of clothes for the fire; at least they wouldn't burn with me in them, the way Candora's had.

I went home and cleaned up, then stopped at Angelina's. It was late, but the crowd was still healthy thanks to the fire. Callie stood in the corner, watching Tony the minstrel mop up some spilled ale. She had her hands on her hips and, although she no longer carried the broomstick, I got the distinct impression she wouldn't hesitate to smack him around bare-handed if he got out of line. Some wags at a nearby table snickered and made snide comments.

I took an open stool. When Angelina came by, I said, "I see Callie's got the upper hand in the relationship now."

"At least until pretty boy earns back the money he stole from her. Not too smart to run out on your girl and only go a couple of streets over."

" 'Smart' doesn't seem to apply much to minstrels," I agreed. "I didn't see you at the fire."

She waved her hand. "I've seen plenty of things burn down

in my life. Besides, I wanted to make sure none of those weird red-rag people came running in here. They need to just go back to the hills where they came from."

"That's harsh."

"*I'm* harsh, in case you hadn't noticed. Are you hungry?"

"Are you harsh?"

"Hang on, then; I'll whip something up." She went into the kitchen, and I watched Callie continue to monitor her ex-boyfriend's progress. He was soot streaked from the fire, as well as red eyed and pale from lack of giggleweed, but maybe sobering up was what he needed. He stopped mopping and looked to her for approval. She pointed to something he'd missed, and he wearily resumed his work. A bearded tanner poured some ale on the floor right in front of Tony's mop, but he said nothing. The tanner and his friends laughed.

Callie flounced over to me, almost shivering with delight at the new balance of power. "And how are you tonight, Mr. LaCrosse?" she said as she kissed me on the cheek.

"Not as good as you, apparently."

"Well, Tony and I have reached an understanding. He's working off the debt he owes me; then we're going to send for Joan Diter and he'll go to work for her."

"Why?"

Callie leaned close and whispered, "Because *he* burned down the Lizard's Kiss. Passed out and knocked over his giggleweed pipe."

"No," I said with mock surprise.

She nodded vigorously. "Oh, yeah. He's lucky nobody died. And now he's going to pay for it. For me, and for every other girl he's ever screwed, then screwed over."

Callie returned to supervising Tony, and Angelina brought me a plate of food. "So how's Liz?"

I gave her the short version, without mentioning the dragons. It still made her eyebrows crawl toward her hairline. "Holy shit, is she okay?" she asked when I was done.

"She will be. She's resting, which is really what she needs. She'll have some scars, but we all have those. And she'll be sore for a while. But she really came through in the end. Don't find many people, men or women, who can keep their cool like that."

"No, you don't," Angelina agreed. "So what about that other thing that was bothering you before?"

I shrugged as I wolfed down some gravy-soaked bread. "Seems kind of insubstantial now. I mean, we'll talk about it, but it matters a lot less than I thought it did."

She mussed my hair the way she'd done to Hank Pinster's oldest boy. "You big softie. I bet you bleed pudding, don't you?"

I finished my dinner, then went upstairs to check my office. Nothing looked different from the last time I'd been there two days ago, when I found old man Lesperitt waiting; certainly no new clients were hiding under my desk. I'd have to see about that fairly soon. Dragon slaying sure didn't pay very well.

I grabbed some of Liz's belongings from our place and returned to the hospital. They still wanted to keep her quiet and isolated, but they let me stretch out in an empty room and gave me something to make me sleep. Which I did, straight through to morning, deep and blessedly dreamless.

They brought me in to see her then. She slept peacefully on clean white linen. She'd been washed, her wrists bandaged and the cut across her thigh tended. With her hair held back by a headband I saw the bruises on her forehead and jaw, the swollen bridge of her nose and her lips cracked and dried from dehydration. If Candora hadn't already been killed in a manner more horrible than anything I could've inflicted, I'd have made the process a long and slow one, worthy of the man who cut Marion up alive.

Still, Liz looked more beautiful than ever to me. I sat in the bedside chair and touched the back of her hand lightly above the bandage. She made a little whimper of contentment but did not awaken.

There was a soft tap at the door. I turned, expecting to see one of the young apprentices or Mother Mallory, but instead a slight figure in an expensive hooded cloak stood there. In the brightly lit hospital this looked especially out of place, and my hand went automatically for the knife in my boot.

The figure pushed the hood back. Princess Veronica said softly, "I didn't mean to startle you. I hope I'm not intruding."

I sat back and glared at her. "You are."

She did not seem fazed. "May I come in?"

"It's your country." My etiquette training did its best to get me to my feet, but my disgust won out and I stayed seated.

She closed the door and stood at the foot of the bed, looking at Liz. Although the princess' hair was immaculate and the dress under the cloak spotless, she looked as tired and worn as I felt. I could imagine the fiery scene with Gary and Argoset after I left. "Is this your wife?" she asked softly.

"What do you care? She's just another immigrant like me. She's not your concern."

She ignored my sniping. "I'm assuming your presence here means the problem we discussed earlier has been resolved?"

"Yes. Two people died horribly, Liz was tortured and . . .

well, let's leave it at that. There are no dragon eggs for your father, I'm afraid."

"I never really believed there were," she said sadly. Her eyes were red and swollen from crying, but her demeanor was calm, even icy. "It was just another fairy tale."

"So what do you want?" I demanded impatiently. Her presence both aggravated and unnerved me a little.

She continued as if I hadn't spoken. "I owe you my life, and I have not honored that debt. But I wish to do so."

"You don't owe me anything, Your Highness. Except the honor of your absence."

"Mr. LaCrosse, within the next few years, my father will die. Either from natural causes or otherwise. When that happens, I intend to ensure Muscodia does not suffer the rule of my brother, Frederick."

"How do you plan to do that?"

"By whatever means are required."

The firm tone surprised me, although it really shouldn't have. It was easy to talk about assassinations and coups, especially when you were a spoiled, headstrong teenager. "And how does that help me?" I said, unable to keep the harshness from my voice. "Or pay your debt to me?"

"I am very smart, and reasonably courageous. I am not very experienced, however, as the events this week have illustrated. When I ascend to the throne, I will need experienced people around me."

The implication hung in the air between us. A tiny smile touched her mouth. "I see you're surprised."

"I see you're delusional," I shot back.

Now she smiled for real. "Mr. LaCrosse, my offer is serious."

"Muscodia needs me?"

"I need you."

"What about Argoset?"

Her smile faded. "Daniel has been reassigned."

"Permanently?"

"That's up to him. His judgment, or lack thereof, has done a lot of damage and gotten people killed. He'll have to convince me that's changed if he wants to regain my favor." It was plain that Argoset's fall had broken her girl's heart as well as engendered her royal scorn.

"I still have his horse," I said.

She waved dismissively. "Consider it a gift. His name's Little Blackie, I believe."

I nodded my thanks. "Will Argoset be upset that you've offered me his job?"

"He would never be suited to the job I'm offering you."

I had to smile now, too. "Your Highness, I appreciate the offer, but I've lost the ability to be a team player. I work better on my own. Besides, you know how sword jockeys are: greedy little men snooping around taverns and whorehouses spying on faithless spouses. We leave a trail of slime wherever we go."

She nodded. "I assumed you'd say that. And I won't push you. But I will seek you out again once I'm queen."

"My answer will be the same."

"Well. I suppose we'll have to see. In the meantime, I hope your wife fully recovers. She is a lucky woman to inspire such devotion."

"She's not my wife," I said. "And I always figured I was the lucky one."

The princess pulled the hood back down over her face and turned to leave.

I said, "But you know what?"

She stopped.

I stood, formally bowed and said, "I can't do anything for Princess Veronica of Muscodia. But if that nice girl Nicky ever needs my kind of help, under the table and behind the tapestries, with something too delicate for official channels . . . she just has to ask."

Her smile was visible inside the hood's shadows. "She appreciates that very much, Mr. LaCrosse." Then she left.

The next morning I awoke in the chair at Liz's bedside and found her watching me. Her right eye was nearly swollen shut, and blood was still caked around her nostrils. She smiled, ointment gleaming on her cracked lips. "This has a familiar feel," she said in a weak, thin voice.

"Except you're on the wrong side of the bed."

"So are you."

My entire body seemed rusted into my sleeping position, and moving out of it took a few moments. "How do you feel?"

"Numb. Are my toes wiggling?"

"Yes. They gave you some concoction to help you relax."

"Any more relaxed and you'll need a ladle to move me. How long have I been here?"

"Only a couple of days. Nowhere near my record."

She reached a bandaged hand toward me. "I owe you an

apology. If I'd told you about Lesperitt the night of the fire, I wouldn't be here."

"You're right," I agreed. "But we don't have to talk about it now."

"Yes, we do."

"Okay. Why *didn't* you tell me?"

She was silent for so long I wondered if she'd fallen asleep with her eyes open. At last she said, "I could give you some story about wanting to take care of things on my own, but the truth is that really . . . I was embarrassed."

"By what?"

"By the fact that I still wanted to believe. That even though the adult Liz knew the truth, the little girl in me still believed dragons might be real. And she had to know. So Little Liz pitched a hissy fit, and Big Liz went along just to shut her up."

I nodded. "And now both of them know they were real."

She shook her head. "No. Not the kind I wanted to find. Not the ones filled with wisdom and power and love. They were just cold, beautiful animals." Tears welled in her eyes. "What kind of idiot insists on believing in gods, anyway?"

"I'm sorry," I said, and meant it. I leaned over and kissed her. Her lips were slippery with the minty healing ointment. "I'm not filled with wisdom or power, but I *do* love you."

She wiped her eyes with the back of her hand. "Ah, you're just saying that to get into my pants."

"Did it work?"

She scooted over on the bed. "Not yet. But it probably will. Now get over here."

I stretched out beside her, let her snuggle close, and we fell asleep together despite the sunlight bouncing off the white walls. Before my eyes closed, I resolved that, as soon as she left the hospital, I would tell her about my past relationship with her late sister. I couldn't very well be mad at Liz over this if I wasn't willing to face the same music myself.

AROUND noon I left her sleeping and headed back to town for lunch. I'd had my fill, literally and figuratively, of the medicinal stuff the moon priestesses called food. I needed something dipped in grease and fried. Before I left, though, I poured Frankie's money into the donation vase. The noise was horrendous in the hospital silence, but no one appeared to investigate.

A whole company of Muscodian troops lined the street outside the Saraden's Sword. They looked tired and ill-mannered, especially the ones not lucky enough to be on horseback. A potbellied captain stood beside the door, while a crowd of onlookers gathered a respectful distance away. I'd seen more crowds in Muscodia during the last week than I had in all my time here, and really looked forward to the day there would again be nothing to gawk at.

The door opened, and two soldiers came out. Between them staggered a disheveled Prince Frederick, looking dazed and half-asleep. The soldiers snapped to attention, and the captain stepped up to the prince with a smart salute.

"Your Highness," he said stiffly, "please allow us to escort you back to Sevlow."

Frederick blinked. "Uh . . . okay, sure." He looked down at his feet. "Whoa, where're my shoes?"

"Boots for His Highness!" the captain bellowed. A junior officer quickly complied. I couldn't tell if they'd brought extra boots just for this contingency or stripped them off a soldier roughly the same size. The two soldiers quickly bent to the prince's feet and had him shod in no time. I suspected they'd done this before. Perhaps this whole company did nothing but chase Frederick around and bail him out of trouble.

As Frederick was guided to a waiting horse, two more soldiers brought out Daniel Argoset. He was in full uniform, and stood stiffly at attention before his counterpart. "Captain Malligan," he said formally.

"Captain Argoset," Malligan replied. Then he reached up and yanked the insignia from Argoset's uniform. "By direct order of King Archibald, you are demoted to private and assigned to my unit."

Argoset swallowed hard, but his voice was steady. "Yes, sir."

Malligan smiled. If he'd spent any time at all with his former peer, he must've enjoyed this immensely. To his credit, the smile was his only gloat. "You're assigned to the rear guard, Private. Am I clear?"

Argoset had just been instructed to clean up any manure deposited on the road behind the company as it traveled. It was a punishment detail, the absolute lowest job available. He simply nodded and said, "Yes, sir, perfectly clear. Where may I find the shovel?"

I left Argoset to his humiliation and continued to Angelina's. There I found Callie's ex-boyfriend asleep on my office stairs, where she could keep him from scurrying out to find giggle-weed. I also heard that Minnow Shavers had inquired about a job; Sharky un-inquired for her shortly afterward. And no one, it seemed, had inquired after my professional services. Neceda was finally returning to normal.

I'd just filled in Angelina and Callie on Liz's condition when

Gary Bunson sat down beside me. His smile was almost wide enough to separate the top of his head from the rest of him. "What are you grinning about?" I asked.

He pulled out a folded piece of black velvet and opened it to reveal a small military medal embossed with the royal seal of King Archibald. "The captain of the guard presented this to me. He even stood at attention."

"You got a medal?" Callie said, making no effort to hide her disbelief. *"Why?"*

Gary pinned it to his chest, and puffed up like a startled toad. "For my quick action in solving the murder of Mother Donna Bennings of the Moon Sisterhood. With the grateful appreciation of the king and people of Muscodia."

"I thought the king didn't approve of the moon priestesses," Angelina said.

Gary was almost beaming. "He may not, but they have a lot of clout and he knows better than to let people go around killing them."

Angelina and I exchanged a look of disbelief. I tried not to laugh. "Gary, the killer came to you and confessed. You basically did nothing."

"Yes, and I did it with alacrity and tact. I have a parchment that says so."

"And your conscience is okay with this?"

Now Gary tried not to laugh. "Eddie, I sold my conscience for a night with a trail whore when I was fifteen. Haven't seen it since, and wouldn't know what to do with it if it turned up." He touched the medal almost reverently. "I also got a raise."

"A raise," Angelina repeated. "A medal and a raise for doing nothing." She shook her head with a grim, humorless chuckle.

There wasn't much else to say. I clapped him on the shoulder. "Congratulations, Gary. That means the next round is on you."

"Hey, sure thing. Angelina, a bottle of your cheapest best stuff." He turned to me. "Want to hear something else weird?"

"Sure," I said.

"Oh, wait: how's Liz? I heard she was in the hospital. What happened?"

"Had an accident making a delivery. She'll be fine. So what else is weird?"

"A sheep farmer from the Black River Hills came into town screaming that a dragon had carried off one of his rams."

"A dragon," Callie repeated. "Like in a fairy story?"

"Yeah," Gary said. "A real fire-breathing dragon. Shiny black scales. Breathed blue fire, he said. Showed up in the middle of the night, scorched his pasture, killed his dog and flew off with a ram."

Now I knew where the creature had been returning from when she found me in her burrow. "That *is* weird," I agreed. "Maybe he just had too much to drink at the hanging."

"He had too much of something. I told him if I heard any more about it, I'd lock him up as a public nuisance."

"Yeah, for the best," Callie agreed. "Anyone who says they've seen a dragon must be a few needles short of a pine tree."

Gary sighed. "Well, I hope we've seen the last of him and those other weirdos, the ones with the red scarves. And anyone from Sevlow, and anyone named Marantz. This used to be a nice, peaceful town."

Gary left; I finished my lunch, then went upstairs to my office. When I went to unlock the door, though, it swung in on its own. Instantly I was flat against the stairwell wall, my boot knife in my hand.

I leaned out just enough to see inside. The waiting room was empty, and the door to my private office stood open.

I silently entered. Nothing seemed disturbed. I went behind my desk and looked out the window. No one on the street appeared to be watching for my arrival. Had I just forgotten to lock the door? Then I noticed the present waiting for me on my desk.

It was a foot-long crossbow bolt, its triangular metal point stuck in the wood, but not with the force of an actual shot. A piece of parchment was tied to the shaft with a red ribbon. I unrolled it and turned it toward the light.

The writing was neat and precise, four words that carried all the meaning in the world. *Not today,* it said. *But someday.* There was no signature, but none was really needed.

I crumpled the note and threw it out the window into the mud of the street. Then I put the bolt in a quiver with my others.

I had one last bit of work to do in the Black River Hills. The next day I left Liz's bedside before sunrise and on my new horse, Little Blackie, headed down trails now familiar to us both. I finished burying Lola, although nature's disposal system had done a good job on the carcass by the time I found it again. Scavengers had also been at Candora's body, but I left it where it was. Feeding the buzzards and crows was more than he deserved.

I carried the dragon's remains to the peak above her burrow and burned them on a small pyre. The wind made it difficult to get the fire started, but once going it didn't take long to consumer the body. Alone with the blue sky, the great forest like a green sea beneath me stretching into the hazy distance, I felt the solemnity of the moment. It marked an end of something large and significant in the world, even though most people would never know it.

As I watched, the remains of whatever organic gas fueled the dragon's fire sent little blue jets of flame through the gaping, blackened jawbones. It was the last time any dragon would breathe forth fire. I felt a twinge of whatever Liz must've experienced as a child, and shared her sad disillusionment. And I shed a tear of my own for Solarian and Lumina.

chapter

THIRTY-TWO

I , ah . . . ," I said, trailing off.

    We sat in my office a few days after Liz left the hospital. I'd brought dinner up from the tavern and lit a candle, making the austere little room vaguely romantic. Fresh flowers sat in a vase on my desk, and a cool breeze blew in from the river. I'd even washed the ale mugs that tended to accumulate in one desk drawer. The sky visible through the window was darkening pink and red, and somewhere a drunk howled at the rising moon. Liz, her fork halfway to her mouth, stopped and cocked her head at me. "You, ah, what?"

I put down my fork, sat straight and looked at her. "I, ah, need to tell you something."

She put her own utensils aside with deliberate care. We were having Rudy's vegetable surprise again; ever since she'd watched Candora work on Marion, Liz had been unable to stomach meat. I understood completely, since I found myself getting twitchy around any open flame, no matter how small; even the candle on the table made me nervous. She said, "That sounds ominous."

"It's not ominous."

"There's not a Mrs. LaCrosse somewhere you haven't bothered to mention, is there?" She looked at me with exaggerated inquiry. The bruises had faded, although her wrists were still bandaged. The cut on her thigh also remained sensitive and forced her to wear dresses, something she generally loathed.

"No, don't be goofy. Who would marry me?"

"You're the one being goofy. 'I, ah, need to tell you something,'" she said, imitating me. "So tell me."

"I'm serious."

"Okay."

I looked out at the sunset. The first stars twinkled at the edges of the pink clouds. A crow, running late, landed in the top of a tree. "You know how you kept the whole dragon thing from me because you worried about how it would sound?"

"I said I was sorry for that. And I meant it."

"I know. The thing is, I've kinda sorta kept something from you for the same reason."

Like me, she could keep feelings off her face, but I knew her well enough to see the rising concern in her eyes. Still, her tone remained light when she repeated, "'Kinda sorta'?"

"Kinda sorta. I didn't lie to you or anything, except by omission, and even then I wasn't trying to keep it from you. I just . . . didn't know how to start the conversation."

"And *this* is how you decided to do it?"

I shrugged. "I'm better at throwing knives."

"So is this great secret something you're ashamed of?"

"No, just something that . . . will be hard to explain."

"And believe?"

"Probably."

She sat back, pulled her napkin from her collar and placed it in her lap. She hiked up her dress to expose the cut to the air per Mother Mallory's orders. It also displayed a distracting amount of thigh. She said, "Does it end with you saying how we can't be together no matter how much we want to be?"

"No. It's really not about you and me."

"Then let's hear it."

Deep breath. It struck me that I was more scared of this than I'd been of the dragon. Yet I not only felt I owed her honesty; I also had taken something fundamental from her that day on the mountain. It can't be easy to know you've lost a god, and I could see the sadness of it burgeoning in her. I felt obligated to try to restore it, to convince her that just because one god proved false, it didn't mean there was no magic in the world. And to believe the story I was about to tell meant she'd have to accept anew the reality of magic, and goddesses walking among us.

Still, it took all my courage to get those first words out. "It's about your sister."

"Jessica?"

That was her older sister, married with a bunch of kids and, now, grandkids. "No, your twin."

It took a moment to register; then her eyes opened wide. *"Cathy?"*

"Yeah."

"Well . . . what *about* her?"

Here we go. "I knew her once."

Under different circumstances, the look on her face would've been funny. *"When?"*

"Years ago. I was . . . well, I wasn't exactly *there* when she died, but I . . . *was* there." I sighed. "It's complicated."

"Then she really *is* dead," Liz said deliberately. It replaced a long-standing question mark with a period.

"Yeah."

She took a moment to absorb it. "And you knew that, and never told me."

"Yeah."

She just stared at me. It was almost fully dark outside now, and the light from the candle reflected from her eyes so that they seemed to burn with contained emotion. It also made her look exceptionally beautiful.

"Okay," I said, unable to bear the scrutiny and silence. "I'll start at the point it all got resolved, which was just before you and I met."

"That sounds like the end of the story."

"It is, but it'll make sense."

She took a drink of ale. A big drink. "And you love me?"

"Yes. And this won't change that, for me at least."

She wiped her lips, burped lightly and said, "You know *I'm* pretty hard to run off, too."

"I'll hold you to that." I took another deep breath, leaned back in my chair and began the long, complicated story of Epona Gray, Phil of Arentia, the scariest dwarf ever and Queen Rhiannon, the sword-edged blonde:

"Spring came down hard that year. . . ."